LEFT TO RUN

BOOKS BY BLAKE PIERCE

EUROPEAN VOYAGE COZY MYSTERY SERIES
MURDER (AND BAKLAVA) (Book #1)
DEATH (AND APPLE STRUDEL) (Book #2)
CRIME (AND LAGER) (Book #3)

ADELE SHARP MYSTERY SERIES
LEFT TO DIE (Book #1)
LEFT TO RUN (Book #2)
LEFT TO HIDE (Book #3)

THE AU PAIR SERIES
ALMOST GONE (Book#1)
ALMOST LOST (Book #2)
ALMOST DEAD (Book #3)

ZOE PRIME MYSTERY SERIES
FACE OF DEATH (Book#1)
FACE OF MURDER (Book #2)
FACE OF FEAR (Book #3)
FACE OF MADNESS (Book #4)

A JESSIE HUNT PSYCHOLOGICAL SUSPENSE SERIES
THE PERFECT WIFE (Book #1)
THE PERFECT BLOCK (Book #2)
THE PERFECT HOUSE (Book #3)
THE PERFECT SMILE (Book #4)
THE PERFECT LIE (Book #5)

THE PERFECT LOOK (Book #6)
THE PERFECT AFFAIR (Book #7)

CHLOE FINE PSYCHOLOGICAL SUSPENSE SERIES
NEXT DOOR (Book #1)
A NEIGHBOR'S LIE (Book #2)
CUL DE SAC (Book #3)
SILENT NEIGHBOR (Book #4)
HOMECOMING (Book #5)
TINTED WINDOWS (Book #6)

KATE WISE MYSTERY SERIES
IF SHE KNEW (Book #1)
IF SHE SAW (Book #2)
IF SHE RAN (Book #3)
IF SHE HID (Book #4)
IF SHE FLED (Book #5)
IF SHE FEARED (Book #6)
IF SHE HEARD (Book #7)

THE MAKING OF RILEY PAIGE SERIES
WATCHING (Book #1)
WAITING (Book #2)
LURING (Book #3)
TAKING (Book #4)
STALKING (Book #5)
KILLING (Book #6)

RILEY PAIGE MYSTERY SERIES
ONCE GONE (Book #1)
ONCE TAKEN (Book #2)
ONCE CRAVED (Book #3)
ONCE LURED (Book #4)
ONCE HUNTED (Book #5)
ONCE PINED (Book #6)

ONCE FORSAKEN (Book #7)
ONCE COLD (Book #8)
ONCE STALKED (Book #9)
ONCE LOST (Book #10)
ONCE BURIED (Book #11)
ONCE BOUND (Book #12)
ONCE TRAPPED (Book #13)
ONCE DORMANT (Book #14)
ONCE SHUNNED (Book #15)
ONCE MISSED (Book #16)
ONCE CHOSEN (Book #17)

MACKENZIE WHITE MYSTERY SERIES
BEFORE HE KILLS (Book #1)
BEFORE HE SEES (Book #2)
BEFORE HE COVETS (Book #3)
BEFORE HE TAKES (Book #4)
BEFORE HE NEEDS (Book #5)
BEFORE HE FEELS (Book #6)
BEFORE HE SINS (Book #7)
BEFORE HE HUNTS (Book #8)
BEFORE HE PREYS (Book #9)
BEFORE HE LONGS (Book #10)
BEFORE HE LAPSES (Book #11)
BEFORE HE ENVIES (Book #12)
BEFORE HE STALKS (Book #13)
BEFORE HE HARMS (Book #14)

AVERY BLACK MYSTERY SERIES
CAUSE TO KILL (Book #1)
CAUSE TO RUN (Book #2)
CAUSE TO HIDE (Book #3)
CAUSE TO FEAR (Book #4)
CAUSE TO SAVE (Book #5)
CAUSE TO DREAD (Book #6)

KERI LOCKE MYSTERY SERIES

LEFT TO RUN

(An Adele Sharp Mystery—Book Two)

BLAKE PIERCE

BLAKE PIERCE

Blake Pierce is the USA Today bestselling author of the RILEY PAGE mystery series, which includes seventeen books. Blake Pierce is also the author of the MACKENZIE WHITE mystery series, comprising fourteen books; of the AVERY BLACK mystery series, comprising six books; of the KERI LOCKE mystery series, comprising five books; of the MAKING OF RILEY PAIGE mystery series, comprising six books; of the KATE WISE mystery series, comprising seven books; of the CHLOE FINE psychological suspense mystery, comprising six books; of the JESSE HUNT psychological suspense thriller series, comprising seven books (and counting); of the AU PAIR psychological suspense thriller series, comprising two books (and counting); of the ZOE PRIME mystery series, comprising three books (and counting); of the new ADELE SHARP mystery series; and of the new EUROPEAN VOYAGE cozy mystery series.

ONCE GONE (a Riley Paige Mystery—Book #1), BEFORE HE KILLS (A Mackenzie White Mystery—Book I), CAUSE TO KILL (An Avery Black Mystery—Book I), A TRACE OF DEATH (A Keri Locke Mystery—Book I), WATCHING (The Making of Riley Paige—Book I), NEXT DOOR (A Chloe Fine Psychological Suspense Mystery—Book I), THE PERFECT WIFE (A Jessie Hunt Psychological Suspense Thriller—Book One), and IF SHE KNEW (A Kate Wise Mystery—Book I) are each available as a free download on Amazon!

An avid reader and lifelong fan of the mystery and thriller genres, Blake loves to hear from you, so please feel free to visit www.blakepierceauthor.com to learn more and stay in touch.

TABLE OF CONTENTS

CHAPTER ONE

Beneath an evening sky dripping with the final glimmers of sunlight, Adele glanced at Agent Masse's trembling hands. His upper lip was beaded with sweat, and his Adam's apple bobbed as he stared down the barrel of his service weapon. Noting her attention, Adele's new partner flashed an uneasy smile followed by a quick thumbs-up. The gesture caused Masse to momentarily release his weapon with one hand, before uneasily readjusting his shaky grip.

Adele resisted the urge to scowl. Her eyes narrowed over her own sidearm, which pointed steadily down the open-air walkway on the second level of the motel. On their right, a thin, rickety white railing—half rust and half steel—provided a precarious barrier between the stretch of hall and the courtyard below. Backup was delayed—something about a gunman at a gas station that had rerouted most of the units in the area. But they couldn't wait. Hernandez had proven slippery in the past. For now, all she had was Masse and her own sense of foreboding.

Adele glanced over the railing at the rectangular pool; the unnaturally blue water reflected the residue of the evening light in crystalline flashes and gentle motion. A diving board on the opposite side occupied the space next to a metal entry ladder dipped into the water. The heavy scent of chlorine lingered in the air, mingling with the proximate buzz of traffic from the adjacent street. Glimpses of stagnant cars could be spotted through the gaps in the motel's separate wings.

"Eyes up," Adele murmured, quietly.

Her back pressed into the popcorn siding of the low-rent motel. She felt a trickle of dust against the nape of her neck, but kept her motions steady as she eased forward, sliding along the wall. A woman stared out from a window across the courtyard, owlishly surveying the FBI agents' approach.

I

Adele glanced at the distant woman and gave a slight shake of her head. The motel tenant ducked out of view behind the window streaked with greasy fingerprints and breath stains.

Agent Masse bumped into Adele, jarring her attention back to room A7. She flashed a scowl at her new partner. "Careful," she muttered in a ghost of a whisper.

Masse raised a placating hand, again releasing his grip from his service weapon. Inwardly, Adele suppressed a groan of frustration. As cantankerous as he was, one thing could be said for John Renee; he despised amateur hour. Now, back in San Francisco, Adele found she missed the tall, scar-faced French agent.

Purely professionally, of course. *Of course.* John was an excellent shot, reliable when faced with danger, and—most importantly—he wouldn't keep bumping into her outside a killer's motel room.

"Would you stop that, please?" she whispered at last after the third accidental knee into her thigh as they both eased up the walkway.

"Sorry," Agent Masse said, a bit too loudly.

Adele stiffened. From within A7, she thought she heard movement. She stared at the door, her pulse in her ears. Then all fell silent.

Adele waited, wetting the edge of her lips, her ears perked, her eyes fixed on the silver door handle beneath the card-reader slot.

Jason Hernandez. Suspected of two counts of barbarous murder. Adele had spent the previous week going over the toxicology reports. Jason had pumped his victims full of methamphetamine before bludgeoning them to death in the living room of their own home.

Allegedly, she thought to herself. Images flashed through her mind. She pictured crimson stains on an ornately patterned Turkish carpet. She recalled the horrified expressions of the cleaning staff who'd found Jason's work. And of course, the crimes had occurred in the Hills. Rich and famous couple murdered? Step aside, homicide, hello, FBI.

Adele nodded toward the door, keeping her weapon raised. Her new partner hesitated.

She tried not to roll her eyes, but in a fierce whisper said, "Key card. Hurry!"

Agent Masse stiffened like a deer caught in headlights. The young agent stared at the side of Adele's face before her words finally seemed to register.

Now moving too quickly, as if to make up for lost time, he hurried past her, rubbing against the rusted white railing facing the pool. His hand darted to his right lapel pocket, where he fiddled with a button.

Adele stared in disbelief.

Masse's cheeks reddened, and he mouthed *Sorry* while finagling the button a bit more. He couldn't seem to undo it. With a wince, Masse holstered his weapon and, now with both hands, he reached up and unbuttoned the pocket. Finally, his gun still holstered, he pulled out the key card the motel clerk had provided. With a still quivering hand, the young agent inserted the card in the door. A small green light flashed over the L-shaped handle.

Masse stepped back, his young face surveying Adele.

She nodded pointedly at his hip.

Again, blank face.

"Your weapon," Adele said, through clenched teeth.

Masse's eyes widened and he quickly unholstered his weapon a second time and leveled it on the door. The windows to A7 were closed, and the curtains blotted out the light.

"He's armed and dangerous," Adele said, beneath her breath. Normally, the second part of that sentence seemed redundant, but with Masse, she couldn't be sure. "If you see a weapon, don't give him the opportunity. Understand?"

Agent Masse stared at her, shivering where he stood, but nodded. Adele swallowed, staving off any of her own nerves. She adjusted her grip, feeling the cold heft of her weapon against her cupped hands. She endeavored not to betray her own discomfort—firearms and all they encapsulated had always been her least favorite part of the job.

Masse took a position on the opposite side of the door. With a significant look in her direction, he reached out with his right hand, his left still holding his weapon, gripped the door handle, and then—

The door banged open. A wild shout emitted from within and someone slammed into the faux wood from the other side, sending Masse reeling.

Her partner fired once, twice—without aiming. Agent Masse was sent stumbling to the ground by the continued momentum of the door. The bullets struck the ceiling. A blur of motion burst from within the motel room, streaking onto the walkway. The blur held something metal glinting in one hand.

A weapon?

3

No. Too small. The figure didn't turn left or right, and instead, with a shout, dove over the railing, lunging toward the pool below. The sound of Adele's curse chorused with the loud *splash!*

Adele trained her weapon and took three quick side-steps of controlled motion toward the railing. Her eyes flitted to the blue pool, then darted to the circling hedges. She leveled her weapon on the retreating form below...

...and recognized him immediately from his sheared head down to the twisting tattoos of two snakes looping over his ears and curling at the base of his neck. The tongues of the snakes intertwined, tied in a knot between his shoulder blades. Jason Hernandez wasn't wearing a shirt. He had a bit of a paunch, and his baggy pants were soaked against him now, but this didn't stop the man from pulling himself with grunts out of the pool, then stumbling away from the edge, dripping wet and gasping as he tried to hop the hedge. He ended up tripping and cracking branches, landing in the brush, before—spitting and cursing in Spanish—he regained his feet and hurried toward the gap between the two wings of the motel, heading for the busy street.

Adele's finger tightened on the trigger, her teeth clenched.

"Stop!" she shouted.

He didn't. Again, she spotted something metal clutched tight in his right hand. A knife?

A clear shot. She had him in her sights. But no—he was unarmed. Most killers didn't *need* weapons though. *Alleged killer,* she reminded herself. Adele lowered her weapon and raced past where her partner was still trying to recover from a motel room door to the face. His nose poured blood and he had a dazed look where he sat massaging his chin.

Adele hurtled past, yelling, "He's getting away!" She sped to the end of the walkway without looking back. No footsteps echoed in pursuit, suggesting her new partner was out of commission for at least a bit longer. Adele set her jaw as she reached the circling metal stairs and flung herself down them three at a time.

Firearms were not her forte. But finding criminals was. She circled the stairs with leaping strides, watching as Jason raced toward the street.

Adele lost sight of him as she cleared the staircase and also moved toward the street. But after a few strides, she pulled up short and hesitated, gasping, next to the browning shrubbery circling the blue water.

Would Jason really use the busy street? People would see him. This part of the city was patrolled rather heavily. Jason would know this. Her mind flipped back to the flash of metal she'd spotted in his hand. A knife? No. A weapon? Too small.

Keys. They had to be.

Her eyes flitted briefly back toward the walkway above. Keys to the motel? No. They'd used a keycard. She turned away from the street, her eyes scanning the length of the second wing of the motel around which the suspect had disappeared. Would he double back?

Car keys—they had to be, right? Jason's truck was in the motel's parking lot; they'd seen it on their way in.

Adele nodded to herself and then, instead of heading for the gap between the buildings which led to the street, she turned and sprinted in the opposite direction. The motel's parking lot was situated behind the buildings, hedged up against a large wooden fence, and bordered on all four corners by new red dumpsters with black lids.

A hunch. But sometimes a hunch was all an agent had to go on.

Adele could hear sirens in the distance, but they were still faint. She was on her own. She glanced back over her shoulder toward the stairs, noticing her partner slowly moving down, a dazed look still on his face as he shook his head. He staggered a bit, blood still streaming from his nose.

Adele exhaled a resigned sigh as she hotfooted in the direction of the parking lot. She hopped another small hedge, grateful for all the time she spent jogging in the mornings. She hurried along the side of the registration office, and then sidled past a chain-link fence and a red dumpster positioned at the back of the offices. The odor of two-week-old garbage wafted on the air and clung to her clothing. She ignored the smell and grunted as a jutting section of fence snagged her suit; a quiet rip, a flash of pain. But she pushed through, ignoring the tear through her outfit.

Adele slid between the chain-link fence and the odoriferous dumpster before pulling up short and staring at the large black truck with jutting mirrors. The vehicle parked halfway between two spots behind a minivan.

The front door to the truck hung open.

Jason was already scrambling into the driver's seat. He shot a look in her direction, then cursed loudly before slamming the front door and jamming his keys in the ignition. She heard a muffled rattling sound, and a string of oaths in Spanish.

She raised her weapon, pointing it at the window. "Stop or I'll shoot!" she yelled.

But Mr. Hernandez ignored her. He continued fumbling with the keys. Finally, at last, the engine revved. Jason stared out the window, his eyes wide in panic. The twisting tattoo of the two snakes seemed to pulse against his skin, and veins protruded from his temples.

He muttered something she couldn't hear through the glass, then shifted into gear. He slammed the gas. There was a squeal of tires, and the truck darted forward, nearly colliding with the office building. Jason cursed inaudibly and readjusted his gear shift before glancing over his shoulder and preparing to reverse.

Unlike the motel, Jason's truck was in immaculate condition. The windows were clean, and the truck itself didn't carry a single chip or dent. Some of the eyewitnesses who'd seen Hernandez follow his supposed victims home had claimed it all started when Mr. Carter nearly rear-ended Jason's truck.

Adele kept her weapon trained and braced herself, shoulders set, feet apart. "Stop, FBI!" she shouted.

"Agent Sharp!" a voice called over her shoulder. For the briefest moment, she flinched and glanced back.

Masse was stumbling through the building nearest Jason—clearly he'd run around the street, going the long way. But now, this meant he was closer to the truck than she was. Masse spotted Jason; the young agent's eyes widened, and he raised his weapon.

"Wait!" Adele snapped.

But Masse unloaded three rounds. Two struck the hood of the truck; the third shattered both windows, piercing clean through one and out the other. None of them hit Jason Hernandez.

But, through the now scattered glass of the truck's window frame, Adele had a good long look at Jason's expression.

He was no longer fiddling with the wheel or the ignition. He stared through the shattered glass, his eyes wide as if haunted, his features pale now. He stared at the smashed pieces of glass, and then his eyeline traced the hood of his car toward the two smoking bullet holes in the front of his beloved vehicle.

"*Puta!*" he screeched. Hernandez scrambled across the seat and flung open the passenger door before stumbling out. He was now on the opposite side of the vehicle from Adele, but closer to Masse.

Adele tried to hold her posture, but growled in frustration; she'd lost line of sight. She moved quickly, still with controlled motions, trying to keep the two quantities within field of vision as she hastily circled the parking lot.

Jason started toward Agent Masse, ignoring the gun waving in his face and Adele skirting around from behind. As she repositioned, Adele glimpsed his expression: Jason's eyes were dilated, blood vessels throbbing in his neck and forehead.

"*Cavron!*" he screeched, glancing from his ruined truck to the FBI agent who'd shot it. He seemed entirely indifferent, or perhaps unaware, regarding the weapon in Masse's still trembling hands.

Adele's earlier cry of "*Wait!*" only now seemed to register with Masse. His trigger finger was still white against the mechanism, but he seemed frozen. He waited, hesitating, glancing between Adele and the approaching form of Hernandez. He hesitated for a second too long.

"No—don't!" Adele shouted, but too late.

Jason surged forward, ducking Masse's line of fire, and tackled the young agent around the waist, sending both of them clattering to the sidewalk.

Adele rushed forward, looking for an opening, her weapon raised. The cold concrete of the parking lot and the safety barrier provided a harsh surface against which Masse's shoulder blades slammed once, twice as he tried to rise. But Jason snarled, punching and scratching the agent's eyes.

"Get off him!" Adele shouted. Then she fired.

Masse loosed a cry of terror. Hernandez, though, grunted in pain, spinning like a top and slamming into the ground next to the agent he'd tackled.

"First one is the arm," Adele snapped, weapon trained on Hernandez. "Keep struggling and the next is going in your chest, understand?"

The sound of cursing and crying faded from Jason's direction where he rolled back and forth, his teeth flashing as they gritted in pain, and he pressed his head against the rough sidewalk. Rivulets of red stained his fingers. Every few moments he would look away from his injured arm and turn toward his steaming truck, shaking his head with a renewed anguish.

Adele sighed, then put her hand to her battery-powered field radio. "We're going to need medical," she said.

She glanced between her partner, who was still shakily getting to his feet, and Hernandez's writhing form. She sighed again. "Better make it two." Then, with a roll of her eyes, she approached Jason, handcuffs emerging from her belt.

Chapter Two

Adele loosed an explosive gust of breath, listening to the quiet creak of hinges as her apartment door closed behind her. Four hours of ridiculous paperwork and interviews later, Adele was glad to be back home.

She flipped a light switch and peered into the cramped space as she rolled her shoulders and winced against a sudden pulse of pain. Adele glanced down at her side and, for the first time, noticed a stain of red on her white undershirt beneath her suit.

She frowned. Wincing again, Adele scanned her small apartment as she went to the kitchen sink, resignedly untucking the front of her shirt from her belt.

A new place. The lease only lasted two months at a time. It had been too expensive to stay in the old apartment. After Angus left, Adele simply wasn't paid enough to keep up rent South of Market, where Angus and his coding buddies had congregated. Now, having moved to Brisbane, she found she didn't mind the change. It wasn't loud—which she had her neighbors to thank for—though the place was little more than a kitchen, a TV, and a bedroom with an en-suite bathroom. All of it, even somehow the TV, smelled a bit of mold.

It wasn't like she spent much time at home anyway.

Adele winced again as she pulled her shirt from her belt and examined the long scratch against her skin. She grimaced in recollection. A gift of the chain-link fence, no doubt.

"Damn rookies," she muttered beneath her breath.

Agent Masse was young. Only a few months out of training. Adele doubted she'd been much better on her first collar, but still . . . that had been a debacle. She missed John. Last time they'd met, though . . . things had grown awkward.

She remembered the late-night swim in Robert's private pool. The way John had leaned in, the way she'd recoiled, almost reflexively.

Adele frowned at the thought and immediately wished she could take it back. Instead, she reached for a clean length of paper towel from the counter and began running hot water. She opened the cabinet over the fridge and snagged a bottle of rubbing alcohol. She dabbed it against the towel and pressed the makeshift disinfectant wipe to her ribs, wincing yet again.

She moved over to the single chair in the kitchen, pressed against the half table between the fridge and the stove, and took a seat facing the wall, dabbing the strong-smelling paper towel against her scrape. At last, as she leaned back, she let out a long breath.

Absentmindedly, she glanced over her shoulder toward the door. Two bolts and a chain lock ornamented the metal frame, remnants from the previous tenants.

The chair creaked as she adjusted herself and leaned one elbow against the table, staring at the surface of the smooth wood. She shifted again, if only for the sake of the noise. The apartment was so quiet. Living with Angus, there would always be a TV show running or some podcast blaring from his room while he worked on a coding project. For the couple weeks she'd spent with Robert back in France, she would often find herself in the same room as her old mentor, enjoying his company by the fire as he read a book or listened to concertos on the radio.

Now, though, in the small, stuffy San Francisco apartment . . . it was all so quiet again.

Adele shifted once more, listening to the creak and protest of the poorly constructed chair. A phrase from her childhood, one of her father's favorites, crossed her mind. *"Simple things please simple minds."* In a sort of phantom protest, Adele wiggled in the chair, listening to the strangely consoling creak of wood one last time, before she gritted her teeth, still pressing her makeshift disinfectant wipe against her wound, and then she regained her feet and trudged down the hall.

"Bloody Renee," she muttered.

Jason Hernandez never would have bolted if John had been there. She missed France. After the interview with Interpol, she'd spent some time with Robert. A nice time—refreshing in its own way. It had given her an opportunity to look for her mother's killer.

Adele pushed open the bathroom door at the end of the hall and stood in front of the mirror. It was a small, cramped bathroom. The shower sufficed as Adele hadn't taken a bath in nearly six years. Showers were far more efficient. The Sergeant—her father—likely hadn't taken a bath his entire life.

She sighed again as she undressed and stepped into the shower, turning on the hot water, but the spray was still lukewarm. Another little flaw of the new apartment. The water pressure wasn't great either, but would have to do.

As Adele stood beneath the tepid drizzle, she closed her eyes, allowing her mind to wander, pushing past the events of the day, of the past couple of months back in the States.

Words played through her mind.

". . . Honestly, it's funny you left Paris, you know that? Especially given where you worked."

She sighed as the water soaked her hair and began to drip down her nose and cheeks in slow uneven pulses, matching the temperamental jets from the showerhead. Yet she kept her eyes closed, still mulling over the words. They echoed—sometimes even when she slept—resonating in her head.

That's what the killer had said.

Back in France. A man who'd sliced his victims and watched them bleed out, helpless and alone. She and John had caught that serial killer, but not before he had nearly murdered her father. He'd nearly killed Adele, too.

The bastard had worshiped her mother's killer. Another murderer—so many of them.

Adele's brow bunched in the stream of water as she clutched her fists and her knuckles pressed against the cold, slick white plastic pretending to be porcelain.

John had killed the serial killer before he'd ended Adele, but that had only left her with more questions. Part of her wished he'd been allowed to live.

Why was it funny she'd left Paris? That phrase haunted her now. She kept running it through her mind. *Funny you left Paris . . . especially given where you worked . . .* Almost like he was teasing her. They had been talking about her mother's killer.

Paris. She was nearly certain now. Her mother's murderer had *lived* in Paris. Perhaps he still did. He would be what, fifty? Adele shook her head, sending water droplets scattering across the shower onto the slick floor.

She gritted her teeth as more lukewarm liquid pulsed in uneven jets from the nozzles.

In a surge of frustration, she twisted the knob the full way, but the water didn't warm. Adele blinked, her eyes stinging against the trails of liquid inside the slope of her cheeks. She stared in anger at the shower knob, the arrow pointing at the culmination of a red slash.

"Fine then," she muttered.

She grabbed the handle and twisted it the other way. Small disciplines compounded over time. The cold water began to arc on her head and sent goosebumps rising on her arms. Adele's teeth began chattering within moments, and the pain in her side faded to a numb chill as the cold water turned frigid.

Still, she stayed in the shower.

The killer had taunted her. As if he'd known something. Something she'd missed. Something the authorities had missed. What was relevant about her workplace? That part bothered her the most. It was almost as if . . . She shook her head again, pushing back the thought.

But . . . what if it was true?

What if her mother's killer was somehow connected to the DGSI? Maybe not the agency itself, but the building. Perhaps there was a proximity. What else would make sense of his words?

Especially given where you worked . . .

The man John had shot had known something about her mother's killer. But he'd taken it to his grave. And the Spade Killer, the man he had worshipped, the man who had killed her mother, was still out there.

The cold water continued to seep down the angled slope of her shoulders, and she drew in small, quick breaths against the sensation, but still refused to move.

She would be sharp next time. They had asked her to join a task force with Interpol on an as-needed basis. But Adele was itching to return to Europe. She liked California, and she liked working with the FBI, especially with her friend Agent Grant as supervisor. But her desire to solve her mother's murder required a level of proximity.

Finally, pushing one forearm against the glass door, gasping, Adele twisted the shower knob.

Mercifully, the freezing water stopped. She stood trembling in the glass and plastic partition for a moment as the water dripped off in quiet taps.

Whoever designed the bathroom had placed the towel rack on the back of the door on the opposite side of the room. It took a few steps to reach it, and though she had a bathmat on the floor to absorb water, she preferred to wait in the shower a bit to dry off before stepping out.

And so she waited, thinking, contemplating, shivering. She thought of another time, soaked in water, also shivering...

A flash of warmth crested her cheeks. She thought of swimming in Robert's pool—John had come over for an evening...

He was insufferable. Rude, obnoxious, annoying, unprofessional.

But also handsome, said a small part of her. *Dependable. Dangerous.*

She shook her head and stepped from the shower, causing the glass and metal door to squeak open and slam into the yellow wall; a few flecks of paint chips fell from the ceiling. Adele sighed, glancing up. Already patches of mold had formed beneath the coating. The previous tenant had painted over it, which had only served to disguise the issue.

Perhaps she should text John.

No, that would be too familiar. An email then? Too impersonal. A call?

Adele hesitated for a moment and reached for her towel, pulling it off and drying her hair. A call might be nice. She reached down to her side with the scrape and winced against the minor injury.

Some wounds healed slowly. But other times, it was best to avoid a wound altogether. Perhaps it was better she didn't call John at all.

Exhaustion weighed heavily on her shoulders as she moved through the house to the bedroom. Her eyelids were already beginning to droop. Three hours of overtime, filling out paperwork and justifying the shooting, had taken their toll.

It was a horrible thought, but Adele was starting to wish for a case in Europe.

Perhaps something that didn't hurt anyone too badly. Just something to get her out of California. Out of the small, cramped apartment. It was too quiet. For some people, the sounds of other human beings moving around, enjoying their lives, assuaged them. It staved off bouts of loneliness.

Adele sighed again, and she moved into her room, donning bedclothes. She reaffixed a bandage on her scrape and tried to push back any further thoughts of animosity toward her new young partner. She flopped into bed and lay there for a few minutes.

In the past, she and Angus would watch TV as they drifted off. Sometimes he would read a book, narrating it line by line out loud so she could enjoy it too. Other times they would just snuggle and talk for a few hours before they drifted off.

Now, though, she lay in her bed. No TV. No books. Just quiet.

CHAPTER THREE

Melissa Robinson moved up the apartment steps, humming quietly to herself. In the distance, she heard the bells from the city. She paused to listen, her smile only widening. She'd been living in Paris for seven years now, yet the sounds never grew stale.

She turned up the next set of steps. No elevators in this apartment. The buildings were too old. *Cultured*, she thought to herself.

She smiled again and took the stairs one at a time. There was no rush. The new arrival she was going to meet had said two o'clock. It was 1:58. Melissa paused at the top of the landing, glancing out the wide window into the city beyond. She hadn't grown up in Paris, but the place was beautiful. She glimpsed the old, yellowed stone structures of buildings older than some countries. She noted the angled pattern of apartments and cafes and crisscrossing streets through the heart of the city.

With another contented sigh, Melissa reached the door on the third floor and politely extended her hand, tapping on the frame. A few moments passed.

No answer.

She continued to smile, still listening to the bells and then glancing back out the window. She could just see the low-peaked steeple of Sainte-Chapelle spiraling against the horizon.

"Amanda," she called out, her voice pleasant.

She remembered the first time she'd come to Paris. It had all seemed overwhelming. Seven years ago, an expat from America, resituating in a new country, a new culture. Knocks on the door had been a welcome distraction at that time. Melissa knew many of her friends in the expat community had a difficult time adjusting to the city. It wasn't always as friendly at first blush, especially not for Americans, or for college-age kids. She remembered her time on an American campus for the first two years. It was as if everyone had wanted to be her friend. In France, people were a bit more reserved. Which, of course, was why she helped organize the group.

Melissa smiled again and tapped on the door once more. "Amanda," she repeated.

Again, there was no response. She hesitated, glancing up and down the hall. She reached into her pocket and fished out her phone. Smartphones were all well and good, but Melissa preferred a bit of an older style. She scanned the old flip phone and noted the time on the front screen. 2:02. She scrolled through the text messages and scanned Amanda's last text.

"I'd be happy to meet you later today. Say, 2pm? Looking forward to the group. It's been hard making friends in the city."

Melissa's smile faltered a bit. She remembered meeting Amanda—a chance encounter in a supermarket. They'd hit it off immediately. The bells seemed to fade in the distance now. On a whim, she reached out and felt for the door handle. She twisted and found that it turned. A click, and the door shifted open just a crack.

Melissa stared.

She would have to make sure Amanda knew about the dangers of leaving her door unlocked downtown. Even in a city like Paris, caution preceded safety. Melissa hesitated for a moment, caught in a crisis of conscience, but then, at last, she eased the door open completely with a gentle prod of her forefinger.

"Hello," she called into the dark apartment. Perhaps Amanda was out shopping. Maybe she'd forgotten the appointment. "Hello, Amanda? It's me, Melissa from the forum..."

No answer.

Melissa didn't consider herself a particularly nosy sort. But when it came to Americans in Paris, she had a sense of kinship. Almost like they belonged to the same family. It didn't feel so much like intruding as checking in on a little sister. She nodded to herself, justifying the decision in her mind before she stepped into the apartment of a woman she'd only met once before.

The door creaked again as her elbow brushed against the frame, causing it to shift open even more. She hesitated and thought she heard voices from down the hall. She popped her head back out and looked up the hallway toward the edge of the stairs.

A young couple moved along the banister, noted her, and instead of nodding or waving, continued on their merry way. Melissa sighed and moved back into the apartment—and then froze. The fridge was open. A strange slant of yellow light extended from the compartment across the kitchen floor.

Amanda was there. Sitting on the floor, facing the opposite wall. Her back was half against the cabinet, one shoulder blade pressed against the wood, the other extending past, her left arm resting on the floor.

"Did you spill something?" Melissa asked, stepping even further into the darkened room.

Wine puddled on the ground beneath Amanda's left arm. Melissa took another few steps and turned to face Amanda, still smiling.

Her smile froze. Amanda's dead eyes stared up at her, gaping over a thick slit in her neck. Cold blood stained the front of her shirt, spilling down to the floor where it had thickened against the linoleum.

Melissa didn't scream, nor did she shout. She merely gasped, her fingers trembling as she struggled to fish out her inhaler. She stumbled toward the door, grabbing her inhaler with one hand and snagging her phone with the other.

After a few puffs of air, she loosed a gurgled groan and, with trembling fingers on her flip phone buttons, she tapped 1-7 for the police.

Still gasping, back against the wall outside the open door to the apartment, she swallowed and waited for the operator to pick up. Behind her, she thought she could hear the vague, fading sound of liquid dripping against the floor.

Only then did she scream.

CHAPTER FOUR

Adele checked her smart watch, cycling through the different screens that kept an eye on her heart rate, movement, music... She inhaled through her nose where she stood in the doorway of her apartment and glanced up at the clock. Four AM exactly. Plenty of time to get in a two-hour run before work. She adjusted the sweatband holding back her hair and glanced over her shoulder toward the sink.

She had left her plastic Mickey Mouse bowl sitting on the metal partition between the sink and the counter. Normally, Adele cleaned up the moment she made a mess. But today, in the small, quiet apartment...

"It can wait," she said to no one in particular. Which, of course, was part of the problem.

Last night had been one of fitful rest, sleep eluding her. Adele stood in the doorway as the digital watch ticked to 4:01. She glanced back at the sink, then muttered beneath her breath and reluctantly strode into the kitchen, grabbed her plastic bowl, and turned on the water with an irritated snap of her wrist. She rinsed out the milky residue in the bottom, placed the bowl in the dryer rack, and headed back toward the door.

Before she could turn the doorknob, though, a quiet chirping sound caught her attention. Adele's eyes darted to the kitchen table. Her phone was vibrating.

She frowned. The only people who would call her this early were her father in Germany, or work.

And she had just spoken to her father a couple of days ago. It was little surprise, then, when she glanced down at the glowing blue green screen depicting a single word in white letters.

Office.

She picked up her phone as the buzzing noise faded. Adele read three simple words in black text flashing across her screen. *Urgent. Come in.*

Adele removed her sweatband and hurried back to her room to change into work clothes. The jog would have to wait.

From the parking lot, through the security checkpoints, Adele only paused once to drop off coffee to Doug, one of her friends on the security team. By the time she reached the fourth floor, and Supervising Agent Grant's office, she could already hear voices through the opaque glass door.

Adele pushed in and pulled up short.

Two large TV monitors set in the wall depicted faces Adele recognized. On the left, over Grant's desk, Executive Foucault, the DGSI supervisor. On the right, situated near a blue-tinted window with a view of the city, Adele spotted Ms. Jayne, a correspondent for Interpol who had first proposed the idea of a joint task force headed up by Adele.

Agent Lee Grant, who'd been named after the two generals in the Civil War, stood behind a metal standing desk, her fingertips steepled beneath her chin, a troubled expression on her face. She glanced up at Adele, waving her in with quick scattered gestures. Agent Grant's office was sparse, with a yoga mat in one corner and a pile of workout DVDs hidden beneath a blue plastic binder next to her desk.

Agent Grant gestured to one of the empty stools in front of her standing desk and waited for Adele to sit. At last, she cleared her throat, regarding Adele with a nod, and said, "They need you back in France."

Adele looked between the TV monitors. Ms. Jayne's and Foucault's gazes were just a bit off, each of them glancing at the various screens at their disposal rather than looking directly into their cameras. Still, Adele couldn't help but search the gaze of Ms. Jayne and the DGSI executive, trying to discern their motives.

"Is it bad?" Adele asked, hesitantly.

Ms. Jayne cleared her throat, and in a clear, crisp voice, said, "Only two victims so far. I'll let Foucault fill you in on the details." Ms. Jayne was an older woman, with bright, intelligent eyes behind horn-rimmed glasses. She had silver hair and was a bit heavier than most field agents. She spoke without an accent, suggesting she'd mastered the English language, but it didn't seem as if it were her native tongue.

On the other screen, Executive Foucault's dark eyes narrowed over a hawk-ish nose; he shook his head and seemed to be glancing down off screen—there was the sound of rummaging papers.

"Yes, yes," he said in heavily accented English. "Two dead. So far. Two Americans," he added, glancing up at the screen. "Or, at least, were Americans."

Adele frowned. "What do you mean?"

Foucault's gaze flitted across the screen one way then the other, not quite lining up with anyone in the room, but suggesting that perhaps he was glancing between portions of his own computer screen.

"Expatriates," he said. "Americans now living in France. Both had visas, but were applying for citizenship, or at least one of the victims did. The other only recently arrived."

Adele nodded to show she'd heard. "So why do you need me?"

Ms. Jayne cleared her throat. Her voice came clear, even through the crackle of the speakers. "We need someone who's familiar with the DGSI, but who America is comfortable investigating their own. The unique nature of the crimes could also use someone with your expertise."

Adele frowned. "What unique nature?"

Foucault replied, "Two dead so far. Throats slit, nearly ear to ear." He adopted a grim tone and continued, "I'll send the files along as soon as I'm cleared by the coroner. Both young women, both recent arrivals. We're investi-gating, of course, and I'm sure our agents will come up with some good leads, but," he frowned again, glancing at his computer screen, "Ms. Jayne seems to think it would be wise to involve you early on. I can't say I fully agree, but it's not my hill to die on."

Adele raised a hand while he spoke, waiting for him to finish. He noticed this, and nodded for her to speak.

"How long between the murders?" she said.

The executive replied without hesitation. "Three days. The killer is quick. It's worth noting there's no physical evidence at the scene."

Adele shifted in her seat, realizing this chair didn't make as much noise as the one back in her kitchen. "What do you mean?"

"I mean there's no physical evidence."

"None?"

Foucault's frown deepened, his bushy eyebrows pressing together. "None at all. No fingerprints, no traces of hair or saliva. No sexual assault that we could find. The cuts alone, according to the coroner's initial report, were strange. Whoever did this slit their necks, but did so without a quavering hand—a practiced motion."

"And what does that mean?" Adele asked.

"If I may," said Agent Grant, speaking for the first time from behind her standing desk, "cuts and slicing wounds carry a sort of signature. Whether the attack was left-handed, or how strong they were, or how tall..."

Foucault nodded with each passing word and cleared his throat. "Exactly. But these particular attacks were done by someone without much signature at all. There's no physical evidence. No sign of a struggle. No forced entry. Nothing suggesting any foul play, except, of course, two corpses in downtown Paris."

"Well," said Ms. Jayne, peering through the screen now. Her eyes seemed to have readjusted for a moment, now fixating firmly on Adele. "Are you ready for your flight?"

Adele flicked her eyes to Agent Grant and raised her eyebrows.

Grant hesitated. "You sure you don't want to spend another couple of weeks with Agent Masse?" she said, her tone betraying no emotion whatsoever.

Adele scowled.

Grant's eyes twinkled in a morbid sort of humor. "I'll take that as a no. Already signed for your leave and reassigned Masse. You're good to go."

Adele tried to suppress the sudden jolt of emotion—she was a professional, after all—but as she pushed from her chair, she couldn't help but feel excitement at the thought of returning to France.

"Is there anything else I should know?" she asked, glancing at Foucault.

"I'll send you the reports," he said with a shrug. "But they're short. As I told you, not much evidence. There is one thing. A strange detail, but certainly important..."

"What?"

"The first victim's kidney was missing."

A strange silence fell over the room for a moment, and the two crackling screens and the two agents in the San Francisco office waited, all of them frowning.

"Her kidney?" said Adele.

"Just so," said Foucault.

"Is the killer taking trophies?"

The executive shrugged, his thick brow narrowing over his sharp nose. "Well, that's what you're here for, isn't it? You provide the answers. It's my job to provide the questions. I'm told Ms. Jayne has already purchased your ticket. First class. Your flight departs within the hour."

CHAPTER FIVE

Adele frowned at her laptop, leaning back in the first-class seat provided to her by Interpol. The plane shuddered as it cut through the sky, but Adele had closed the adjacent blind, allowing the glow from the computer screen to illuminate the cramped portion of airplane cabin.

She found herself twisting the strap to her laptop bag nervously where it rested in the empty seat next to her, surveying the information on the screen again. Once she read a case file, she rarely forgot the details.

She settled in, leaning against the curving white wall of plastic, her eyes flicking from paragraph to photo.

Two dead so far. Three days apart. A rapid pace, even for a serial killer. No physical evidence of any sort. A missing kidney in the first victim and a pending coroner's report for the second. Would she also be missing a kidney?

Young women, both. Expats—Americans now living in France. Recent arrivals, too. Both killed so quickly they hadn't even reacted. That was the only explanation for the clean nature of the cuts. No jagged slices, no signs of a struggle. One moment, the young women had been alive, in their own apartments, the next, seemingly as if by a ghost, they had been snuffed out.

Adele doubted the women had even seen it coming. Not much to go on—not yet anyway. Still, she kept the window blind low, listening to the churn of the engines as they hurtled through the air. Her eyes narrowed as she scanned the case file again and again . . . and again.

She'd been able to connect to the Charles De Gaulle Airport Wi-Fi, and her eyebrows twisted down as she looked at the most recent message from Robert

Henry, her old mentor and friend. It said: *Sorry, dear, I won't be picking you up. They sent another agent.* Then he'd included a series of emojis and smiley faces.

She paused, then typed: *No problem. I'll see you at the office. Who did they send?*

No response. Adele shook her head as she exited the walkway and entered the main terminal, greeted by the odor of overpriced coffee and stale pastries from the airport restaurants. Her eyes flicked along a series of shops; one for curio items, and another a bookstore. Adele pushed her phone back into her pocket, moving quickly through the airport toward baggage claim. Last time, she'd been paired with John—likely it would happen again. But they'd left things awkward after the last visit. While she and Robert had messaged each other every few days in the month since she'd been in France, John hadn't reached out once.

Neither did you, a small voice reminded her.

But she pushed it away with a slight shrug. She reached the baggage claim and watched as the luggage circled the metal slatted conveyor belt; she waited patiently, but still never fully managed to shake the anticipation clotting her chest.

At last, she managed to retrieve her bag, waiting for a space to clear around the claim.

She found herself brushing her hair behind her ears and straightening her outfit even while she approached customs and waited for the border agent to survey her special detail passport and papers. *Get a grip,* she thought scathingly. Why was she so concerned about her appearance all of a sudden? John or not, why did it matter? Adele was taller than most woman, but not unusually so— her long, dirty-blonde hair framed features that hinted of her French-American heritage. Exotic, some said. A single mole stippled the top of her lip, a source of insecurity as a teenager, but no longer.

Adele thought of the last night she'd seen John, swimming in Robert's private pool on his estate. The way John had been at the start of the evening, followed by how he'd behaved toward the end. He had tried to kiss her, hadn't he? Had she misinterpreted the gesture? Whatever the case, when she'd pulled back, he'd been offended. He'd left shortly after.

In defiance to her burbling emotions, Adele messed her hair, intentionally disheveling her bangs. Then, setting her jaw, she wheeled her suitcase through customs and out into the receiving area of the airport.

Her eyes scanned the crowd, looking for the tall, lanky form of her previous French partner. But as her gaze looked over the waiting crowd, there was no sign of John. Her smile—which she hadn't realized was displayed—became rather fixed as her gaze settled on a suited woman standing against the tinted glass of the window facing the streets outside the airport.

Her smile faded completely as she recognized the woman's pursed lips and her silver hair pulled into a bun. The woman resembled a no-nonsense supply teacher, or perhaps a nun out of smock. Not a single strand of hair was out of place, and even the wrinkles along the edge of her eyes seemed to stretch as if attempting to stand to attention.

An agent she'd worked with before . . . But not John.

This particular agent had been Adele's supervisor back when she'd worked for the DGSI. She also had been demoted, an unfortunate scenario whose blame had been placed solely on Adele's shoulders. Every ounce of scorn and impatience displayed itself in every crease and glint in Agent Sophie Paige's eyes, but at last, she raised a hand and gave a quick jerking gesture in Adele's direction.

Not a wave, but more a beckoning call like a master calling their pet hound. Adele stood frozen for a moment, feeling people jostle past her as they moved to greet waiting family or friends. The still air swelled with laughter, the sound of bodies embracing, the quiet murmurings of exhausted travelers retreating from the airport and hurrying with relief toward waiting cabs or cars on the curb.

For the briefest moment, Adele had to resist the urge to turn right around and march back onto the plane, leaving Sophie Paige and her scowl standing by the window.

But at last, she mustered up the residue of her courage, quickly brushed her hair back into place with furtive motions, and moved toward the waiting form of her past supervisor and new partner.

CHAPTER SIX

Removed from the center of Paris, in the northwestern suburbs of the Ile-de-France region of the capital, Adele kept her eyes forward as the car pulled up to the fourth floor of the DGSI parking structure. The afternoon drive had proceeded in complete silence; now, Agent Paige brusquely exited the vehicle, calling something over her shoulder about meeting with Foucault. She left Adele alone to meander her way through security to her old mentor's office.

Stepping into Robert's office was a relief.

Adele could feel her shoulders sagging as if a weight were lifted as she stepped through the door with a quiet knock on the frame. The day's travel weighed heavy, but her spirits lifted as she scanned the familiar room. The walls still carried the same framed pictures of old race cars and beneath them shelves of dusty books with cracked leather covers. Two desks now sat in the room. The second desk had been placed by the window with an upright leather swivel chair behind it. On the desk a small, golden nameplate read, *Adele Sharp.*

Hearing a man clear his throat, she redirected her attention to the first desk and its occupant.

Robert Henry was already standing. He often stood when a woman entered the room. The short man was straight-backed with a long, curling mustache oiled and dyed black. He wore a fine-fitting suit, which Adele guessed had been tailored specifically for him. Robert came from wealth; he didn't need the job at the DGSI, but he enjoyed it. Perhaps this was the reason he had one of the best records at the department. Robert had once played soccer for a semi-professional team in Italy, but had returned to France when he'd been recruited by the French government long before DGSI existed.

The small French man examined Adele for a moment, but his eyes twinkled, betraying the smile which hid behind his lips.

26

"Hello," said Adele, unable to resist a smile of her own.

Robert Henry smirked now, flashing a row of pearly whites missing two teeth. Adele had heard many stories to how he'd lost the teeth, each of them more far-fetched than the other.

They held eye contact across the room, watching each other for a moment.

Then Adele said, "You use too many emojis." Some of her bad temper from earlier began to fade in the face of her old mentor and friend.

Robert sniffed. "I consider it an art form."

"Mhmm," said Adele. "Weren't you the one who told me the advent of cartoons was the death of culture?"

Robert set his shoulders and with a prim wiggle of his chin replied, "A genteel man knows how to admit when he's wrong."

Adele's smirk turned to a good-natured grin. Robert Henry had been like a father to her for many years. Her own father wasn't a fan of affection, but Robert was the sort who went out of his way to make sure Adele felt welcomed and comforted. Robert owned a mansion, but he lived in it alone, and often welcomed the opportunity to have guests. Adele would be staying at his house for her time in France.

"Took you a while," said Robert, glancing at his watch. The glistening silver timepiece looked like the sort of item that might've belonged on a banker's wrist. Robert adjusted his cuff links and nestled the watch beneath the edge of his perfectly pressed sleeve.

Adele leaned her suitcase against the doorframe, placing her laptop bag on the floor. "Whoever scheduled my flight gave me a three-hour layover in London," she said. "Then it took some time getting the car—we had to walk to the other side of the airport. Someone more petty might think she did it on purpose just to frustrate me."

Robert frowned. "She? Who did Foucault pair you with?"

Instead of answering, Adele strode across the room and extended her hands, embracing the smaller man. She wasn't particularly tall, but Robert was still three inches shorter. She hugged her old mentor, and felt a warmth through her chest. He was smaller than she remembered, though. Almost...frail. Though Robert dyed his hair and his mustache, Adele couldn't shake the notion he was aging. She separated from her old friend and smiled again. "We'll be working out of your office, I hear," she said.

Robert patted her on the shoulder in a comforting way. "Yes—that's yours." He nodded to the desk with the name plate.

"You put it by the window. I appreciate that."

"I remember how you liked the view last time you were here," said Robert with a shrug. He lowered his hand and moved back to his own desk chair, emitting a quiet groan as he lowered himself, settling with a soft sigh.

"You all right?" asked Adele.

Robert nodded, waving away any further questions with a dismissive gesture. "Yes, of course. The old bones just don't move like they used to. I'm afraid I won't be in the field with you."

Adele gave a noncommittal nod. "Figured you wouldn't be. We just need someone to keep track of things back here, anyhow."

Robert was no longer smiling. His gaze seemed heavy all of a sudden.

"You're not sick, are you?" Adele blurted out. She wasn't sure where the question came from, but it ushered forth before she could stop it.

Robert smiled and shook his head. "No, not that I'm aware of. But," he tapped his fingers against his desk, and then glanced at the computer screen across from him, "I'm learning how to use it better. Email is hard. But I figured, well, for your sake . . ." He trailed off, glancing at her.

Adele felt a flush of gratitude. She knew how much Robert despised technology. Despite the number of emojis he used in his texting, he'd been stubborn on the advent of computers. Still, she had demanded Interpol allow Robert to be a part of her team. That was the deal she'd made with Ms. Jayne when hashing out the contract.

At the time, she'd heard whispers and rumors that the DGSI was trying to edge Robert out of his position—a mandatory retirement. She felt a flash of frustration. The thought of anyone taking Robert's job was unconscionable. They'd built DGSI's homicide division, in part, with his efforts. He had made a name at other agencies long before the DGSI had even formed, which had attracted many new recruits. Adele respected most of the agents who worked for France's intelligence agencies, but there were none she respected more than Robert. He was clever in an intuitive sort of way, and he was rarely wrong. The last case in Paris, he'd insisted the killer had natural red hair, and he'd noted the vanity of it. She hadn't been sure, but in the end, it had proven an accurate deduction.

Still, she remembered her interactions with Executive Foucault. The frown on his face when she requested Robert's help. The agency was trying to whittle back personnel. Now, though, with his help on the Interpol attaché, she'd tied Foucault's hands.

"I need you," she said, simply. "You're the best at what you do."

Robert shook his head, sighing as he did. "I don't know if that's true, dear," he said, his voice creaking all of a sudden.

"It is. Don't worry about the computers; you'll figure it out. I'm sure. We just need someone to touch base with, to coordinate from back here. I wouldn't want anyone else."

Robert nodded again, his expression still glum. "I'm old, Adele. I know I might not look it." He ran his hand through his clearly dyed hair. "But this agency, this place, I think it's for the younger folk now."

Adele's brow dipped. "Why are you saying these things?"

Robert waved a hand. "It's not important. I'm grateful. Likely, if you hadn't asked for me, I would've been out of the agency within the week."

Now Adele's frown turned to a scowl. "You heard that? Did someone say they were trying to get rid of you?"

Robert just shook his head. "I am an investigator. I'm not meant to be stuck behind a desk. Sometimes you just know these things."

"You're thinking too much. You're invaluable—trust me. And besides, if you go, then I go."

Robert smiled at this comment and tapped his fingers together. "Fair enough. Computers aren't my forte, but I'll try my best. But you still haven't said, who did the executive pair you with? John?" His eyebrows flicked up ever so slightly. A small glimmer of a smile edged the corner of his lips, but Adele shook her head, quieting his expression.

"Agent Paige," she said with the gravity of a judge's gavel.

Robert stared at her.

She shrugged.

He continued to stare.

"I didn't ask for it," she said.

"Sophie Paige?"

Adele glanced back out the door, checking that the hall was clear, then nodded. "Looks like. She was about as happy as I was."

29

"Doesn't Foucault know your history?" said Robert, his voice rising.

"It's fine," Adele replied in a hushing voice. "I don't know what the executive does or doesn't know. But it is what it is."

"And what about John?" Robert demanded.

Adele waved a hand airily, as if the thought hadn't really crossed her mind. "You mean Agent Renee? Well, I think he's working another case. That's what Paige said."

Robert's manicured eyebrows hung low over his eyes like dark clouds threatening a storm. "Paige," he said with a grunt. "Now I know why Foucault didn't tell me."

Adele hesitated. There was something in his tone she couldn't quite place. "What do you mean?"

Robert was still frowning at his fingers, though, and Adele had to repeat the question. His eyes darted up at last. "Oh, I mean, nothing, or—except, he knows how I feel about you. And Paige hasn't exactly been the warmest towards you since the incident."

Adele paused, studying her old mentor. She knew Robert would take her side. But there'd been something more to his tone. Something behind his frown that she didn't quite understand. "Have you had words with Paige since I left?" she asked, slowly.

"Words? No." He trailed off as if preparing to add more, but then he seemed to decide against it and gave a quick shake of his head, latching his fingers together and folding his thumbs on top of each other. "No, nothing like that. I'm sure both of you can be professional though, yes?"

Adele shrugged. "I can if she can."

"*Magnifique*," he said. "I hope you slept on the plane, though. Foucault wanted to meet the moment you landed."

Adele nodded, her lips pressed firmly together. "Agent Paige is already in his office," she said. "We're to start right away?"

Her old mentor nodded as he pushed out of his chair and moved with stiff motions around the edge of his desk. "Leave your suitcase here," he said. "I'll send someone to take it to my home. Come now."

Robert took her by the arm, looping her hand through the crook of his elbow, and escorted her to the elevator. Robert was old-fashioned, and there were some who thought of him as pompous. But to Adele, his behavior only summoned a fond amusement.

They waited for the quiet ding of the elevator and stepped into the compartment. For the briefest moment, Adele's finger hovered over the button for the second floor—John's office would be there. Was he in? No—now wasn't the time. There wasn't a gap of three weeks between kills like the last time. Three days. That's all that had passed between the killings. A rapid, startling pace. A pace that might only get worse.

Adele pressed the button for the top floor and, with Robert next to her still holding her elbow, she waited as the elevator carried them up and toward the office of the executive.

Paige sat by the window, a familiar comfort in the way she reclined in the office chair. Executive Foucault himself peered out from beneath a hawk-like brow, gnawing on one corner of his lip and shaking his head.

Adele and Robert stood, waiting, watching. Foucault's eyes fixed on his computer screen and his expression only darkened. "This is it?" he asked, glancing up. "Nothing new?" His eyes darted to Agent Paige, whose own gaze bounced to Adele as if redirecting the executive's ire.

Adele hesitated. Sunlight streamed through the open window of the executive's large office—the gusting air ushered out some of the scent of cigarette smoke, but the odor still clung to the walls.

"I just arrived," Adele said, hesitantly, unsure if she was being blamed for something. "I was planning to settle at Robert's . . ." She trailed off at the look on Foucault's face and then cleared her throat. "Honestly, I slept on the plane. We can start this afternoon. I'd like to see the crime scene of the second victim."

Foucault nodded, waving a hand. "Yes," he said, his thick eyebrows narrowed over his dark eyes. "That would be best. We don't have time to wait on this one, hmm? No." He nodded toward Paige. "You two have worked together before, yes?"

Paige continued to sit in silence by the window. She nodded once. Adele also nodded.

After a few moments of awkward silence, Robert intervened, clearing his throat. "A strange one, this," he said, quietly.

Adele kept her eyes fixed on Foucault, but nodded in agreement.

Robert grunted as the attention in the room shifted from Adele to him. "The victims must have known the killer," he said. "A friend? Maybe a family member?"

Adele turned her face slightly, rolling her head against her shoulders. "Maybe. Or maybe the killer snuck up on them. A landlord? With a key?"

Robert hesitated for a moment and silence reigned once more. At last, he said, "What do you make of the missing kidney?"

"You've been over the files?"

"Second report isn't in yet." Robert paused, inclining an eyebrow toward Foucault in question.

The executive nodded. "They're working on it, but it's taking some time. Full report should be in soon."

Robert nodded and this time addressed Foucault, moving across the room to peer through the open window into the street below. A small, pink-painted cafe occupied the street across from the DGSI.

"I did read the first report," he said. "Only the kidney missing. Why do you think that is?"

Paige and Foucault both stayed silent. But Adele glanced across the room toward her mentor, watching the way the afternoon sunlight illuminated the side of his face and cast shadows against the carpeted floor.

"Trophy collecting?" she said.

"Perhaps," said Robert. "Makes sense."

"What else?"

Robert shrugged and his gaze snapped to Foucault behind his desk.

The executive's frown deepened. "That's what you're paid to find out," he said. His eyes darted between the three agents and he reached out, patting the side of his computer. "We need more information, and you don't have much time to provide it."

Adele noted the quick way in which *we* became *you*. She paused, then said, quietly, "I've been thinking about the victims. Both of them expats, yes? Growing up, I had some experience with that community—not much, as my mother was local. But some American friends at school whose parents relocated for work."

She paused. "They're a vulnerable community. Isolated a lot of times—barriers in language and culture. Perhaps the killer is using this to get close to them. Exploiting loneliness or a pressure to please the host country."

Foucault took this with a nod and shrug. "Explore all possibilities," he said. "Just," he paused, "don't make it personal." He turned from Adele. "Agent Henry, you'll be staying here, I presume?" Foucault's gaze flicked to the smaller man.

Robert rubbed his mustache. "I'll leave the field work to the youngsters, I think."

Foucault returned his attention to Adele. "Second crime scene?" he said. "It's still under our supervision."

"I'm ready to start if she isn't too tired," Paige said, speaking for the first time since they'd entered the room. The comment seemed innocent enough, but something about it raised Adele's hackles.

Now that the attention was once again on her, Adele inhaled softly.

Americans in France, expats—she felt a kinship with them; a camaraderie. Adele knew what it was to move from country to country, to reestablish roots, to build a life once more.

But these lives had been built only to end with bloodstains on the floor of their apartments. No physical evidence. No sign of a struggle. No sign of breaking or entering.

Now wasn't the time for rest.

"I'm ready when you are," said Adele, already turning toward the door.

CHAPTER SEVEN

Adele ground her teeth in frustration, tapping her fingers impatiently against the woodwork of the door frame that led into the apartment. She glanced at her watch for the tenth time in the last thirty minutes and her eyebrows lowered even further over her eyes, darkening her countenance as a flash of impatience jolted through her.

"Christ," Adele muttered. She frowned as she glanced up and down the street, tracking the flow of vehicles. She kept trying to spot any government issues, but found her attention drawn only to the loaner she'd parked against the curb by the empty meter. It was still afternoon, with the sun high in the sky, dipping only slightly in the horizon.

Adele and Sophie had taken separate vehicles, as Adele would be heading to Robert's straight from the crime scene.

She leaned against the railing leading up the concrete steps and turned back toward the front door of the apartment. For a moment, she considered entering on her own. But generally, protocol dictated two agents were required on scene in tandem. On her first day back on the job in France, Adele didn't want to stretch boundaries. Still, Agent Paige was making it difficult. Already, she was nearly thirty minutes late.

Adele let out a low growl. She'd made arrangements with Robert to take her luggage to his house, and then driven straight to the crime scene. The drive had taken twenty minutes. Paris was one of the few cities with next to no stop signs. It was rumored there was one stop sign, somewhere; Agent Paige must have found it and not known how to proceed.

Nothing else explained why Adele had been waiting on Paige for half an hour.

34

She glanced along the street, toward the gap between the blocks of buildings. She swallowed, staring toward the open path across the street, with hints of green hidden within. Something she loved about Paris had been the little passages and hidden gardens ready to be explored as if through some labyrinth crisscrossing the hunched buildings. The French had a special word for those who walked aimlessly, enjoying the side roads and gardens: *la flânerie*. Adele couldn't remember the last time she'd relaxed enough to walk aimlessly. And now certainly wasn't the time.

With a final puffing breath of frustration, Adele turned to the doors and moved to buzz the bottom button marked *Landlord*. He'd been instructed to let her in. With or without Paige, Adele was determined to see the crime scene of the second victim.

Before she could push the buzzer, though, there was a quiet screech of tires. Adele glanced over her shoulder and spotted a second SUV with black tinted windows parking behind her own vehicle. Agent Paige's silver hair appeared over the top of the doorframe as she exited the driver's seat, taking her sweet time about it. The older agent paused on the curb, then snapped her fingers as if realizing something, turned back to her car, opened the door, and began rummaging around inside.

Adele stared; it took nearly a minute before Paige found whatever she'd been looking for, and then once more, at a snail's pace, began to move toward the stairs to the apartment. She gave a noncommittal grunt in Adele's direction.

Adele suppressed her temper. She would have to work with Paige for the duration of the case, and starting off on the wrong foot wouldn't help anything. But it almost seemed like her assigned partner was intentionally dragging her feet on this one.

"I thought we agreed to come straight here," said Adele, trying to keep her tone neutral.

Paige shot Adele a long look out of the corner of her eye. "Yeah? I'm not usually in a hurry to waste my time. The crime scene monkeys have already been over this. Not sure why we're here."

Adele turned fully now, looking away from the apartment doors and the buzzers to face her partner. "We're here," she said, gritting her teeth, "because I want to examine the crime scene myself. Is that all right with you?"

Paige picked at her fingernails, flicking whatever she found onto the sidewalk. "You're not going to discover anything new."

"Maybe not, or maybe so."

Adele could smell Agent Paige's perfume, though to call it perfume would have been a stretch. Her partner smelled of soap; not scented soap, but rather a sort of plain cleansing odor that hearkened of hygiene and simplicity. Agent Paige wore no earrings, nor jewelry of any kind. She had a strong profile with a roman nose and sharp cheekbones. Adele remembered her first year at the DGSI, working under a taskforce with Agent Paige—she'd been intimidated by the older woman then, and, judging by the twisting swirling in her gut, the sensation hadn't faded.

Adele had never visited Sophie's family, but she knew from discussions with other agents that Paige had five children of her own, all of them adopted. And yet, in Adele's experience, she'd never seen the woman miss a day of work. It had taken some digging, when she'd been at the DGSI, but by the sound of things, Agent Paige's husband stayed at home, taking care of the kids while his wife worked long hours for the government.

Paige returned Adele's look of annoyance, and in answer, Adele reached out and slammed her thumb on the buzzer for the landlord. It took a moment, then the doors buzzed. Sophie pushed open the front door, moved in, and allowed it to swing shut behind her.

Adele had to hurry forward to jam her foot in the gap, catching it before it closed fully.

Adele stared in frustration at the back of the older agent's head. Again, not a single hair was out of place. Paige's clothing was neatly pressed, her suit jacket a charcoal gray, matching her pants.

Adele had never particularly enjoyed her old supervisor's company. The last time she'd interacted with the woman, on the previous case in France, Paige had caused trouble.

"Excuse me," said Adele, keeping her voice low, "do we need to talk?"

Paige acted like she hadn't heard, though, and continued toward the stairs.

Adele took a few hurried steps to catch up with the older woman, and she reached out, gently placing a hand on the other agent's forearm. As if she'd been scalded, Paige whirled around, a snarl on her lips. "Don't touch me!" she snapped.

Adele's eyes flicked to the woman's holster beneath her parted jacket. She lifted her hand, raising it in a placating gesture. "Apologies."

"What do you want?" Paige said, scowling. "We're doing it your way, aren't we? We're here wasting time instead of talking to witnesses."

"What witnesses?" Adele said, biting back further retort.

"The American. The one who found the body."

Adele shook her head. "She found the victim, but she didn't *see* anything."

Paige pursed her lips. "It would be a better use of our time than going over an empty crime scene. You read the report, didn't you? No physical evidence. There's nothing for us here."

Adele huffed, shaking her head. She reached out as if to steady herself, gripping the wooden banister of the railing that led up the apartment steps.

She could hear the jingle of keys and the sound of footsteps approaching as the landlord made his way across the hall. She glanced past her partner, over the banister and through the wooden rails, to spot an old, bald man with a bit of a paunch and a stained sweater moving toward them.

Adele lowered her voice, trying to keep calm as she said, "You can contact the officers with the American. They're on standby. Tell them to bring her here, if you want. We'll interview her after; better here than the station, anyway."

"Fine," said Paige. "Maybe I will." She reached for her phone and fiddled with it for a moment.

Adele waited as the landlord approached, hoping this was the last heated exchange for the moment. It wouldn't do to look unprofessional in the face of public speculation.

The landlord glanced between the two women, seemingly ignorant of the bad blood. He adopted a simpering, oily smile and said, "I can show you to the room." He paused for a moment, his smile still stretching his lips like taffy. "Just out of curiosity..." He paused, as if waiting a rehearsed number of seconds. Then he said, "When will I be able to rent out the apartment? There are bills to pay—"

"I'm Agent Sharp," Adele interrupted. She studied the man. "This is Agent Paige." She reached into her pocket and flashed her badge, as well as the Interpol credentials Robert had given her.

The landlord waved them away without glancing toward either ID. Paige was still glancing at her phone, ignoring the man.

"I can show you," he repeated.

Adele gestured with a hand up the stairs and allowed the landlord to take the lead, following him at a slow pace as he breathed heavily, moving up the stairs one at a time. When they reached the third-floor landing, he clicked the keys into the lock and twisted, pushing the door open. Adele examined the keys, then glanced at the back of the landlord. "You didn't enter the apartment a couple of days ago, did you?"

The landlord regarded her, and then after a moment, his face adopted a horrified expression. He immediately began shaking his head wildly, causing his jowls to jiggle. "No," he insisted. "Certainly not. I never enter the apartments. The keys are just for emergencies."

Adele raised her hands. "Does anyone else have access to a set of keys?"

The landlord shook his head firmly. "Only the apartment tenant. And myself. And I don't use them," he repeated.

Adele nodded to show she'd heard, watching as the man pushed open the apartment door and stepped aside, gesturing for the two agents to enter.

The agents ducked under the crime scene tape crisscrossing the door. Adele moved onward and glanced at the tile floor.

Already, most the blood had been cleaned up. Photographic evidence had been taken of the scene, and previous investigators had come through to catalog everything. Adele glanced around the kitchen; she noted a few stains of blood against the cabinet next to the fridge, as well as along the tile floor. She moved over the stains and glanced at the fridge. It was closed now.

Besides the closed fridge door and the missing stain, the crime scene looked exactly the same as the photos. The body had long since been taken to the coroner, and the final report would be forthcoming soon enough.

She hated to admit it, but there wasn't much to be seen. No physical evidence. Just liked she'd been told.

They'd already dusted and scanned for fingerprints all along the counters, the fridge, the body. And still, nothing had shown up. Nothing besides the victim's own fingerprints.

The second victim had been found with her back against the cabinets, facing the fridge. This meant whoever had attacked her had done so quickly. There had been a bit of blood spatter, but not much. There'd been no signs of defensive wounds on the body. No struggle whatsoever.

"Do you think she knew the killer?" Adele asked, quietly.

Agent Paige said, "Maybe."

Adele stepped daintily over the faded pool of blood. She walked to the fridge, and, using her pocket to sheathe her hand, she grabbed the handle and pulled it open. There were still groceries in the fridge. Old sandwiches rested in the crisper, and a large jug of milk sat nestled next to a dozen eggs. Otherwise, the fridge was mostly bare. Adele regarded the cabinets where the woman had been found, sitting on the floor in a pool of her own blood.

She examined the wooden block of steak knives next to the sink. All the knives were accounted for. They'd been scanned for blood and cleared. The killer had taken his weapon with him. They still didn't even know what he had used to kill the woman.

Adele reached up, opening the freezer. There were two trays of ice, a tub of ice cream, and some frozen pizzas. The ice cream container was stained with melted, then refrozen, streaks on the side, and one of the trays of ice was completely empty. Adele pursed her lips; it was a personal pet peeve, but she hated when people put empty ice trays back in the freezer. She glanced at the ice cream container, and then her eyes flitted to the frozen pizzas. Cauliflower. She wrinkled her nose, but felt a sudden flush of embarrassment as she studied the food.

What had she been expecting to find?

She eased the freezer door shut and turned back to survey the room. There was no indeed physical evidence. She regarded the sink and noted a slow drip. She moved over and twisted one of the handles. The drip continued, one droplet at a time. *Tap, tap.* Droplets struck the metal basin.

"Is the witness coming?" Adele said, glancing over at Paige.

The older woman was still watching the skyline through the window. She grunted, "On her way."

Adele cleared her throat. "What was her name again?"

"Melissa Robinson. Also American—she found the body."

Adele set her lips. "How do you think we should approach questioning?"

Agent Paige shrugged again. "You're the Interpol operative. I'm just here following your lead. Do what you want."

Adele hesitated, staring across the crime scene. She nodded once, then, in as diplomatic a tone as she could summon, she said, "I think we need to have a chat."

Paige finally looked away from the window and raised a silver eyebrow.

Adele approached carefully, coming to stand in front of the older woman, though part of her wanted to hide in the corner of the room. The scent of soap was even stronger than before as she met her partner's gaze. "This doesn't have to be painful, but I have a feeling you're not putting in as much effort as you could."

Paige betrayed no expression for a moment. At last, she shrugged and said, "I'm not in charge of your feelings. Maybe you should do a better job controlling them."

Adele stared at the older woman. "I don't believe this is helpful."

"The number of things you're unable to believe isn't my business," Paige said coolly. She carried the attitude of someone delighting in the frustration of another. Adele's mounting temper seemed only to further fuel Paige's enjoyment.

"I didn't know it was you," Adele blurted out at last.

Agent Paige's expression became fixed.

Adele glanced back toward the door, and was glad to see the frame empty, suggesting the landlord was further down the hall. She lowered her voice all the same and said, "I didn't know. I just saw someone had moved one of the accounting documents out of evidence. I thought it was a clerical error. When I reported it to Foucault, I had no clue—"

"Stop," Paige snapped, gritting her teeth.

The quiet, quizzical expression of complacency had faded now, like ice melting over a pool, revealing the boiling anger beneath.

"I'm serious," Adele said, "if I had known—"

"You did what you did." Paige was scowling now. Her hands, at her sides, trembled against her gray suit. "They demoted me. I'm lucky I still have my job. Matthew was arrested. They questioned him for nearly a week!"

Adele winced. "I'm sorry. All I saw was missing evidence. I didn't know—"

"God damn what you don't know," Agent Paige snapped. She slammed her finger into Adele's chest, pushing sharply against the younger woman. "You should have come to me. I was your supervisor! You went behind my back, like a little rat."

Adele stepped back, reaching up and rubbing at her chest, wondering if she'd find a bruise come morning. She shook her head and said, "You moved evidence to protect your boyfriend. I didn't know what had happened. I didn't even know you were dating a suspect—"

"He wasn't a suspect when we started," Paige snapped, but then trailed off, biting the words with a snarl. "It's none of your fucking business who I date, understand? And they cleared him. He didn't do it."

Adele nodded, trying to keep her posture nonthreatening. "Good. I'm glad. I didn't know that at the time. All I knew was that someone had moved evidence. If I had known it was you, I would have talked to you. I definitely would have. You didn't tell me, though. I just saw it missing—"

Sophie snorted and waved a hand at Adele. "Not everything has to be catered toward precious little Adele," Paige snapped. "Not everything is about you."

Adele ground her teeth, and she wanted to protest further, but the words wouldn't come. The situation had been a bad one. Agent Paige had been lucky to keep her job. Her relationship with Matthew, an accountant with the DGSI, hadn't been public knowledge at the time. Adele hadn't known her supervisor was dating a suspect in the death of a prostitute. In the end, Matthew had been cleared. But Paige had blamed Adele for reporting the missing evidence. It had turned out Paige was trying to cover for her boyfriend; in the end, though, it had come to light that Matthew had been sleeping with the prostitute. Adele suspected Paige hadn't known this when she'd hidden receipts and documents suggesting Matthew's involvement.

Adele had seen the evidence missing, though, and had immediately reported the vanished files. After that, Sophie Paige had been investigated as well as Matthew. Her boyfriend had been cleared of murder charges, but had been fired from the DGSI. Paige would have been fired, but Foucault—for some reason Adele didn't understand—had gone to bat for her and kept her on, demoting her in the process.

"I don't like you," Paige said, simply, all pretenses gone now, her expression once more a scowling, stony one. "I'm not ever going to like you. I didn't ask for this assignment. I have to bear it. As do you. Now how about you stop wasting my time by dragging me to crime scenes that have already been investigated? Did you find anything new?" she demanded.

Adele hesitated, glancing back toward the kitchen; she was loath to admit she hadn't. So instead, she said, "When's the witness coming?"

"You're insufferable," Sophie snapped. She turned back to the window and stared out into the city. Adele, her hands trembling from anger, moved to the door and into the hallway, preferring to wait outside for the witness to arrive, rather than spend another moment with Agent Paige.

CHAPTER EIGHT

Adele was startled from her reverie by an officer in uniform tapping her shoulder. She glanced back, turning from the window in the hallway outside the victim's apartment.

"Excuse me," the officer said, quietly.

Adele raised an eyebrow to show she'd heard.

The officer cleared his throat and smoothed his mustache. "The witness refuses to come inside. She says she'd rather talk on the sidewalk. Is that all right?"

Adele glanced at the man, then toward the open door to the apartment. For a brief moment, she was tempted to leave Agent Paige and go talk to Ms. Robinson on her own. But at last, she sighed and nodded. She pointed toward the open door. "Would you mind telling my partner?"

The police officer nodded once, then circled the banister, heading for the door. He gave a polite wave toward where the landlord still waited at the end of the hall, keys in hand. For all Adele cared, he could wait all day. They wouldn't be renting out the place anytime soon. Not yet at least.

She moved back down the stairs, taking them two at a time, hoping to have a couple of moments to speak with the witness without Agent Paige's presence clouding her thoughts.

She reached the ground floor, pushed open the door to the apartment building, and noticed a third car, this time a police vehicle, waiting at the curb. Adele glanced at the front of the vehicle, where a second officer sat on the hood. She had a cigarette in her hand and looked to be lighting it, but when she spotted Adele, she quickly tucked her lighter back in her pocket and flicked the cigarette toward the grate beneath the car's front wheel.

The officer pushed off the hood just as quickly and nodded toward the back seat of the vehicle.

"She refuses to get out," the officer said. "I can make her, if you'd like—"

"Of course not," Adele retorted. "She's not a suspect." She moved toward the rear of the vehicle and peered inside. A dimple-faced young woman with curly brown hair sat in the back. She couldn't have been older than Adele. Perhaps early thirties.

Adele tapped on the door and looked toward the officer expectantly. The officer waved apologetically and then reached into her pocket and clicked her key.

The police car lights flickered; there was a quiet *ticking* sound of the locks. Adele tugged on the handle and opened the door. She peered inside the cabin, ducking low and meeting the eyes of the American woman.

"You're Melissa Robinson?" she asked.

The curly-haired woman nodded once. "Yes, I am," she replied in accented French.

"English or French?" Adele said. The woman hesitated, frowning, and began to speak, but Adele interrupted and said, "How about English? Easier for both of us I'd imagine."

The seamless way Adele switched from nearly perfect French to flawless English seemed to take the woman with the curly hair back a bit. "Are you—" she began.

Adele said, "On assignment. It's a long story." Normally people didn't understand what it was to be American, German, and French. The idea of having three citizenships was lost on most and Adele didn't want to get into it.

She heard footsteps behind her, and with a weary collapse of her shoulders, she glanced back to notice Paige approaching, glaring in her direction.

Adele returned her attention to the police vehicle once more. She still didn't enter the vehicle, figuring it might be perceived as threatening, so instead she leaned forward, her arms pressed on the top of the door, in a sort of sheltering posture, hoping the way she positioned herself would communicate protectiveness to the woman within.

Adele cleared her throat and said, "I'm very sorry you had to come back here, and I'm sorry that we wanted to bring you back upstairs. That was my oversight."

Melissa Robinson nodded, smiling in a small, sad way as if accepting the apology. Adele felt a bit of weight lift from her chest at the American's expression as she continued, "But I was wondering if perhaps you could tell me anything about the victim. Her name was Amanda, is that right?"

"Yes," Melissa said, her voice quavering.

Adele continued to lean in, but she could now hear more footsteps, and could feel Agent Paige coming even closer.

Melissa's gaze flicked from Adele, over her shoulder toward the approaching agent.

"You mind giving us a moment?" Adele said, tight-lipped, to her partner.

Agent Paige leaned against the front of the vehicle, though, peering into the back without greeting the witness. "Go right ahead," she said. Paige made no move to leave. The two officers watched the agents, but stayed where they were on the sidewalk.

With a frustrated sigh, Adele turned back, keeping her expression as pleasant as possible. "Is there anything else you might be able to tell us about Amanda?"

Melissa shook her head almost immediately. "Nothing," she said, stammering a bit. "I barely knew her. We were going to meet for the second time today."

Adele frowned. "Today?"

"I'm sorry, I mean yesterday. It's been rough ... Yesterday, early on, before she ... when she died." The woman shook her head again, wincing, and she glanced back through the window, up toward the third floor of the apartment building.

"I'm very sorry to hear that," said Adele. "But do you mind helping me out; what do you mean you were going to meet yesterday?"

"I mean," said the woman, "that we met at a supermarket briefly, but for the most part only ever spoke online."

"Online?" said Paige, gruffly, leaning past Adele and shouldering her out of the way so she could peer into the back seat. "What do you mean online?"

Melissa glanced between the two women. "I mean on the Internet. We have a chat room for expats from America. She wanted to meet up; it can be lonely sometimes in a new country if you don't know anyone."

"There are a lot of you here?" Agent Paige said. Adele didn't like the disapproving tone in her partner's voice. Paige issued a soft snort of air, but she kept herself mostly in check. "Don't like the home country, is that it?"

Melissa fidgeted uncomfortably, twisting the seatbelt in her hands. She still had it attached, even though the car was parked. Adele didn't blame her; sometimes people latched onto anything for a feeling of safety.

The woman shifted again and seemed unsure whom she ought to address. At last, she settled on looking at Adele. "We don't dislike our country. At least, not all of us. Not really. There are a lot of reasons someone might move away. Culture, changing jobs. I can't tell you how many hours most of us had to work back home. Sometimes it feels like in America you just live to work. In France, it feels like there is more of a life. Plus there are so many different people you can meet; a common history and architectural beauty..." She trailed off, shaking her head slightly. "I'm sorry, I'm rambling. Don't get me wrong; I do like America too, sometimes," she added quickly. "But everyone has their priorities and tastes. Some people love to travel. Some people want to start over. I can't imagine it's that strange."

Adele shook her head. "It isn't," she said, "but you said you met Amanda briefly before. How?"

Melissa brightened at this. "I... I met her while shopping. We..." She hesitated, her tone slipping. And she swallowed. "We met in a checkout line at Le Grande Epicerie de Paris..."

"The grocery store?" Adele asked.

Melissa's eyes were sad, but a bit of humor crept into her tone as she said, "It's—it's a bit of a joke among our community. The USA section at the store only carries things like peanut butter cups, popcorn, beef jerky—a funny interpretation of what Paris believes are the staples back home..." Melissa hesitated, then shrugged. "It's not uncommon for Americans to shop there. Some of us find it ironic; others..."

"Like the peanut butter cups and beef jerky?"

Both women smiled. But Melissa's faded first. "I'm one of the moderators of our online community. I heard Amanda checking out, speaking to a friend in English. I'm-I'm the one"—her voice cracked, but she pushed through—"who invited her to our group."

"Moderator?" Agent Paige said.

"She keeps the community running," Adele replied quickly, then looked back at Melissa.

Melissa interjected. "I'm one of ten. There are quite a few moderators. I don't usually deal with new members, but Amanda was ... she seemed so friendly."

Adele nodded sympathetically and allowed an appropriate amount of time to pass before asking, "Is there anything else you can tell us about her?"

The woman shook her head. "I'm afraid not."

"The victim had a strange injury," Agent Paige said, carefully. "Do you know ..." She hesitated, as if trying to find a delicate way to put it, but then shrugged and continued, "... why her kidney was missing?"

Melissa's eyes widened in horror, and she stared past Adele now, transfixed by the older agent. Melissa stammered and shook her head, but she turned away again, staring out the window. This time, she didn't turn back.

Adele exhaled deeply, but then waved at the two police officers, gesturing back toward the vehicle. She stepped from the street onto the curb and called out, "Thank you for your time, Ms. Robinson."

Agent Paige followed after her. Muttering beneath her breath, and stepping up the sidewalk, Adele whispered, "What's wrong with you?"

Paige frowned. "Careful who you're talking to."

"Are you trying to scare our witness?"

"No, I was asking a valid question. I waited until the end of the interrogation."

"She's not a suspect." Adele glanced toward the figure in the back of the police car once more and tried to suppress her frown. "It wasn't an interrogation. We were questioning a witness."

"Be that as it may, I waited until the end of the questions to ask her. It's an important point. We still don't know why the kidneys are missing."

Adele couldn't disagree with this, but she still felt a sense of frustration. At her partner's comment, though, her eyes widened. "Wait, what do you mean *kidneys*? More than one? I thought only one kidney was missing."

Agent Paige looked at her fingernails. "Yes, one. But also from the second victim."

Wait," Adele said. "*Both* of them were missing a kidney? How come I wasn't told this sooner? When did you find out?"

Agent Paige waved airily. "I just received the call a few minutes ago. I wonder why they called me instead of you." Adele glared at her, and Agent Paige shrugged and began to move back toward her vehicle. "We should check back at headquarters and see if we can get the social media platform to release the information about this expat group."

Adele continued to stare at her partner. "Were you even planning to tell me about the second kidney if I hadn't asked?"

Paige was already opening the driver's door of her car. "I'm telling you now. They emailed the report. I'll send it along in a minute."

Adele braced herself, shaking her head. The two police officers were already getting back into their vehicle, preparing to take Amanda back home. Adele stood between the police vehicles and the old apartment building. It was starting to feel like she was in over her head. The killer was still out there. He killed at a three-day pace. That meant he could strike again within the next forty-eight hours.

She shivered at the thought and tried to avoid looking in Agent Paige's direction. The sight of the older woman only set her blood boiling.

Still, perhaps Paige was right about one thing. They needed to talk with the online forum service provider to figure out if they could get information about the users. Adele wondered about the reasons why Americans were coming to France. Amanda had been polite about her thoughts of America, but perhaps there were others who weren't so fond of their home country.

Did that have something to do with it? Maybe the motive for why the two victims had left American to come to France would be a connecting point. Adele watched the two vehicles pull from the curb; first Agent Paige's SUV, and then the police car.

Still frowning to herself, Adele moved back over to her own vehicle. She felt her phone chirp, and glanced down as she slid into the front seat. An email attachment had been sent by Paige.

Adele wondered again if Paige was intentionally going out of her way to sabotage the investigation. But of course, if Adele went to complain to Foucault, she would never hear the end of it. She couldn't afford to make an even greater enemy out of Paige. Right now, it was a matter of petty nuisance and annoyance, but further escalation could prove dangerous.

Vaguely, Adele wondered how that woman had five adopted kids and a husband. She seemed insufferable.

She sighed through her nose, opened the email attachment, and began to scan the reports. They would have to send a request to Foucault to get permission to approach the social media company for information on the expat forum. Right now, it felt like a race against the clock. What tied these two victims together? Why were they both missing kidneys?

Adele examined the photos and felt a shiver up her arms. The cuts had been small; the incisions clean. They'd been done hurriedly, though. On both victims, the incisions were matching.

Adele texted Robert: *Meet you at the office. Something came up—housewarming will have to wait.* She lowered her phone, tossing it over onto the passenger seat, then buckled up, put the keys in the ignition, and set the car in gear, pulling away from the curb and heading back toward the DGSI headquarters. Questions swirled through her mind, and the sense of urgency pressed on her like a cloud.

With matching incisions, it meant it was the same killer, then. There had still been a possibility it wasn't serial. But now, that notion seemed far-fetched. It was the same person killing these women. The only question was why? For pleasure or compulsion? Or some other reason? And when would they kill again?

CHAPTER NINE

Shiloah Watkins stood by the door to her new apartment, adjusting the security chain. She felt a buzz in her pocket and sighed, pressing her hand against the rectangular form of her phone. She didn't need to check to guess it was her mother texting for the millionth time about the two murders in the city. An entire ocean separated them now, but her mother only seemed *more* interested in Shiloah's business. An echo of her mother's voice nagged in her head, and Shiloah checked the locks again, then turned away from the door and moved through the small hallway in the direction of her bedroom.

She paused by the bathroom door and glanced in, noting her towel had fallen and was now bunched up beneath the rack. She muttered softly to herself and approached the towel, lifted it, and hung it again.

The shower itself was notably devoid of shampoos, and only had a single, whittled yellow bar of soap.

She'd only been in France for a few days now and had yet to muster the courage to go grocery shopping. Shiloah reached up and tugged at her hair, she emitting a grunt of disgust as her fingers rubbed against the grainy texture.

It was a scary thing, coming to France. She'd only graduated with a bachelor's in linguistics two months before. Now, she'd be working as an English tutor.

Shiloah moved away from the towel rack and over to the sink, peering into the mirror and studying her expression. She had always possessed a fondness for France—ever since a study-abroad program two years ago. Now, she hoped to live here permanently.

Shiloah heard a quiet buzzing from her pocket and reached down, pulling her phone out. As she'd expected, there were three missed calls from her mother.

She resisted the urge to roll her eyes, but then noticed another red number next to a blue blip on the screen. She frowned. The messenger app displayed a notification from the Yankees in Paris.

It was a silly title for a group, but a couple of blogs she'd read—in preparation for *the big move*—had suggested the online community as a way to make connections in the new city.

Shiloah scanned the group and noticed a message from one of the moderators. They'd accepted her application to the group. There would be a get-together sometime in the next week.

It took her a moment to translate the message. A lot of them could speak English perfectly well as they were from America for the most part, but preferred to communicate in French to help acclimate new members. Shiloah struggled with a couple of the words, but managed to finally translate the message and determine the location and time of the coming meet-up.

She typed, *"Thank you. See you then!"* and turned from the bathroom door, heading toward her room.

She again brushed her hair behind her ear, wincing as her knuckles trailed against her bangs. Three days without a proper conditioner did that to someone. In the past, her mother had often sent her soaps and shampoos in care packages to her dorm room. A lot of her friends often joked that twenty-two was the new fifteen, but in her case, Shiloah was now in another country, living on her own for the first time with no dorm mates to speak of.

As she turned, walking toward her bedroom, trying to put thoughts of her dry hair behind her, she heard a quiet tap on the door.

Shiloah frowned and turned.

Another quiet tap.

"Hello?" she called out.

A pause, and for a moment she thought she'd been hearing things.

But then a voice replied, "Maintenance."

Her frown deepened. She hadn't requested any maintenance. Still, she supposed perhaps this was routine for new tenants. "Coming!" she called.

She opened the door and reached for the chain. Her hand hovered for a moment before she unhooked it. She thought of the murders her mother had read about in the news.

Her hand lowered for second, and she pressed an eye to the peephole, peering out into the apartment hallway and noticing a man standing there in uniform with a name tag she couldn't quite read. He wore a yellow hat and carried a toolbox which now rested on the banister.

The man had a young face boasting no facial hair. He almost looked as if he might be her age. For some reason, this put her a bit more at ease. Shiloah adjusted the chain and slid the bolt before twisting the knob and pulling the door open.

"Hello," she said in French.

The young man in the maintenance uniform nodded at her.

She now read on his chest the name Freddie. She wrinkled her nose. It wasn't a particularly French name. "Did the landlord send you?" she asked. She kept the door open, wide enough so it wasn't rude, but she still stood in the way, one hand braced against the frame in a sort of protective posture, preparing to shut it if she sensed anything awry.

But the man was smiling now. He made eye contact, held it, and said, "Yes, just routine. I'm supposed to check on the pipes. I hear there's been a leak."

She frowned and began to shake her head, but then hesitated. "Not aware I am that of," she said, slowly. "I did—no, sorry, did *not*—hmm, yes, did not ask for anything." She struggled to find the words in French, but managed to eventually complete the sentence to her satisfaction.

The young man gazed at her in an expression of confusion. He had a very pleasant face with nearly feminine features. His cheeks dimpled when he smiled, and the slope of his nose was smooth and cherubic. He displayed kind eyes with the suggestion of crow's feet at the corners; perhaps he wasn't as young as he first looked.

"I do believe it was the downstairs complaining about a leak coming from your bathroom," he said in slow French. Obviously he detected her accent, and was trying to communicate as best he could. He spoke the language perfectly, but with a bit of a regional dialect—like the difference between a Texan and a Californian. His words came in a musical, disarming sort of way.

Slowly, Shiloah pushed the door open a bit more. He made no aggressive moves, his hands now at his waist, his toolbox still resting on the banister.

"Someone downstairs said there's a leak?" she asked.

He winced apologetically and nodded. "Through the ceiling; there's mold. I can come back later. I'll go talk to the landlord if you want."

She paused, then quickly shook her head. "No, that won't be necessary." The last thing she needed was to cause trouble on her first week as a tenant. After all the trouble she'd gone through for months arguing with her mother about the move, she couldn't stomach the thought of being evicted.

She stepped aside, smiling at the dimple-faced man. The crow's feet in the corners of his young eyes bunched up as he returned the expression. *Yes,* she thought to herself, perhaps he wasn't as young as he first seemed.

He had long hair pulled back in a ponytail beneath his hat, and he stepped past, nodding at her as he maneuvered into the apartment. He really was quite handsome.

The man hitched his belt, hefting the toolbox, and pointed toward the hall. "Bathroom?" he asked.

"Yes. Just that way."

He tipped his hat politely. "You're sure this is okay?" he asked. "I'm happy to speak with the landlord. I can come by later. Maybe when you're not here if you'd prefer."

Shiloah thought about it for a moment. She knew what her mother would say. But she also knew what her friends would think of her. Coming to live in another country was anything but the action of someone who made decisions out of fear. She set her feet and jutted her chin, summoning courage in her chest. "No, I'm fine. Thank you for coming. The bathroom is the first on the right. It should be clean. I've only just arrived."

"Oh?" he asked, raising his eyebrows at her. "To Paris? I'm so sorry, I don't mean to be rude, but you speak with a bit of an accent."

She shook her head. "No, that's not offensive at all. I just moved from the United States; Illinois. A few days ago."

The man gave a little chuckle. "Oh, in that case, a special welcome to you. Say, if you'd like I could tell you some of the best places to visit in Paris. It's a wonderful city, this."

Shiloah found herself relaxing, and she moved over and shut the door behind her. She hesitated, but decided not to lock it. Then she gestured toward the bathroom again, and he moved on, whistling quietly beneath his breath.

She regarded him for minute from the doorway as he set down his toolbox and opened the cabinet beneath the sink; he began adjusting some of the plastic couplings. Not only was he handsome, but he was built especially well too. She found her eyes lingering, moving up and down; then, just as quickly, she felt her cheeks warm, and she quickly decided to move away. "I'll be in my room. Let me know if you need anything."

He didn't say anything and returned to whistling beneath his breath while he worked. It was a very pretty song.

Returning to her room, Shiloah sat down at her desk chair listening to the quiet clatter and tap of metal tools against porcelain. The sound of whistling seemed to echo in rhythm with the tools. For the next few minutes, she listened quietly, but then glanced down at her phone as another buzz caught her attention.

It was a new message from the moderator of the expat community. Shiloah frowned. It said something about being careful. There was a killer in Paris targeting American women.

Shiloah paused for a moment. The sounds from the bathroom continued, still ushered out by a quiet whistling. She felt a cold shiver as she reread the message. *The killer is targeting Americans.* She swallowed, and then moved from her bedroom.

"Excuse me," she said, hesitantly. "Perhaps it might be better if you do talk to the landlord. Maybe you could come back tomorrow. I'm so sorry. I don't mean to be a bother, but I just want to make sure . . ."

She trailed off as she approached the bathroom door. The quiet tapping of the tools and the whistling had a soothing effect, but as she entered the doorway of the bathroom, her comments faltered in her throat.

The bathroom was empty. She could still hear the whistling, and the toolbox sat open on the floor. It didn't have any tools in it, though. In fact, as she stared into the case, she realized it wasn't a toolbox at all. Her eyes narrowed as she peered down, and she couldn't quite understand what she was seeing.

"What in the . . ." she began, and then her eyes flitted to the sink. There, resting on the porcelain counter, was a small recording device. The sounds of whistling and tapping continued to emit from the small, black speakers.

54

"Freddie?" She began to turn, the slow blossom of fear now numbing her chest and causing prickles to rise across her spine. Before she could turn fully, though, she felt hands suddenly grab her from behind and hold her neck.

She felt a hot flash of pain across her throat.

And then, she felt nothing.

CHAPTER TEN

Adele sat by her desk, facing Robert across the small office space. She fiddled with her nameplate, and every few seconds she refreshed her computer. Her email browser was open, and tech had instructions to send any new information directly to her. Adele had decided Agent Paige wasn't an ideal middleman for leads in the case.

Adele continued to click impatiently, watching her inbox refresh. But still, no news on the social media front. The account info had been approved by Foucault, but it was taking some time to get what they needed. In France, there was no call for judge's warrants. But there was still a reasonable expectation of privacy and all sorts of red tape that often had commercial implications.

Adele continued to hit the refresh button in near-perfect synchronization with the old clock Robert had on his wall.

Robert had a taste for old-fashioned things. He liked philosophy books and art and tea. A lot of his tastes were predictable, but others weren't. He also enjoyed woodwork; this particular clock he'd bought from a carpenter in the heart of France. It never told the time properly, but it was quite beautiful to look at and, Adele had discovered over the last few hours sitting in the office, it was also very loud.

Tick, tick, tick. Tap. *Tick, tick, tick.* Tap.

The second hand would move, and eventually Adele's fingers would follow, refreshing her email.

She sighed in frustration again as her inbox remained empty, culminating in grayed out words. Vaguely, Adele thought of her mother, allowing her absent-minded thoughts to meander where they would. Would she have time to further look into her mother's case? The words still haunted her. *Funny that. Especially given where you worked . . .*

Adele thought about Agent Paige. It wasn't unusual for DGSI operatives to have connections with all sorts. In Agent Paige's circumstance, her boyfriend, whom she'd been seeing while also married, had been investigated for the murder of a prostitute. And while he'd been cleared of charges, that didn't mean all agency connections were aboveboard.

What if the man who had killed her mother had ties to the police force? Or even the DGSI itself? But the more Adele thought about it, the more she considered the greater possibility: the killer had been bullshitting her. He'd been a murderer. Why did she trust what he had to say?

Adele sighed heavily again and tapped the refresh button a few times.

Again, no new information.

She suppressed a surge of curse words bubbling to her lips. The thought of swearing made her consider her father. Adele traced the edge of her desk. Perhaps she should call the Sergeant. Maybe she'd even have time to visit him in Germany. She hadn't talked to him since the investigation had started. But the last time they'd spoken, her father hadn't seemed to like the idea of her investigating her mother's case. His exact words had been, "Stop wasting your time hunting ghosts. You'll only lose yourself."

But Adele couldn't let it go. She wouldn't.

She refreshed again.

A line of black text appeared at the top of the inbox.

Adele felt her heart jolt. Further thoughts of her parents were chased from her mind, ushered away by the ticking hand of the woodwork clock. Quickly, she clicked on the email and scanned the contents.

She read them again and called out, "Robert, are you seeing this?"

Her mentor also sat before his computer, pretending to study the screen— and while he had attempted to earlier in the day, Adele knew for the last few hours he'd been secretly reading the paper files he'd had printed and squirreled away in his desk drawer.

His eyes flicked up from where he was looking into the desk drawer. Robert cleared his throat and flashed a toothy smile, revealing the two gaps in his pearly whites. "Yes," he said instantly. "I mean, I am if you are. What exactly are we seeing?"

Adele sighed, got up, moved over to his computer, and noticed he wasn't logged in. She logged in for him, typing the password he used for everything for the last decade: *1234*. And then she clicked on the email from the tech department.

"They found a link between the victims in the user info," she said.

Robert gazed up at her, adjusting his mustache with quick and furtive gestures of his left hand. "Users? Were they drug addicts?"

Adult studied him for a moment, raising an eyebrow.

He held up his hands. "Just joking," he said.

She rolled her eyes. "Users from the online forum Yankees in Paris—the expat community."

Robert nodded. "What connection?"

Adele pointed, directing his attention toward the attached folder below the main body of the email. She opened the folder and said, "See? Looks like both victims were speaking to the same man."

Some of the confusion on Robert's expression faded. The idea of a common connection between victims wasn't foreign to him. The internet talk and the technology frustrated him, but when it came to old-fashioned detective work, there was none better.

"They had a contact in common?" he asked. "Is this his name? Sam?"

Adele shook her head. "That's the agent who sent the email. No, here, see? In these messages they had on their accounts. It's a Gabriel Waters..." She paused. "Gabriel Waters," she repeated. "That name hasn't come up, has it?"

Robert slipped a peek into the drawer beneath his desk. Then, with a resigned grunt, he pulled the manila folders out and began rifling through. He ignored Adele's pointed look and finally he settled on opening a file and scanning the contents.

At last, he shook his head. "No one by that name."

Adele continued to scan the information over Robert's shoulder, leaning against his chair and furrowing her brow. "He's also an American expat. See, look, here are the messages."

Robert followed her finger, and after a few moments reading, he whistled. The screenshots from the messenger account painted a damning picture. "Dear Lord," Robert said. "He just sent that, on the Internet? Doesn't he have any shame?"

Adult chuckled. "Starting out, it was just friendly chatting, but down here," she pointed to the end of the message chain and winced. "At least they pixelated it."

Robert leaned in, peering at the photo, and then his eyebrows shot up. "Is that—is that a man's . . ." He turned to Adele now, scandalized. "People actually upload private photos of themselves onto the Internet? Don't they know others can see this?"

Adele patted her old mentor on the shoulder, moving back to her computer. "My dear, dear innocent friend. What you can find on the web would shock you. Whatever the case, this Gabriel Waters knew both our victims. And he sent explicit photos before they died."

Robert continued to stare at the screenshots on the computer.

Adele said, "They also sent his address." She reached her own computer and double-checked the email had also made it to her phone.

Robert eyed her across the room. "Are you going to take her?"

Adele adjusted her sleeves as she pulled on her jacket. "Suppose I should, shouldn't I? It's what I would want her to do."

Robert said nothing, but just tilted his head toward the door.

Adele breathed heavily, but then threw her hands up. "I guess I'll try to take the high road, you know? Damn low road is mighty appealing."

"Stay safe," said Robert.

"Same to you."

"Adele," said Robert, calling out from where he now leaned back in his chair behind the large desk.

She glanced back and raised a questioning eyebrow.

"If he tries to . . . show you anything, don't hesitate to shoot him, understand?"

Adele paused, and then her eyes widened as a small spurt of laughter escaped her lips. "If he flashes me, I'm sure Foucault will see it as a justified shooting. Not to mention Ms. Jayne."

"Damn right," said Robert.

Still chuckling, Adele moved away from the door and disappeared down the hall, heading toward Sophie Paige's office to retrieve her partner and go question Gabriel Waters.

She wasn't sure what she dreaded more. The car ride with Paige or the thought of confronting someone connected to the murders of two young women.

CHAPTER ELEVEN

The car ride to Mr. Waters's home proceeded in absolute silence. Neither Adele nor Agent Paige uttered a word for the duration of the winding journey through the tightly wound avenues and streets of Paris, passing the Disney Store and Pomme de Pain. Gabriel lived about thirty-five minutes from the DGSI headquarters, and the further they went, the thicker the clusters of buildings became. Large trees jutted from the sidewalks. The buildings were like one great block of apartments, all in a row, with little division between, spanning the entire boulevard. Delivery trucks and public buses lined the sidewalk as well, parked or idle. A single restaurant Adele didn't recognize, made entirely of glass on all sides, was situated across from various business set on the opposite side of the street, facing the tenements.

At last, Agent Paige pulled the vehicle to a halt outside a blocky gray apartment set in the arrondissement near the Champs-Elysées. She parallel parked between two vehicles next to an advertisement pillar across from a gated hedgerow, hidden between two chains of buildings.

At the end of the arrondissement, in one of Paris's many hidden gardens, Adele glimpsed a couple of children playing on a pink bicycle, pulling each other around and around the cobblestones between the hedges under the watchful eye of their mother, who stood in the doorway of a terrace.

The street was busy, but otherwise, Gabriel Waters's apartment complex seemed quiet enough. Adele studied the address on her phone and then looked back up at the building.

"This is it," she said. "Says here he works in maintenance."

Agent Paige unbuckled her seatbelt and turned off the engine. She had insisted on driving and Adele had decided it wasn't worth contesting the point.

The bad blood between them, instead of slowly dissuading over time, seemed only to be getting worse. Now, though, Adele felt a flicker of fear. She thought of the last time she had chased down a criminal with a new partner. That time, the suspect had dove off the motel balcony into the pool. Bullets had been fired—they'd been lucky no one had died.

Adele shifted and looked at Agent Paige. "Do you have my back?" Adele asked, quietly.

Paige watched the younger agent for a moment, but then said, "Do you have mine?"

"Yes. Of course."

Paige shrugged. "Follow protocol and we'll both be fine. This," she said, glancing at her phone, "Gabriel Waters is an American. Maybe you should take lead."

Adele wasn't sure if her partner was offering her an olive branch or shoving her in front of an oncoming bus. Still, at least they were talking. That was some measure of improvement. Adele and Agent Paige both exited the vehicle, slowly closing the doors to avoid making noise.

Adele examined the large gray section of the long row of crowded buildings. The painted concrete had chipped in places and the side-alley garden grass was overgrown around the terrace steps. A pile of mail rested before the front door, yet to be collected. "Think he's home?" asked Paige, her hand going beneath her jacket and resting on her holster.

Adele shrugged and continued toward the side of the alley. She peered around the hedge, toward the windows. The window in the middle of the alley above the cobblestones was open, allowing a quiet breeze to waft in.

"I think he is," she said.

They took the concrete steps up to the patio, and in a quiet voice, Paige asked, "Does he have a family?" For the first time, there was a note of concern to her tone. The older agent looked uncertainly across the sidewalk in the direction of the hedge-garden, toward the two children playing on the bike beyond the black gate. She hesitated, then said, "Give me one moment."

Before Adele could protest, Paige moved off the steps and hurried, with long strides, up the wide avenue, through the pedestrians, towards Mr. Waters's apparent neighbors.

Adele hesitated, uncomfortably standing silent on the front steps, glancing at the buzzers. As far as Agent Paige's talk about protocol, abandoning her partner in front of a suspect's home hardly fit the bill. Adele watched as her partner talked with the mother on the overlook terrace, and waited as the woman quickly ushered her children up the steps and into the apartment. Adele couldn't hear above the sound of traffic, but it seemed as if the mother were thanking Paige before shutting the door. Adele continued to watch as her partner returned, the concern in her eyes having faded. Behind her, the windows were being shut and curtains drawn.

"Didn't know it was habit to inform the locals," said Adele, her eyes fixed on her partner.

"Just buzz the door," Paige snapped.

"No," Adele said, "in answer to your earlier question. He doesn't have a family. And he lives on the ground floor." Then she turned and unsnapped the holster to her weapon but didn't draw it. Gabriel Waters was only guilty of sending lewd pictures and texting terrible pickup lines so far. The fact he had a connection with two women was concerning, but not damning.

"Ready?"

In response, Paige impatiently reached past and buzzed Gabriel's number. A pause, then a staticky voice. "Yes?"

"DGSI!" Paige shouted. "Open up!"

Adele thought she heard a quiet static-polluted curse over the intercom, followed by the sound of thumping footsteps. A pause, then a buzz. The door clicked open.

Adele's eyebrows rose slightly as she stepped into the apartment with Paige in tow, the sound of traffic fading a bit.

The green door to their immediate left opened a second later; Gabriel Waters glared out. "What?" he demanded.

The man had features that would have been handsome if accompanied by even the barest form of personal hygiene. But the stubble on his face made it down his neck and up his cheeks. His hair stuck out at odd angles and he had a bit of a paunch. There were beer bottles scattered around the couch behind him, and the TV was blaring. A bag of chips rested on top of a pile of fitness DVDs.

Agent Paige frowned at the man from the apartment hallway. "Are you Mr. Waters?"

He replied in French, a thick accent making it difficult to understand. "Yes, what is it?"

Adele switched to English and said, "I'm with Interpol. My name is Agent Sharp. We would like to ask you a few questions if you don't mind coming with us."

The moment she spoke English, the man's eyes flicked away from Paige and regarded Adele. He had seemed annoyed at first, but at Adele's words, his face turned pale. He began to shake his head, backing slowly away. "This is a mistake," he said in English. He had a clear American accent. "Whatever you think I've done, I want to assure you," he said, trailing off, "it's just..." He glanced between the two women.

Agent Paige said, "Don't move," in a low growl.

But Waters looked back at Adele. "You're American?" he asked.

Adele nodded. "Yes, but I'm here with Interpol investigating—hey!"

Before she could finish, Gabriel Waters let out a squeak of fright and began to back away. As he scarpered, he knocked over the DVDs and the chips, shaking his head and waving his hands.

"I'm afraid you need to come with us!" said Adele. She found herself slowly drawing her weapon. The man took one long look at her, then spun on his heel and bolted.

Adele and Paige shouted in unison and burst toward the door. They both tried to enter at the same time and ended up blocking each other instead. Adele backed off and Agent Paige pushed her out of the way with a snarl and barreled into the unit. She broke into a sprint, racing after the man down the hallway.

Instead of racing the same direction, Adele turned, pulled back out of the door, through the front entry, down the porch, and toward the side of the apartment where she had spotted the open window.

A second later, she watched as Gabriel Waters threw himself through the window and let out a loud grunt of pain as he landed on his ankle on the cobblestones between the hedges. He turned toward Adele, yelped, and began sprinting around the side of the apartment toward the back. He lashed out, toppling two bins and sending a stack of splintered wood scattering across the ground.

Adele kept her weapon holstered and hotfooted after him, shouting for him to stop—cries which he ignored.

A pause. Then Agent Paige also emerged through the window. The older woman moved quickly, with agile motions, dropping nimbly to the cobblestones. Paige leapt over the toppled bin and shattered wood and sprinted after Gabriel Waters, who was heading for a brick wall in the back of the alley garden.

Adele and Paige were nearly neck and neck, both of them shouting directions, both of them racing toward Gabriel's frightened form.

Adele put on an extra burst of speed, but Gabriel made a sudden juke to the left, which Adele tried to follow. The garden was kept in as nearly poor condition as Gabriel's apartment, and Adele spotted the tangled hose too late. Her foot caught and she struggled to maintain her balance, but the distraction sent her tripping over a hedge protruding from a pile of mulch.

Adele rolled away from the shrubs, somehow maintaining her footing. Mr. Waters was slow, though, lagging from a limp to his right ankle from jumping out of the window. A nearby horn honked loudly—whether due to traffic or the spectacle, Adele didn't know.

Each step of the suspect accompanied a curse. Waters tried to wheel away from Paige, but found Adele had cut off his escape back to the front of the apartment. He turned and flung himself at the wall, trying to drag himself up the brick structure. But his injured ankle wouldn't follow his commands.

Agent Paige surged forward, kicking out his injured leg, then shoving him to the ground with a quick jab, and her weapon snapped from its holster. "Stop moving!" she screamed.

Gabriel tried to rise, but he found Paige's foot in the center of his chest, holding him down.

He licked his lips, glancing at the gun. "This is all a mistake," he said in frantic English. He tried French when Agent Paige didn't lift her foot. "This is a mistake," he repeated, but Adele's reluctant partner only pushed her foot harder against him, eliciting a groan of pain and stemming the tide of words, English or otherwise.

Paige growled, "Don't move, and keep your hands where I can see them." The older woman glanced over to where Adele approached, then back at Gabriel. "A step slow," she said, with a smirk.

"Good job," Adele muttered through clenched teeth. "I'll cuff him if you keep him down."

Gabriel was larger than both of them, but the threat of the gun and their combined presence made it a quick collar, and soon, they had him in handcuffs, leading him out of the alley garden and toward their parked vehicle.

"Mincy," said Gabriel, whispering quietly, "my cat. Someone needs to feed her."

Adele thought for sure Agent Paige would scoff at this, but instead, her partner pushed Waters forward and said, "I'll let an officer know."

The two of them reached their vehicle, pushing Gabriel in the back, his hands still cuffed as Adele called in on the radio, reporting the arrest. Eventually, they pulled away from the curb, circling the arrondissement. Adele noticed the mother in the adjacent unit to Gabriel's, peering through the window, staring after them.

Adele returned her attention to the rearview mirror, examining the suspect. He didn't have the look of a killer. He looked like he hadn't showered in a week; his shirt had stains, and she could almost smell him from here.

She felt an uneasiness as she regarded him.

This man had spoken with both of the victims before they'd been murdered. He had to know something.

CHAPTER TWELVE

Agent Paige wiggled Mr. Waters's phone beneath his chin and then dropped it. The suspect protested with a shout as his device thudded against the surface of the metal table. "Careful!" he exclaimed. "You'll break it!"

Agent Paige pointed an accusing finger at the phone, glaring through slitted eyes. "That's what you used to communicate with them?" she demanded. "What's the password?"

The phone rested on the table, glinting beneath the naked bulbs pulsing white throughout the room. Adele shifted uncomfortably, standing against a wall mirror at the back. Slight cracks ornamented the plaster beneath the mirror, and flakes of white paint were scattered on the ground under her feet, but Adele kept her eyes focused on Mr. Waters, studying the suspect.

He still had the look of someone who hadn't showered in a week, but his teeth, she noticed, were in immaculate condition. Whenever he opened his mouth to speak, she noticed a glare of resplendent white.

"The password," Agent Paige insisted. She jabbed her finger against the metal table again, and loomed threateningly over Gabriel Waters.

The American shifted uncomfortably, his hands still cuffed behind him, encircling the metal chair. He shot a pleading look over at Adele.

Adele paused, then said, "I'm not gonna lie to you, Gabriel, it isn't looking good."

Mr. Waters's eyes darted between the two agents, and he nervously licked his lips. "I-I can explain," he stammered, then trailed off. "What, what exactly is it you think I've done?"

He spoke in a sly, hedging sort of way that immediately put Adele on guard. She said, "I can't help but notice your English is better than your French. How long have you been living outside Paris?"

The man shrugged one shoulder, and then winced as his handcuffs scraped against the back of the metal chair. "What does it matter?"

Adele clicked her tongue. "I'll tell you what matters. How long have you been here? There's some discrepancy with your papers."

Mr. Waters stared at the phone on the table, grinding his perfect teeth. Agent Paige waited like a gargoyle, her ominous shadow cast by the naked bulb in the ceiling.

"I . . ." he began, hesitantly. "I just . . . I didn't do it. Whatever you think I did." He trailed off again, glancing up with a desperate look in his eyes.

"Two women were murdered," Adele said, biting off each word with venom. "You contacted both; don't play with us. We know you had something to do with it." She pushed off the wall and moved over to join Paige by the table, flanking Waters's other side.

But at her comments, the suspect looked up sharply. "Wait, hang on, what did you say?"

"You heard her," Paige growled in careful English.

Mr. Waters shook his head wildly and his voice went up an octave. "Murder? I didn't have anything to do with murder. Hold on—no, I'm serious, what are you even talking about?"

Adele pointed at his phone. "Amanda Gardner. Stephanie Riddle," Adele rattled off. "Both of them American. Young. Pretty. Is that how you like them? Their kidneys were missing. What do you do with them? Eat them?"

Gabriel Waters's face had turned the same color as the white walls, and at the comment about the kidneys, his lips took on a greenish tinge. He rapidly shook his head now, shifting violently back and forth in his chair as if his whole body were trying to protest the accusation.

"Hang on, hang on, just one second—no, that's not it. I swear, I didn't know anything about killings. Kidneys? God . . . Just harmless chatting was all. I didn't—Christ—didn't *kill* anyone!"

Paige jutted her finger into the side of his cheek, her forefinger indenting his flesh. "So you do admit you had contact with them?"

Gabriel growled in frustration, trying to move his head to avoid the offending finger. "I have contact with a *lot* of women, okay! It might happen that some of them were killed, but that had nothing to do with me. Yes, I'm American so some of the women I talk to are American! So sue me. There's no crime in texting someone."

Adele gritted her teeth. "No, but there is a crime in murdering them and taking their organs. You're expecting me to believe that it's just a coincidence the two women you were talking to ended up dead?"

By now, Waters was sweating. Quiet droplets of perspiration slipped down the inside of his cheek and twisted toward the tip of his chin. "Hang on; I can explain."

"I'm waiting," Adele said, scowling. She felt sick to her stomach, but couldn't quite say why. The crimes were gruesome, but she'd seen worse. Something about Waters's reaction, though, left her feeling ill. Almost...almost as if he were telling the truth.

She shook her head, trying to suppress the sense. He *had* to be the killer. He had to be. "Why did you run?" Adele snapped.

Waters jerked his head away from Paige's jabbing finger again. "Is this bad cop, bad cop? Just give me a second. Let me think."

But Paige leaned in on the other side and snapped in French, "No thinking! Tell us. You ran. That's an admission of guilt."

The perspiration grew worse, and Gabriel Waters's lips were now trembling. He let out an involuntary squeak and fluttered his eyelids. "I-I..." he stammered, "I just—I don't know what to say. But it's not-it's not what you think. I didn't run because I killed anyone! I didn't even know you were there about the women I'd been chatting with. Yes," he added quickly, "I did talk to a couple of American girls—I talk to a *lot* of Americans. I have twenty conversations going right now!"

He pointed toward his phone with his chin. "Sometimes it works, sometimes it doesn't. I don't even know who you're talking about. If two of them are dead it's the first I'm hearing it."

Adele crossed her arms over her chest, taking a step back and studying Waters from a distance. He cut a pathetic silhouette against the mirror behind him. The door to the interrogation room was shut, and he was trapped with the two agents. Gabriel Waters had the look of a liar, but he at least seemed to be telling the truth about the women.

"What's your password?" Adele said.

Waters shook his head. He opened his mouth, but didn't speak, and instead shook his head again.

"What is your password?" Adele repeated, enunciating her words.

He muttered something beneath his breath, but then a bit louder, after clearing his throat, he said, "If you let me type it in..."

Reluctantly, Paige fished a key from her pocket. "If you try anything," she said, snarling, "I will shoot you dead."

Mr. Waters wagged his head, but waited patiently, almost eagerly, for the agent to unlock his cuffs. Adele listened to a quiet click then a rattle; Gabriel Waters's right hand emerged from behind his back. His left followed, still dangling with the cuffs. He wiggled it toward Paige expectantly, but she glared in return.

"Your hands are free," she said. "The cuffs stay on. Open the phone."

For a moment, Waters glanced toward the door. Adele tensed, her hand moving to her holster. But then Waters sighed and he lifted his phone; with his free right hand, he tapped in the password.

He handed it over with a slight droop of his hand toward Agent Paige. Then, as the suspect massaged his free wrist, Paige took his phone and began scanning through it.

After a few minutes, she snorted in disgust and held it up so Adele could see. "He's not lying," she said. "He has at least fifty message chains with women. Their names seem American. Most the texts are in English."

Adele looked at Mr. Waters. "Why are you communicating with all these women?"

Gabriel flashed a white smile, shamelessly eyeing Adele. "Why do you think? A man can get lonely sometimes, you know? It isn't like French women are super excited to be with an American. So I have to sometimes go fishing someplace privately stocked, if you know what I mean."

Adele wrinkled her nose. "I'm not sure I want to. Fishing metaphors aside, you're telling me it's purely coincidence you were texting both Amanda Gardner and Stephanie Riddle when they died?"

Again Waters shrugged. "Like she said, I text a lot of women. If they're American and in Paris...they can get needy," he said, with a significant tilt of his eyebrows. "There's no predicting what a lady will do when lonely. There aren't *that* many Americans in Paris—especially not of," he cleared his throat, "noticeable assets and age. If someone else is taking shots at the same community, that's none of my business. I'm not killing *anyone*."

Agent Paige continued scrolling through the messages, her eyebrows ratcheting up with each passing second. She snorted, and Gabriel glanced up, frowning at the expression on her face.

She smirked. "Have you ever heard of using a razor?" she asked in an innocent tone.

Gabriel clenched his teeth briefly, and his frown became fixed. "Can I have my phone back?"

Agent Paige smirked again, but at last lowered the phone to the table. Gabriel reached out to grab it, but Paige snared his wrists, twisted them back, despite his protests, and cuffed him once more.

"Honestly, as kinky as this is," Gabriel said, "I'm telling you the truth. I'm really broken up over their deaths; Michelle and Susan..."

"Stephanie and Amanda," Adele shot back.

"Whatever," he said. "I'm serious, it's real sad to hear about."

"Oh," said Adele, "you sound very sad."

Gabriel began to roll his eyes, but caught the gesture and cleared his throat. "Whatever. I'm just telling you, I had nothing to do with any murders. I like a little cookie on the side, so sue me. You're wasting your time."

"Cookie on the side?" said Agent Paige, snorting in disgust. "Is that what they call it in America? Cookie?"

Adele glanced between her partner and their suspect. "Hang on," she said, raising her hand. "If that's true, why did you bolt? When we showed up, you took off. Explain that."

Gabriel had been starting to look more relaxed and annoyed. But at this, he slunk lower in his seat once more, his shoulders straining from where they twisted behind his back. He glowered at the table and muttered again beneath his breath.

Adele tapped her fingers against the glass mirror behind her, trying to regain his attention. "Look at me," she said. "Why did you run? You could have been shot."

Agent Paige leaned back too, putting one arm akimbo in an impatient posture.

Gabriel glanced between the two of them and shifted in his seat once more, still slouched low. At last, barely loud enough to hear, he said, "It was when I heard your accent that I bolted." He looked over at Adele with narrowed eyes.

She returned the glower. "Why?"

"Not a fan of Americans?" said Paige, raising an eyebrow. "Your phone says otherwise. Want me to read you some?" Paige cleared her throat; her accent in English was strong, but Adele could still make out the words well enough as Paige read from the phone, "*I want to lick you all over and lather you with honey. Just imagine, the thought of my rock hard—*"

"Okay!" Gabriel said quickly. "I get it, I get it. That's private property, isn't it?"

Adele shrugged. "You're in France now, friend. Mind telling why you bolted?"

Again he hesitated, and Agent Paige read, "*. . . the thought of your lips, covering me and bringing breath from my lungs and filling the—*"

"Fine! Look, I may have had a little bit—a *very little bit*—of trouble back stateside. I didn't kill anyone. It's really nothing at all. Really."

Adele shared a look with Paige. Adele said, "You had trouble with the law in the US? For what?"

Gabriel glared at Paige still flipping through his text messages. "Practicing medicine with a suspended license," he said.

"You're a doctor?" Adele asked.

"Kind of," he said in a sullen reply. "I mostly do dental work."

"So you're on the run." Adele raised an eyebrow as Gabriel twisted uncomfortably in his chair.

"Sounds bad if you put it like that. I had a little bit of trouble is all. Look, this is all being blown out of proportion. I didn't kill anyone."

Adele studied him, then shook her head. "I don't believe you."

He gaped. "What do you mean? I told you everything you wanted to—"

"We looked up your name. You're not in any American database."

With one last glare across the table and a defeated sigh, he said, "Try Marcus Short. I'm not interested in catching a murder rap."

Adele felt a final twinge of regret. She was nearly certain now; they'd caught a criminal, just the wrong one. "You're using a fake name? Marcus Short. If we look that up, what are we going to find in the database? Save us some time here."

He paled again and shifted in his seat. "It wasn't a big deal," he repeated, shaking his head. "Out of proportion. Not a big deal."

Adele turned away in disgust and glanced back at Paige. Her would-be partner shrugged.

"Stay here," Adele said, expressionless. "I'm going to look up what you have to say. But if you're lying to me . . ." She pointed a firm finger toward their suspect.

Gabriel, though, was no longer paying attention. He had nearly melted in the chair now, and was scooted so low his head was nearly in line with the metal back support. Adele could see the panic in his eyes as he considered the implications of what came next.

If he was telling her the truth, he would be in trouble. If he fled the US, avoiding warrants or fines, France would most likely extradite. Especially to play nice with Interpol. But also, if he was telling the truth, it meant he wasn't a killer.

Reluctantly, she opened the interrogation room door and moved out into the hall, heading for Robert's office with reluctant, uneven steps. The background check wouldn't take long if the name he'd provided was accurate.

They were back to square one. Adele knew Agent Paige wouldn't let her hear the end of it. But worse, it meant a killer was still out there.

CHAPTER THIRTEEN

"Check it again," said Adele, then added, "please."

Robert readjusted in his chair behind his large oak desk. The quiet ticking of the wooden clock above the door was followed closely by clacking from the computer's keyboard. At last, Robert paused, then looked up. "There is indeed a warrant out for Marcus Short."

Adele felt her chest tighten. The last vestiges of hope faded to a resigned inevitability. "Are you sure?" she said, though her heart wasn't in it. Adele moved away from the door and circled the desk to peer over her mentor's shoulder.

Robert scowled in mock offense. "I'll have you know, I'm becoming quite adept with these things. Computers aren't so tough after all." He affectionately patted the side of his monitor.

"That's not the computer," said Adele. "It's the screen. But your point is taken."

A picture of Gabriel Waters was displayed on the screen next to the name Marcus Short. As she scanned the information, she reached out and scrolled with the mouse. "Suspended medical license," she murmured, her mood souring even more.

Robert jerked the mouse away from her, though, and said, "All right, grabby hands, just tell me what you need..."

"Scroll down a little. When was the warrant issued?"

Robert glanced down at the bottom of the screen. Then whistled. "He's been wanted for the last two years. Looks like his story checks out." Robert winced and glanced over his shoulder at Adele. "Sorry."

She grunted in disgust, then moved away from the desk once more. Adele could feel Robert watching as she moved back over to her own desk. Instead of sitting, she plopped down on the edge of the desk and crossed her legs before folding her hands in her lap and staring out across the room.

"Well," she said, "that's it. Back to square one."

"Ever wonder why it has to be a square? I mean ... why not an oval? Or a cube?" Robert asked, still looking at his computer screen.

Before Adele could reply, Agent Paige appeared in the doorway. Adele stiffened as the agent cleared her throat. "Well," Paige said. "That was a waste of time."

Adele frowned. "You check the records too?"

Paige nodded, barely concealing a self-satisfied smirk. "His story checks out. Plus, he has a solid alibi for the night of Amanda's death. Not our man."

Adele's knuckles whitened where her hands clasped each other in her lap. "No," she said, "I guess not."

Paige glanced from Robert to Adele. "Any other brilliant leads?" she asked, cheerfully.

Adele glared. "Hey," she said, "I'm trying here. You have a better idea?"

Agent Paige leaned against the doorframe, crossing her arms and pressing her fingers against the sleeves of her gray suit. "You're the Interpol attaché. What's your brilliant plan? Any other wannabe Casanovas you'd like to arrest?" She smirked. "Not getting lonely, are you?"

Adele narrowed her eyes at the older woman. "It was a solid lead and the right call."

"Right call?" Paige snorted. "How was that the right call? We arrested a man for showing his junk to a couple of women."

"No, we arrested a man who fled when we approached him for questioning. And like I said, if you don't have any better ideas—"

"You know what your problem is?" Paige said, matching the frustration in Adele's tone.

Adele pushed off her desk and stood to her feet, hands loose at her side. "No, what?"

"Ladies," Robert interrupted, also rising from his chair. The shorter man didn't cut an imposing figure, but he kept his tone calm anyway, speaking gently. "Please," he said, "there's no need for this."

Paige rounded on Robert. "You stay out of this," she snapped. "If I need the advice of an old fossil, I'll ask."

"Hey," Adele retorted, stepping toward Paige, "watch it! Show some respect."

Paige's narrowed eyes leveled back on Adele, and she made a tsking sound through her teeth. "Is this how he taught you to investigate? I shouldn't be surprised. You're still trapped in an old way of thinking. If we find out someone else died, it will be *your* fault. Both of you!"

"There's no need—" Robert began.

But Agent Paige didn't let him finish. "No need?" She jammed a finger at Adele. "You know what this bitch did?"

Robert flinched, and his expression darkened. "Careful," he said, scowling for the first time.

"No, you be careful," Paige snapped. "You're in bed with a snake. Is that what you do up at that mansion of his? Get in bed?" She whirled back on Adele, her eyes flashing.

Adele hadn't realized it, but she'd taken another two steps, her hands bunched at her side; she now stood only an arm's length from the older woman.

Paige's eyes narrowed. "What are you going to do about it?" she demanded.

"Shut up," Adele snapped. She was tired of playing this game. Tired of trying to be polite, trying to deflect frustration. Agent Paige was going out of her way to be a complete liability. Adele refused to stand by, watching as Paige insulted Robert.

"I don't take orders from you," Paige growled. "Even though you might want me to."

"I told you," the sound of gritted teeth stressing the words, "I never meant for any of that to happen. I saw evidence missing and I reported it. What should I have done?"

Paige went stiff again, as she had the last time the subject had been breached. "You nearly cost me my marriage. You cost me my job."

Robert cleared his throat. "The same way you're trying to get me out?" he asked.

A silence fell for a moment, and Adele glanced over in confusion, looking between Paige and Robert.

Paige, though, turned toward the window, not meeting Robert's gaze, a look of guilt flashing across her face. But just as quickly, the expression vanished, and she glared at Robert. "Foucault trusts my opinion. And I provided it. What he decides is up to him."

Adele continued frowning, trying to keep track. "Robert, what's she talking about?"

Robert's face was still creased. "It's not important," he said.

But Adele didn't let it go. "No, tell me."

Robert didn't speak, but Paige turned back to Adele. "I guess you and I aren't so different," she said with a sneer. "Foucault asked my opinion a few months ago about areas where the department could get better." She shrugged, stretching her mouth and turning the corners of her lips down in an infuriatingly noncommittal way. "I may have mentioned your old mentor here is out of date. Obsolete." She slowly enunciated the last word, emphasizing and dragging out each syllable. She didn't blink now, staring at Adele as if challenging her to make something out of it.

Adele could feel her blood pulsing in her ears. Her hands were still bunched in fists. "You're the one who's been trying to get Robert out of here? Just to get at me?" Adele was shouting now. "What's wrong with you?"

Paige sniffed. "Not everything is about you."

Adele's voice became a shout. "I can't believe Foucault assigned you to me. You're the worst. John was unprofessional, but he at least knew how to work a case. You—you're useless. You're worse than useless. You're a liability!"

Paige laughed, a short, unpleasant barking sound. "John? You want to know about John? The moment he heard you were coming back, he jumped at the first case they offered. Something in *finance*, of all things. He didn't want to work with you!" She watched Adele, as if looking for some bitter fruit to pluck. At a flash in Adele's eyes, Paige smirked, and continued, "That's right. You didn't know. But John didn't *want* to work with you. He begged for the first case they had. Leaving me stuck with you; he *chose* to avoid you. So much for your precious Agent Renee."

Adele hesitated, shaking her head. She was so mad her hands were trembling. She had never wanted to punch anyone in the office before, but now, she could feel herself rehearsing it in her mind.

"Adele," Robert said, quietly, "it's not worth it."

Agent Paige jutted her chin up defiantly, her own hands at her waist, but also clenched, as if preparing for Adele's reaction.

A brief moment of sanity reigned as Adele wondered if Paige was telling the truth about John. Had John really taken another case to avoid working with her? Her mind flashed back to the last time they had talked. It had been awkward, sure. But did John really hate her so much?

She felt a flash of shame and quickly transitioned to the easiest emotion. Anger. But, as words burbled up and her fists continued to tighten at her side, there was a sudden chirping sound.

Adele hesitated. The chirping was soon accompanied by a buzzing noise. Then another one. Three ring tones echoed in the room. Adele, Paige, and Robert all glanced down at their pockets, fishing their phones out.

It was as if, for the moment, a spell was broken.

Adele stared at her phone, then answered. As she listened, she could feel the blood leaving her face. After a moment, she closed her phone.

"Told you we were wasting our time," Paige said, growling. She turned and stomped out of the room, and Adele heard her hit the elevator button.

Adele stood in Robert's office for a moment, glancing at her old mentor. "Third," she said, nearly breathlessly. "A third murder."

Robert stared back. "You want me to come with you on this one?"

Adele hesitated, a numb prickle across her skin as the anger and shock continued to course through her. "Yeah," she said at last. "Couldn't hurt to have your eyes. They haven't moved the body."

Robert nodded. "Let me get my jacket.

CHAPTER FOURTEEN

Adele stood in the quiet, cloistered apartment complex, allowing the silence to speak to her in pauses and stuttered breaths. This unit was more rundown than the last and occupied a more affordable part of the city. Adele's eyes flicked to the open door yawning into the hall. A single chrome locking chain dangled toward the floor, swaying back and forth. Adele stared at the chain and then glanced over to the body.

She was young. No more than early twenties. Her throat slit in the same way as the other victims. The pool of blood spread out around her in the hallway. Adele stepped down the hall past Robert.

Two police officers stood in the apartment door, preventing rubber necks and overly curious residents. Agent Paige postured in stony silence on the opposite side of the bathroom, regarding the floor.

The partners had taken separate cars to the crime scene, and Adele had decided she would act as if Paige wasn't even there. Time for the high road had faded the moment Robert had been dragged into it.

For her part, as Adele studied the bathroom, she felt a chill trickle down her spine.

He had dropped a third body. In less than two weeks, he had murdered three young women. Adele looked down at her phone where she'd received the woman's preliminary information. Shiloah Watkins. Another American girl—a recent arrival on a visa *de long séjour* by the look of it.

Adele studied the poor girl for a second, but then flicked her eyes away, refusing to let her emotions rear their ugly heads. Robert had often told her emotions were best reserved for commiseration, or talking with a victim's family. But at a crime scene, they only distracted.

It was hard to completely suppress them, though, especially with Agent Paige lingering nearby like a ghoulish shadow. Adele avoided looking at the gray-haired agent and tried to completely block her out as she scanned the body once more.

No sign of struggle. No defensive wounds. Nothing under the fingernails. Nothing to suggest she'd been alarmed, or even scared. How was he doing it? How was the killer gaining their trust? How was he getting in?

She glanced toward the door with all the locks. There had been no forced entry. She let out a sigh of frustration and scanned the body once more.

"Right side," Robert grunted.

She glanced over at the shorter agent and noticed where he was pointing. She dropped to a knee, and, faintly, with the edge of a pen she pulled from her pocket, she lifted the woman's shirt.

Just past the belly button, against the tanned flesh, she immediately spotted the incision. "Missing kidney," she said. "Right one. Same as the others."

Paige moved closer and peered down at the body. "Any sign of it?" she asked in a cool tone.

Robert had already departed and Adele could hear him in the kitchen now; the fridge door opened, by the sound of things, then the freezer. Then Robert called from the other room, "No. He took it with him, like the last two. There's no reason he would leave it behind."

Adele stepped into the hall and peered toward the kitchen. "Trophy hunting?" she called out. "It's starting to feel like something different. Why the same kidney every time? What's he doing with them?"

The question lingered in the air, unanswered. Adele had her own theories bouncing around her mind. But no confirmation. Nothing beyond theory and three dead girls.

Adele got back to her feet, pushing off her knee and emitting a quiet whooshing sound. She stared down at the body, trying to focus.

"Only twenty-two years old," said Adele, swallowing. "She got here three days ago. Three days. How did the killer stalk her? How did he figure out where she lived? There's no way he could've established a friendship, a rapport, over three days, is there? Unless she knew him from before. Maybe he's an exchange student," Adele said suddenly, opening her eyes.

Robert appeared down the hall again. "Possibly." He looked pensive as he approached.

For her part, Paige's eyes were fixated on the young girl's face. Adele was reminded that Paige had five children of her own. She wondered about their ages.

"I'll be back," Paige said through tight lips. Pale-faced, she moved hurriedly out of the bathroom, down the hall, and out the apartment door.

Adele shared a look with Robert and her mentor shrugged once. They both turned back to the body. Now that Paige had left the bathroom, Adele felt she could focus a bit better. She scanned the tiled room. Only a single container of soap, but no shampoo.

She pointed it out. "Didn't have time to shop?" she asked, glancing at Robert.

He was studying the shower and the sink. "Newly moved in," he said. "She doesn't seem the neglectful sort. Had vegetables and fruit in the fridge."

"Right. Good little American girl. But a lot of locks on that door."

Robert glanced over. "I'd noticed. Do you think that's the sort of thing a young girl considers?"

Adele shrugged. "I suppose so. Especially if you're new to a city."

But Robert hesitated. "A college girl, bold enough and brave enough to come to another country to study. Do you think the first thought she might have is her own safety? I'm not saying it's not important. But do you think that's the first thought she would have when arriving? To find a place that would be safe? A place with excess locks on the doors?"

Adele frowned. "What are you getting at?"

"I'm saying, for someone like this, not all the decisions were made by her. Protective parents?" he said. "Maybe a protective boyfriend?"

Adele hesitated, then ran her eyes over the bathroom once more. "Protective might mean sheltered. Sheltered might mean we're dealing with someone who wasn't used to the real world. Didn't know how things were supposed to go. Maybe too trusting."

Robert pursed his lips. "Trusting. You think it cost her? She's only been here three days. How did the killer get in? No struggle; did you check the fingernails?"

"The first thing I looked at," said Adele. "No defensive wounds. He crept up from behind. Was he maybe waiting for her? Had a key? Did you run files on the landlord from the last place?"

Robert nodded once. "Nothing besides a few parking tickets."

"So how is he getting in?"

Adele glanced around the bathroom once more but then paused, frowning. She noted a towel hanging over the rack, but a small pool of water in the center of the bathroom floor between the tub and the sink.

"Look at that." She pointed.

Robert followed her attention, frowning at the puddle.

Adele appreciated that he didn't ask what she was talking about. The moment she pointed it out, she knew he would detect the anomaly too.

"Why is there water only in the middle of the floor?" Adele said, softly. "The sink is here, and the shower there. How do you get water smack dab in the middle of the floor?"

Robert approach the bathtub and glanced down. "Hasn't been used recently."

Adele glanced at the sink as well. "Do you think she flicked the water by accident? Maybe spilled something?"

Robert got to a knee, glancing down. He hesitated, shot a look toward the door, then dipped his finger in the water and quickly lifted it. He licked his pinky and winced for a moment, as if anticipating something bitter. But then he shook his head. "Just water."

"Strange," Adele said. She sighed and moved out of the bathroom, through the apartment.

The third victim heralded a threat. The killer wasn't done. He hadn't stopped at one or two. Which meant he wouldn't stop. If he continued to kill at this pace, the body count would rise at an alarming rate.

Adele glanced at her mentor. "We have to catch this guy, Robert."

He nodded.

At that moment, Adele heard a soft noise from up the hall. She held up a hand as if to say, *Give me a moment,* and she moved toward the apartment door, peering into the apartment stairwell.

Adele moved into the hallway, following the source of the noise. She glanced up and down the open corridor, her eyes tracking the windows. Her gaze flitted along the banister, around the curling oak rail, and rested on the two police officers stationed at the stairs, standing just behind yellow caution tape.

Adele noticed neither of them were talking. They seemed bored, staring out across the hall or peering through the window on the third floor.

She glanced around again, but could still hear the noise. Like a quiet muttering. Or, perhaps, sobbing.

Adele frowned at the nearest officer, and he looked in her direction. His cheeks flushed, as if embarrassed. He glanced back, noticed she was still watching him, and then, with the most surreptitious of movements, he jerked his thumb toward the stairs and tilted his head ever so slightly, causing his hat to skew a bit. He stood straight again, adjusted his hat, and stared ahead, refusing to meet her eyes.

Adele scanned the hall for Agent Paige, but her reluctant partner was nowhere to be found. Adele moved toward the stairs the officer had indicated, and she took them one at a time, carefully. The sounds had faded at this point but Adele couldn't shake a slow, ominous feeling creeping up her chest.

She reached the top of the stairs; instantly, she spotted a form hunched by the nearest window, staring out into the street below. The form's shoulders trembled, and Adele heard a quiet sniffle followed by a hand wiping across the person's nose.

Then a quiet cuss, and the person lowered their hand and continued to stare out into the street.

Tentatively, palm still on the railing, Adele approached. She froze; one foot still on a step, the other on the floor's landing. The various metal doors lining the hall were closed, depicting silver numbers. Adele shifted uncomfortably, but all sound had faded at this point. Agent Paige stood by the window, wiping her eyes.

For a second, Adele thought to turn back and hurry away. Whatever was going on here, Adele doubted her presence would make it any better.

She felt a flash of sympathy as she regarded the older woman. But at the same time, she wasn't sure how to react. Why was Paige crying? As if in response to the thoughts themselves, Paige turned slightly, glancing toward Adele.

The moment her eyes cleared and she made out the person at the top of the stairs, her frown turned into a downright scowl. Her eyebrows were so low over her eyes, Adele thought she might sprain something.

"I..." Adele began, unsure where to go. "I was just coming to check..." She trailed off again. "Are you all right?" she settled at last.

At the question, though, instead of softening, Paige's expression only hardened. The older woman no longer reached up to touch her face or wipe her eyes. Tears were still evident on her chin and along the tracks of her cheeks. Her eyes were red, but she stared proudly ahead as if daring Adele to make something of it. "I'm fine," she snapped. "Go away."

Adele hesitated again. Everything in her wanted to comply with this directive. But at the same time, she couldn't shake the feeling of sympathy swirling in her gut. As much as she disliked Agent Paige, the thought of seeing anyone upset bothered her. But also, another part of her, the investigator, had its curiosity piqued.

"You didn't know the victim, did you?" Adele asked, carefully.

Paige's glare became a hateful stare, and in one wild moment Adele thought the older agent might pull her weapon and fire. But at last, Paige said, "No."

Adele raised her hands. "Sorry. Well, we're going downstairs again. I didn't mean to bother you. Just," she coughed, "come when you're ready. If you need anything—"

"I don't. Not from you."

Adele nodded and turned, trying to suppress the flush now creeping up her own cheeks. No matter how much she tried, Agent Paige didn't seem interested in working together.

She took the steps one at a time, again quietly, trying to make as little sound as possible. But she'd only taken three steps before Paige muttered, "You think he's so bad, don't you?"

Adele hesitated. She didn't want to turn back. But then again, the part of her that still held compassion, even sometimes for killers, couldn't just leave. Agent Paige was cantankerous, impossible to work with, and downright vengeful, but still, another more nurturing part of Adele didn't want to just abandon her partner. It wasn't the right thing to do. She could only imagine the Sergeant's horror at the thought of leaving one's fellow officer without support. Then again, her father would've laughed at the notion of anyone crying on the job. Still, Adele had to pick and choose which parts of her father's philosophy to embrace.

With a weary sigh, she turned, her hand gripping the railing, her feet twisting on the stairs. She stood where she was, half turned, glancing over her shoulder.

"Excuse me?" Adele asked.

Paige was once again staring out the window, her breath fogging the glass. Adele could see the left side of her face; her silhouette cut a glowering form.

"You think he's awful," Paige repeated, "this killer. He's killed three. He just killed that girl down there. You think he's a horrible person."

Adele paused. Was this a trick question? She hesitated, then said, "He's causing a lot of pain. I do think he's a bad person. And I think we need to stop him from doing anything else."

Paige turned now, rounding on Adele in fury, her eyes blazing. "He is awful. A monster. He's despicable, irredeemable, horrible. Everything about him is loathsome. If I could, I'd shoot him dead right now."

Adele hesitated again. She wasn't sure what Paige wanted from her. "All right, well, hopefully you don't just shoot him if we find him. We do have to follow protocol, you know . . ."

Paige gritted her teeth. "You don't get it, do you?" she demanded. "You know what he did that's so terrible? He killed someone, yes. But you know who is going to feel the most pain? It's not that girl down there. That beautiful, young, bright-eyed girl. She had her whole life ahead of her. But you know who's going to feel the pain, because it's not her. The dead don't feel pain."

Adele again moved uncomfortably.

"Her mother," Paige snapped, pointing down the stairwell toward the open apartment door. "She's American, yes? She's in this country, but I bet you her mother was scared. Her mother would've done everything to talk her out of coming here. I bet you she wanted to keep her child close, so she could keep an eye on her. And at the very least, I bet you she spent every day calling, texting. The officers found her phone; they said there were five missed calls. Her mother was trying to reach her."

"That's terrible. I can't imagine—"

"No, you can't!" Paige snarled.

"I'm sorry, but I don't understand. You seem angry at *me* about this. I didn't have anything to do with—"

84

"That's not the point! You think the killer's awful. And you're right. But you're no better."

Adele bristled at this now, still confused, but angry as well. "Hang on, how am I—"

"Do you even know what your actions caused?" Paige demanded. "Are you completely vapid? Is there anything going on in that little cheerleader head of yours?"

"Paige, I'm afraid I don't know what you're talking about. And I have to ask that you—"

"What did you think would happen? You told Foucault about me. You told him about me and Matthew!"

Adele pulled up short. Up until now, Paige had seemed loath to explicitly engage in any mention of the events that had transpired between them five years ago.

Adele shifted. "I told you, I just saw evidence missing, and—"

"And you should've come to me. Your direct supervisor."

"Maybe. No, really, I mean it. I'm sorry. I really, truly am. I didn't know what was going on. I was young. I am sorry."

"Sorry doesn't take it back. If the killer from downstairs told you sorry, would you forgive him?"

Adele passed a hand over her face, and again wanted to turn back and leave. Her left foot took a slight step, moving down one stair. But she stood there, one hand still gripping the railing, the other dangling uselessly at her side.

She could practically feel the attention of the officers below, watching, cataloging. She didn't like to be the center of attention, especially not in circumstances like these. She again inwardly cursed Foucault for pairing the two of them. Perhaps it was the DGSI executive's quiet protest of Interpol's arrangement. Maybe he didn't like the coordination between the agencies—perhaps someone higher up had approved it against his wishes. Adele also wondered about John. He wanted to avoid working with her. Adele brushed aside both these thoughts with a steady exhale, focusing on the moment.

She needed to head back downstairs, to continue the investigation. "I don't know," said Adele.

Agent Paige didn't say anything, but judging by her posture, the defiant way her cheekbones pressed against her skin and her jaw clenched, Adele surmised the woman wouldn't take this answer with satisfaction.

They lingered in silence for a moment, and the pressure to give a more complete response weighed on Adele. At last, she said, "I don't think it's my place to forgive anyone we investigate. My job is to bring them to justice. And if they were forgiven, I still wouldn't trust them. People like that can't be allowed in society. They'll just hurt others more. It's like you said, a mother lost her child today. What could be worse than that?"

"Exactly," Paige said, jumping on the words as if she'd been waiting for just this. Spittle flew from between clenched teeth. "When you went to Foucault and you told him about Matthew, what do you think my husband thought? Did you think it wouldn't get back to him also? He was told. They questioned him. In front of my daughters. My sons."

Adele swallowed against a suddenly dry throat, trying to keep up. "I'm sorry, are we talking about the killer, or—"

"Yes! We're talking about him. We're talking about you! You're just as bad. He took a daughter from her mother. But you did the same. You cost me more than you can imagine."

Adele shifted. "I'm sorry, but I thought that your husband stayed with you. That's what I heard..."

"He did." Paige paused, staring out the window. Her expression softened, if only for a moment, but when she turned to regard Adele once more, the look of hatred returned. "He stayed. He's a strong man. But my daughters? My oldest is twenty-three. Her twenty-year-old sister does everything she says. They won't talk to me. Haven't talked to me in years. She was eighteen at the time and moved out. She doesn't return my calls. She won't ever forgive me for what I did to their father. You took my daughter from me. For five years now I haven't spoken with her." Paige's voice cracked for a moment, but this small veneer, the shattering of her rage, only seemed to propel her to further fury. She clenched her fist and pounded it against the glass. "You think you're better than the killer, but you've done the same. You cost a mother her daughter. My second oldest also left; moved in with her sister. I made a stupid mistake, I admit that. My husband understood. You, you cost me my career. I'll never advance now. You cost me my daughters. I'll never forgive you for that."

Adele just stared, trying to keep up. She wasn't sure what to say, certain, in that moment, that no matter what, her words wouldn't change anything. She was beginning to understand the extent of Paige's loathing.

"I didn't know," Adele said, softly. "I'm sorry."

Paige turned away again, her shoulders sagging a bit, as if the sudden explosion of anger had worn her out. She was shaking her head, her silver hair shifting. "You just don't know," she muttered.

Adele turned and began to move back down the stairs, abandoning any thought of further conversation. There was nothing she could say that would make Paige feel better. Nothing that could restore their partnership. Nothing that could make the woman forgive her. Perhaps, now, it made sense why she'd been going after Robert's job. Adele felt a cold shiver through her heart. Maybe a selfish emotion, but in that moment, she felt a flush of fear at what Paige would do if given the chance. Adele had never had someone hate her this much. Paige blamed Adele for the loss of her children. Five years without speaking to her oldest daughter . . . Adele felt a surge of guilt, but tried not to focus on it.

She left Agent Paige and moved past the officers at the base of the stairs. Neither of them looked in her direction. Adele surmised this probably meant they'd heard every word.

"It's just . . ." she began, slowly, but then she abandoned the utterance with a shrug and moved toward the lower window, glancing at the street outside.

She peered out into the busy road, watching as cars drove by. She tried to focus on the job; the one thing that helped her focus, that realigned her thoughts.

Had the killer used a car? Had he walked?

Adele continued to stare into the street, her eyes flitting along the glass and stone, the old buildings and the new crammed together. She examined the pedestrians, moving about, some of them carrying shopping bags, others trundling along carts and still others laughing or talking as they moved with groups up the Boulevard. She could just glimpse the edge of a *plage* along the Seine—an artificial sand-free beach along the river stippled with red and white umbrellas.

Her eyes moved to the nearest businesses and settled on a furniture store, with large block letters displaying announcements for sales and golden stars attempting to attract the eye of potential customers.

Adele tried not to focus on the obvious. In her job, it was important to focus on the things that weren't so clear.

Vaguely, she thought of the small puddle of water. The apartment had been warm. Someone had turned on the heat. Which made Adele frown for second. Why did that seem important? The puddle of water, the warmth—why was that relevant?

She thought of the blood staining the floor, and the young woman dead by the doorway. The slit in her side, her right kidney missing, just like the other two.

Adele continued to stare at the furniture store, her eyes tracing the glass windows. There had to be a clue she was missing. Some break in the case. Adele refused to believe the killer would get away with it.

Then she stiffened.

Her eyes zeroed in on the furniture store. More specifically, on the two security cameras placed in the top of the window, facing the street.

"Please be recording. Please be recording," she muttered to herself. She heard footsteps behind her, and Robert's voice called out, "Adele, are you—" He paused, and Adele heard him quicken his stride. "What is it?" he asked, recognizing the look on her face. "Is everything okay?"

Adele didn't point. She just stared, and she knew Robert was good enough to spot the cameras on his own.

She waited for a few moments before Robert also froze next to her. "Oh," he said. "You think they're on?"

Adele's mouth felt suddenly dry. "Half the time they're just for show."

Robert began to tug at her arm, pulling her past the officers behind the caution tape. "I guess we can find out," he said. His eyes were narrowed now, calculating. Adele liked it when he got like this. Very little escaped his attention.

Adele fell into step, following after Robert, ducking beneath the caution tape. The two officers bid farewell with quick nods. Adele glanced up the stairs in the direction of Agent Paige. She could just see the bottom of the older woman's feet, where she continued to stand by the window.

Adele didn't call out, though. Some relationships couldn't be repaired if both parties weren't willing. This partnership was a liability.

"Shall I fetch her?" Robert asked softly.

Adele acknowledged her shorter partner, but shook her head once. "Give her some time."

Robert nodded. And the two of them took the stairs, moving out the front of the building and heading over to the furniture store with the security cameras.

CHAPTER FIFTEEN

They sat in Robert's office, both staring at the computer behind Adele's desk this time. Initially, they had tried accessing the files from Robert's computer, but somehow, he had managed to download a virus. On the other side of the room, a tall IT operator with long, rock star hair pulled back in a ponytail was tapping away at Robert's keyboard, trying to clean the hard drive. For Adele's part, she examined the security footage on her laptop again. She stood, allowing Robert to sit in her chair, both their backs to the window.

Agent Paige had come with them at the discovery of new evidence. She lounged in the doorway, seemingly loath to enter the room. This suited Adele just fine. The more distance between them, the better as far as she was concerned.

They watched the video again, then again.

"You think it's him?" Robert queried, then answered his own question. "Has to be. Fits our time frame perfectly." He pointed at the screen, tracking the figure as they played the video clip on loop.

The only figure besides an elderly couple exiting the building in the allotted time frame was a man in uniform. He carried a toolbox in his right hand, which swung mildly with each stride. He seemed of average height, but had a cap over his head. He had longer hair, though not quite as long as the tech working on Robert's computer. Besides the hair, they couldn't make out anything about his face beneath the brim of the hat. The man also wore gloves.

The grainy footage played again on loop. The video almost seemed to taunt them as the toolbox swung nonchalantly by his waist. Adele watched as he entered the apartment. Then the tape fast-forwarded, and about an hour later, judging by the timestamp, he exited the building. Still carrying the toolbox, still with his hat over his face, his head hung low, his gloves on. "Anything?" Adele asked, quietly. Robert continued to frown, studying the screen.

"Nothing," he said, "I don't see anything."

"Hang on, play it again," Adele said.

For the fourth time, Robert restarted the clip, and they both watched.

Yellow hat, average height, longish hair. No visible features, no reflection in the glass. No one else entering or coming from the building except for an elderly couple.

"Nothing," Adele echoed Robert's word. "Come on," she said through clenched teeth. "There has to be something ... there's always something."

Robert continued to stare. "One hour he was in there. That's long enough to talk his way in, kill her, cut out her kidney. But he had to move fast."

She didn't even bother glancing up, but Adele could see Paige out of the corner of her eye shaking her head.

"Why the toolbox?" Robert cut her off, frowning. "If all he needed was a knife, to get the kidney, to kill her. Why the toolbox?" She watched as her old mentor jabbed a finger at the screen, pointing adamantly. "See, see I knew it. He switched hands."

Adele hesitated, "Excuse me?"

Robert jammed his finger against the screen again. "He switched hands. The toolbox. When he's entering, he's carrying it in his right hand. But look, look." He waited, pausing for the video to repeat its loop and come back around to the part where the killer exited the building. "Look; left hand. He enters right hand. Exits left hand."

"Okay, I'll give you that," Adele said, "he switched hands with the toolbox. So what?"

"Everyone has a preferred carrying hand. Just watch anyone carrying groceries in from the store. Every single person has a preferred carrying hand. He preferred carrying the toolbox in his right hand when he entered the building. But then coming out, he's holding it in his left hand."

"So," Adele said, "now, he wants to treat it delicately. When he leaves, he's taking more care with the toolbox. Look, he's not even swinging it as much."

They played the image again, and both of them nodded in turn. Adele heard a shifting sound, and a creak of the floorboard; she noticed Agent Paige now moving further into the room, as if lured by the curiosity of it all.

"It's the kidney," said Adele, nodding once in certainty. "He has the kidney in that toolbox."

Robert shifted. "So he is right-handed, and he has the kidney in that tool-box. What's the significance of that? You don't think he eats it..." Robert trailed off, allowing the horrible question to linger.

But Adele shook her head quickly. "No, I actually don't." She stared at the screen now, her cheeks heating. "The apartment was warm. I don't think he did that. I think the victim wanted the heat on. It was probably chilly; I don't know. But that tells me one thing—why didn't that water evaporate on the bathroom floor? It was there for hours. A thin glaze of a puddle. How come it didn't evaporate? Even most of the blood had dried except for the thickest parts. So why was the water still there?"

Robert tapped his fingers against the desk now in a quiet drumming sound.

"Ice," Adele said.

Robert looked up at her and he began to nod.

"There's ice in that toolbox," Adele said. "Some of it was moved, displaced by the kidney. That ice ended up on the floor and melted slowly. At the second victim's crime scene, I remember opening the freezer. There was a tray of ice missing its cubes. Maybe he needed extra. This time, I'm confident he brought his own." She turned, tapping a finger on the image of the grainy toolbox.

"At the second scene he needed more ice?" said Robert.

Adele shrugged. "I don't know if he took it because he forgot to bring some of his own, or if he just wanted more. But I bet you he had something to do with the missing ice."

"But if there's ice in that toolbox..." Robert said, trailing off, "that means he's not taking the kidneys as trophies. He's keeping them viable!"

Adele shook her head resolutely. "What was his name—Mr. Waters, he said he was on the run back in the US for operating with a suspended medical license, yes?"

Robert nodded. "You don't think he has something to do—"

"No. That's not what I'm saying. My point is, I was looking into it a bit. The underground market, for faux doctors and those operating outside the law, or outside hospitals, at least, is much bigger than you might think. He took the kidney and had ice in his toolbox because I don't think it was a toolbox. It looks like it. But I think it's a cooler. What if he isn't a psychopathic killer, but just someone stealing organs?"

Robert stared at her. "Sounds pretty psychopathic to me."

"You know what I mean. What if he isn't in it for the pleasure of the kill? There's been no mutilation to the bodies. He doesn't seem to have a sexual thrill. He doesn't spend much time with the body as far as we can tell. That would explain no physical evidence. He doesn't get off on fear, either. Which would explain no defensive wounds. They don't even see him coming. He doesn't enjoy the kill. It's a necessity for his business."

Robert hesitated. "That would explain why they're nobodies. Recent expats, people trying to escape one life but yet to establish a new one. Vulnerable. Many of them without connections or friends. They would be alone half the time in their apartments. Except for philanderers like Mr. Waters, there hasn't even been time for them to establish romantic relationships. Girls, alone, without connections, barely able to speak the language, trying to make friends in a big city like Paris. They're the perfect victims."

"I think," Adele said, hesitating, "what if all of this is organ harvesting? A black-market operation? What if he sells these kidneys?" She fell into silence as a slow, ominous prickle tingled down her arms. A serial killer might get scared—might call off an attack or go into hiding. Like her mother's killer. But someone killing for profit? There was no telling if they'd ever stop.

CHAPTER SIXTEEN

At that moment, Adele heard a groan. She stared resolutely out the window, refusing to look back toward Agent Paige.

But Paige approached, causing the floorboards to creak as she did. She snorted again, as if determined they respond to the noise. "Organ harvesting?" Paige snapped. "Are you two stupid? It's a serial killer. And you're talking about a black market of organ harvesting? Conspiracy theories in the DGSI offices. You're getting old," she said, and Adele knew she was directing her comment toward Robert. "And you, well, it's not like I would expect anything better."

Adele closed her eyes, breathing quietly, trying to count to ten in her head. Part of her wanted to shoot the woman. But she supposed it might not be the most advised option. Still, punching Paige sounded very enjoyable at that moment.

She glanced down and noticed Robert reaching out and patting her on the leg in a gentle, calming motion. He pressed his hand against her knee and held it there as if trying to anchor her in place.

"Do you have a better theory?" Robert said, coolly. Adele knew he wasn't so much offended on his own behalf as he was on hers.

"No," said Paige. "I don't need a new theory. We are dealing with a psychopathic killer, preying on young women. Who cares what he's thinking? Killers are always thinking stupid things. And you, both of you, are wasting our time. Interpol or not, you're working in the DGSI, and you're jumping to the wild conclusions of a first-year rookie!"

Adele turned at last, glaring at the woman. "Shut up," she said, her temper boiling.

"Oh? Good one," Paige retorted.

"I said, shut up!" Adele shouted.

Paige's eyes narrowed. She flashed a crocodile grin. A smirk devoid of joy and fueled only by malicious pleasure. "You're inept and impossible to work with."

"I'm impossible to work with?" Adele said, stunned. "You're unconscionable!"

Paige grunted and turned. "I've had enough of this bullshit. I'm reporting you to Foucault. I can't work with stupid and her lecherous old sugar daddy."

With a spring in her step, Paige hurried out of the room, up the hall. Robert lifted his hand, and he nodded toward the door. "Probably best you're in that room when they have that conversation."

Fuming, Adele extricated herself from the desk and hurried into the hall as well. She adjusted her sleeves as she raced after Paige, her blood pulsing in her ears with throbbing pumps. She strode down the hallway and ignored the elevator, watching the door slide shut as Paige entered. Adele made a beeline for the stairs, hurrying up them three at a time. She passed a couple of coworkers but ignored them, despite their nods of greeting.

Just before she reached the top floor where Foucault's office was, she heard the *ding* of the elevator above her. The noise was accompanied by the sound of sliding doors, then quick, hurried footsteps.

Adele cursed and put on an extra burst of speed until she was practically racing up the final steps, then turning down the hall toward the executive's office.

She glimpsed the opaque glass door; wooden chairs and a bench faced the room. Adele glimpsed white painted walls and a thin carpet before spotting Paige rushing to the door, and then the sound of rapid knocking as she tapped her knuckles hurriedly against the frame.

Adele set her jaw and strode down the hall. She heard a voice call from inside the opaque office, and Paige tapped even more insistently.

The voice called a second time, and Paige opened the door, pushing it in. She paused in the doorway, glancing toward Adele, and her eyes narrowed. She shut the door firmly.

Adele immediately heard shouting from Foucault's office. She raced forward, catching words like, "...inept..." "...useless..." and "...fire her, Thierry!"

Instead of knocking, Adele grabbed the handle, flung open the glass door, and stepped in. Executive Thierry Foucault sat behind his large desk. He had a headphone in one ear, and a glass of wine in his hand. A cigarette was smoking in an ashtray.

The smell of nicotine smoke lingered on the air, mingling with the odor of expensive cologne. Adele had been in the office before, and at the time, the windows had been propped open, and the air hadn't been so pungent.

The room was soon polluted with sound as well, drowned in shouting as Adele and Paige both tried to be heard. For a moment, Foucault just stared at them, his eyes dancing between the two like someone watching a tennis match.

The executive of the DGSI shifted uncomfortably in his seat. He had a hawk-like nose and dark eyebrows. His hair was slicked back, and if Adele hadn't known better, she would've guessed he was some sort of banker.

Now, though, she was shouting at the top of her lungs, trying to be heard over Agent Paige. "Unreliable!" she was saying. "Completely unacceptable! Undermining the case from the very—"

Paige, not to be outdone, increased her volume. "Inept! Sending us on wild goose chases! A complete fool!"

"—hateful and spiteful from the start," Adele insisted, grinding her teeth and glaring at Paige now. "Uncooperative to a degree I've never seen before!"

"—stupid," Agent Paige snapped, "harebrained theories—"

At last, Executive Foucault lowered his glass of wine, pulled the earbud from his right ear, and, with a growling tone, shouted, "Enough!"

Both agents fell silent, staring at their boss. He breathed heavily and gave a small cough. He reached out, grabbed his cigarette, put it to his lips, and pulled a long drag. He held it for a second, his eyes closed, and then he exhaled, breathing a jet of smoke toward the closed windows.

Adele shifted uncomfortably. Foucault noticed this motion and scowled. Agent Paige smirked.

The executive regarded the two of them and said, "I had hoped...by pairing you two, you would be able to work out anything between you. I can see now I was mistaken."

"Work out?" Agent Paige snapped. "This loathsome weasel is impossible to work with!"

For her part, Adele ratcheted her eyebrows up. "Get your finger out of my face."

"Quiet!" Foucault thundered

A tentative silence fell again. Both of them were heated, but still, for the moment, Adele reminded herself where she was and who sat behind the desk.

Foucault was a powerful man with powerful connections. If she wanted to continue working with Interpol, and through DGSI and BKA, pissing off the director of the French agency wouldn't be a good start. She swallowed back the next series of retorts and stared directly at Foucault, refusing to look at Agent Paige.

The executive took a long drag from the cigarette again and then smooshed the butt into the ashtray, causing the last bit of white and yellow paper to rend across spreading ash.

He breathed a couple of times, then said, "Clearly, pairing you two was a mistake. Paige, I'll find you something else come morning. Agent Sharp," he said, "I'll assign you a new partner." Then, with a frown he added, "I might also suggest the DGSI was operating just fine before you got here. I don't like what this signifies for future operations. If you can't manage a team of one person, a single partner, I'm not sure what sort of role you'll have in cases to come."

"Sir," Adele said, scandalized, "Agent Paige is the one—"

"Enough!" Foucault snapped, cutting her off. "I wasn't asking for excuses. I was telling you how it is. You can't even manage one partner; I don't know how Interpol expects you to navigate the treacherous waters of multiple agencies across the world. I'm going to have to take a long hard think about this program if things continue like this, understand?"

Adele could feel her cheeks heating up, and she didn't have to look to sense Paige's delight. But she fixed her gaze on the executive and with as much strength as she could muster, she nodded her head once. "I understand."

Everything in her wanted to add more, to repeat how this was Paige's fault, to point out what the older woman had done since they started. She'd been a nuisance at every turn. But judging by Foucault's expression, she doubted he would hear it. And, the more she thought about it, she realized there had to be some sort of personal relationship between Foucault and Agent Paige. After the incident with Matthew and the missing evidence, Paige had only been demoted. Foucault had been in charge then, too. Any other executive would have fired Paige, if not pressed charges. Clearly, there was a history between these two. Though, as Adele glanced at Foucault, she didn't think it was intimate. Still, now wasn't the time to figure it out. She filed the question away for further consideration.

Agent Paige cleared her throat. "Thierry, maybe it would be better if *I* took the lead on this case, and you assign Sharp something else."

"Agent Sharp," Foucault said, "is working with Interpol. I'm not interested in starting anything on that front. Sorry, Sophie, but you're going to have to wait. And you," he said, glancing at Adele again, "are going to need to wait for me to find you a new partner. Can I rely on both of you to play it professionally from this point forward?"

Again, Adele wanted to protest, to defend herself. But at the same time, there was a level of truth to his words. She had a responsibility to the BKA, to the DGSI, and to the FBI. She had a responsibility to Interpol not to rock any boats. And while Paige was insufferable, it was up to Adele to manage unruly partners. She was in her early thirties, and this was the age where careers were either made or destroyed. Glancing at Foucault, she knew this wasn't a man to cross. So she nodded her head in deference, then said, "Am I free to go?"

Foucault grunted. "I never asked you to come. Just don't slam my door this time."

Stiffly, Adele turned and marched, straight-legged, out the door. She quietly shut the door behind her, resisting the urge to linger and eavesdrop through the glass.

As she stepped into the hall, she exhaled, breathing a sigh of relief. It felt, for the first time, like a ball and chain had been unlocked from around her ankle. Hopefully, she could move freely for the first time in days.

She shook her head in a physical gesture of relief. Adele thought of the three victims, of the killer with his toolbox. Despite what Paige thought, Adele felt certain that organ harvesting had something to do with it. The water on the floor and ice—the toolbox as a cooler, the missing kidneys... Someone was killing people to harvest their organs. But where should they go from here? What was the next step? They still didn't know who that fake maintenance man was. What connection did he have with the three women? All of them had been expats. There were online forums and groups where they connected. Perhaps that was where they would start. To investigate anyone who might have a connection to those groups. Maybe they weren't the killer, but they could easily be supplying information to the actual culprit.

Adele adjusted her suit and straightened her sleeves again. She marched straight to the elevator and pushed the button. Paige could take the stairs this time. Adele had to find an organ harvester.

CHAPTER SEVENTEEN

Adele stared out the window, watching the corpulent rain clouds lumbering across the gray horizon. The bleak skies matched her mood. She could hear Robert at his computer, which was once again clear of viruses. She'd spent the last thirty minutes listening to the tech rep admonishing Robert and giving him a series of instructions to avoid infecting his computer again.

Adele had very little doubt the computer would likely be inoperable within the week. Still, she could hear her old mentor tapping away and murmuring quietly to himself. She glanced over her shoulder in his direction, and said, "Anything?"

He didn't look up, and instead smoothed his mustache and yawned, exposing the two missing teeth in the upper part of his smile.

"Still nothing," he said. "Nothing related, at least. No missing kidneys as far as I can tell. There was a case three years ago where someone's lungs were taken, but it was done sloppily. Not professional. They were useless once the police caught up with him."

Adele shivered. "Well, thanks for that image," she said. "Let me know if there's anything relevant."

Robert waved and returned his attention to the screen. Adele glanced back into the gray skies. She pressed her hand to her pocket with her phone, waiting impatiently for it to buzz. She'd contacted Ms. Jayne, who'd promised to have her own people at Interpol look for connections to organ-harvesting outside of France.

The way clearance worked with Interpol's files, only one of the French agents had access to old cases at a time. Adele and Robert had flipped a coin and he'd won—though she suspected he'd cheated. But now, Adele had to sit and wait for her turn to go over the old cases.

"Almost done?" she asked.

Robert shrugged. "Only a few more hours," he said. "Then you can have the security key."

Adele sighed. This license with Interpol was still in a testing period. She hoped, eventually, the more trust she garnered, the easier it would be to access files. For now, though, a few hours was a long time to wait and stare out a window.

At last, sensing her disgruntlement, Robert glanced up from his computer. "If you want," he said, "you can take a break. You look like you need it."

Adele studied the rain clouds and watched as the first few droplets appeared as hazy streaks against the sky. She had once found herself caught in a rainstorm, right on the verge of the raindrops, fleeing it. Angus hadn't believed her when she'd told him, but Adele still swore to this day that at one point the back half of her car had been tapping with rain, while the front windshield had been completely clear.

"Nowhere to go," she said with a shrug.

Robert waved distractedly at her, once again his attention fixed on the computer. "The swimming pool is open back at the house. Or you could go for a jog." He trailed off, muttering to himself. Adele glanced over; it seemed as if he was again riveted by whatever he was reading.

"Just make sure to text me if there's anything important," Adele said.

Robert waved distractedly and continued to study his computer screen, scrolling with his mouse. "Fascinating . . ." he murmured.

Adele rolled her eyes, pushed out of her chair, and exited the office.

As she approached the elevator, she felt a prickle up her spine, and she glanced over her shoulder, half expecting Agent Paige to be watching her every move. But there was no one in the hall. The disruptive agent had been assigned a new case, and Adele would have to wait for her new partner.

She thought of Robert's comment about the pool back at the mansion. The last time she swam in the pool, she had company. But that had been nearly a month ago. A month since she last spoke with John.

Adele found her hand moving absentmindedly to the elevator's buttons. She pushed the down arrow, waiting for the compartment to arrive. She entered the elevator and pulled out her phone. Absentmindedly, she scroll down to a contact: *Dad*. She stared at the screen for a moment, and then tapped the button.

At the same time, as the phone emitted a quiet ringing noise, she reached out with her other hand and pushed the button for the basement. She didn't really feel like taking a break, but right now there was nothing for her to do. Perhaps she could meet up with an old friend.

She sighed as her phone continued to buzz. At last, before the elevator reached the bottom floor, there was a quiet clicking noise, the sound of static, then a voice. "Sharp?" her father's voice buzzed through the speakers.

Adele frowned. Her father often referred to her by their last name. It had been something he'd done since she was a child. Secretly, she suspected it made him feel more like he had a boy than a girl. Her father had always wanted a boy. In recent weeks, he had done better at calling her by her first name, but turning over a new leaf often took time. Especially in her father's case; she had it on good authority he hated leaves, and trees, and anything green in the world.

"Dad?" she said.

"What is it?" his buzzing voice replied. A quiet pause in the elevator, then, as if realizing perhaps he'd been too blunt, he said, "It's," he cleared his throat on the other end, "good to hear from you. How are you doing?"

Adele suppressed a smile. At least he was trying. "I'm doing fine, Dad. How are you?"

"Oh, can complain, but won't," he said.

Adele waited, and so did he.

At last, he cleared his throat. "Do you need anything?"

"Christ, Dad, we've been over this. Sometimes I'm just calling to catch up."

"Oh," he said, clearing his throat again, "right. Well, yes. I'm, to be honest with you, I'm actually in the middle of something, but, actually, I suppose it could wait. A few minutes."

To most, a few minutes of their father's time every week might not seem like much, but Adele knew it was a great improvement. "Thanks," she said. "Is anything going on back home? How's the job?"

The one thing the Sergeant cared about most besides politics was his job. "Fine," he said, "fine. Of course, had some trouble the other night. Couple of drunks came in and one of them overdosed in the entry hall. Wasn't pretty. Which, I might add, is why you should always stay clear of—"

"Dad, I'm not doing drugs. Are you watching anything good?"

She knew her father spent a lot of time watching TV, but he hated to admit it. The Sergeant hadn't looked fondly on those who watched TV when she'd been growing up, but in his old age, in an empty house, there were only so many model sets and crosswords one could do.

"Oh," he said, "you know how it is. Mostly the news. How—how is your job?"

Adele smiled faintly and glanced at the phone. The elevator dinged, and the sliding doors opened at last. She stepped off into the basement, glancing down the long hall. Before she could turn back and reconsider, the elevator made another noise, suggesting someone had called it back upstairs, and the doors slid shut. The compartment rattled, leaving her alone in the abandoned hallway of the DGSI basement.

"Oh," she said, "not great. Getting a new partner, which isn't bad."

There was silence, and Adele frowned at her phone, wondering if she'd lost reception. After a moment, though, a staticky voice said, "Hello, dear, I can't hear you. You're breaking up."

Adele tilted her head, pressing her phone tightly against her face. "Sorry, Dad. I'm in a basement. Reception is bad."

"Sharp? I can't hear you. I'll call you later. Soup is getting cold."

"That's fine," she said, shouting in order to be heard. "Take care, Dad!"

She paused, then heard, a muffled, "Goodbye, Sharp." There was a quiet click and then silence.

Adele turned away from the elevator and stowed the phone in her pocket. "Progress is progress," she murmured out loud to no one in particular. The only times they argued now, when her father was trying, was when the topic of her mother's killer came up. The Sergeant knew Adele still intended to bring the murderer to justice, but he wanted her to leave the case alone.

Adele put the thought from her mind as she moved through the abandoned hall toward John's old makeshift speakeasy. He had set up a distillery in the basement, which would've surprised her in anyone else, but given what she knew about the tall, scar-faced agent, she supposed it was somewhat predictable. John didn't often play by the rules, but he was a reliable partner when times got tough.

Hesitantly, she rested her hand on the door to the interrogation room. She noticed it was cracked. For a moment, her heart fluttered in her chest and she felt a flash of excitement.

She swallowed the emotions, though, wondering why she was acting like a schoolgirl. Adele reached out, gripped the door handle, and began to ease open the door to John's bachelor pad. The hinges creaked, and Adele's excitement culminated, but then fell.

The room was empty.

She felt a flash of disappointment. But she suppressed the emotion just as quickly and looked around the room.

There was a cup resting on the speakeasy's desk. The distillery, with all its pipes and flasks and beakers, looked like it had been used recently. A couple of droplets of clear liquid dangled from the edge of a spigot, over the floor, which had a single splash on the varnished wood.

Adele glanced up and down the hall, but there was no sign of her former partner.

The floor was dusty in the hall, and various footprints ran up and down the space; some were hers from the previous day, and others were larger. Vaguely, Adele wondered if John brought other people down here too. This thought bothered her. She moved back into the old interrogation room, swinging the door shut.

She inhaled the room, smelling the odor of liquor and the faint hint of dust. She glanced over to the wall where there hung pictures of John with the Commandos Marine—special forces similar to US Navy SEALs. John often spoke highly of his old crew, but she had never met any of them. There had always been a sadness to John when he mentioned them.

Agent Renee wasn't a particularly sentimental man, and those two photos of his old crew were all he had on the wall. There were no pictures of a family or a wife or kids. As Adele moved into the room, she reached out for the cup on the counter. She examined the inside, decided it was likely clean, and poured herself a drink from the distillery.

She then took her ill-gotten gains and collapsed onto the lumpy couch beneath the unframed photos. The couch was more cushion than support; she melted into it and breathed a deep sigh, leaning back against the cushions.

Adele inhaled the scent of the alcohol from her glass. It stung her nostrils, and she lifted it to her lips, taking a sip. It nettled as she remembered it had, and her eyes watered briefly at first, but it was smooth going down.

After the first sip, Adele felt alert. After the second, she felt a flash of contentment. And after the third, she closed her eyes and settled back, embraced by the cushioned couch, allowing her thoughts to wander.

She considered the case for a moment. This had to have something to do with organ trafficking. She was nearly certain of it. But she'd been wrong before. Foucault had struck a nerve. If he withdrew support for her connection with Interpol, the whole operation would likely collapse. This was a trial run. Ms. Jayne had hired her as a liaison between the three agencies and the three countries. A shared asset between the FBI, the BKA, and the DGSI. But if Executive Foucault thought she wasn't up to the task, or decided to take Agent Paige's side over hers, the whole operation could end before it even started.

Adele shifted again, throwing her legs up on the couch now and taking her shoes off, knocking them with her right foot onto the floor, listening to the dull thumps as they landed on the ground. She stretched, exhaling as she lay against the couch, and then took another sip from the glass, her head elevated against the cushion of the armrest.

She needed to be in France. Her mother's killer was somewhere in France. Maybe in Paris, maybe not. Wherever he was, he had gotten away with it.

Adele took another long sip, wincing against the strong flavor. She found she could breathe clearly through her nostrils now.

Adele tried to consider her father's aversion to her mother's case. Why did he care so much what she investigated? It wasn't like he even cared about her mother before she had died. Had he?

She thought of her father's house. He kept the home they'd lived in when she'd been a child back in Germany. Adele had left at the age of twelve to move in with her mother in France. But her father still kept the family pictures. He kept her room the same way, and the last time she'd been there, she had even seen her stuffed animals on the old bed.

Those weren't the actions of a man who didn't care. So why did he want her to ignore her mother's case? Didn't he want justice realized? Surely they had loved each other once upon a time.

Adele breathed deeply, pushing the thoughts from her mind. It wouldn't do to be scatterbrained, to split her focus. Robert was currently looking into other organ harvesting cases in France. She wondered what he would come up with. They needed a lead. A solid one. But where would that come from?

As Adele thought, her mind began to slow. She lowered her glass and placed it on the floor, half empty. She listened to the sound of the quiet bubbling from the distillery; beyond that, there was no other noise. Even the vents down here were quiet.

No footsteps, no quiet mumble of voices, no buzz of electricity or clack from a keyboard. In silence, Adele slowly drifted off to sleep.

She awoke to a quiet creaking sound.

Slowly, Adele opened her eyes—her training kicking in—keeping them half slits, surveying the room before announcing her consciousness. She still lay on the couch in John's bachelor pad.

The door, however, was open.

She spotted a tall silhouette in the door, staring at her; then, just as quickly, the figure turned and exited the room, easing the door shut behind him, quietly. As the door clicked, Adele's eyes shot open, and she bolted upright.

Chapter Eighteen

"Hang on!" she called, her voice quieter than anticipated as the sleep slowly left her and she regained her motor skills. She heard the sound of footsteps in the hall, and her frown deepened.

She swung off the couch and surged forward, rushing to the door and flinging it open. Adele stepped into the hall and peered down it, her eyes fixating on John Renee where he headed for the stairs with long strides.

"John!" she called out.

The agent froze, one hand on the banister, a long leg extending up four steps, his foot pressed into the marble. The other, though, remained at the bottom of the stairs as he seemed to have momentarily frozen. She heard a vague swallowing sound.

Adele cleared her throat. "John," she repeated.

"Oh," said John, with a would-be nonchalant shrug. Hesitantly, he began to turn, and his dark eyes surveyed her across the hall. "How are you doing, American Princess?"

He still carried an air of indecisiveness as he twisted on the stairs. His lopsided smile stretched his face, and Adele noticed the burn mark along his neck and up the underside of his chin. He wore a loose, unbuttoned black shirt, and his forearms were more defined than she remembered. He had a handsome face, which in the past she'd likened to that of a James Bond villain. Now, he seemed caught on the stairs, half turned to leave, and half stuck in place like a child with his hand caught in a cookie jar. He looked uncomfortably at Adele, studying her like the same child determining how much trouble they were in. His lanky form and broad shoulders did little to offset the discomfort written across his face.

Adele strode across the hall, a feeling welling inside her that she couldn't quite place: part frustration, part happiness, and part rejection.

"What was that?" she demanded, jutting a thumb over her shoulder toward the doorway. John glanced at her thumb, then toward the door, a stupid look on his face.

"Oh, what was . . . I don't . . ." He trailed off, jumbling his words, and ending with another shrug of his large shoulders.

Adele's eyes narrowed. She came to a halt in front of him, her chin angled so she was looking into his eyes. He was a head taller than her, well over six feet, and yet it was him, not her, quailing in that moment. "You saw me, and you left!" she exclaimed.

John paused. He seemed to be considering his words and frowned slightly, his dark eyebrows like gashes in granite, angling over his brooding gaze.

"I," he hesitated, "I saw a pretty figure sleeping on the couch," he said, pivoting quickly, now adopting a wry grin. He gave a nonchalant shrug, seemingly relaxing. "You know you snore when you sleep."

Adele scowled. "I do not. And don't bullshit me; pretty figure indeed. Why didn't you stay to talk?"

John gave an emphatic role of his eyes. The uneasiness from before seemed to melt beneath his returning confidence, his posture now one of relaxed indifference, like a tomcat slinking through an alley. He smirked and wiggled his eyebrows, "Did you want me to come in while you were sleeping?"

Adele glared at him. "Cut it out. Why have you been dodging me?"

John's smirk faded slightly, and Adele caught a glimpse of something authentic in his eyes. Just as quickly, though, he mastered his expression and grinned again. "Well, Adele Sharp, I didn't know you were into that sort of thing, I'll keep it in mind for future reference."

"Why did you duck me?" she said, jabbing a finger into his chest now.

He winced and daintily withdrew her hand. "All right, hang on there, jabby. No need to dent my chest. Look, I came down for a drink, saw you sleeping, decided not to disturb you. What's the big deal?"

"You've been avoiding me," she repeated. "Agent Paige said the moment you heard I was coming back you took a case—"

"Oh," said John with a snort, "forget what that vampire says. You can't trust the woman. Take it from me, I think she's sleeping with the executive."

Adele hesitated. She didn't think the same, but wanted to stay on task, so she didn't correct him. "John, I'm serious, why have you been avoiding me?"

John let out a long breath, his chest deflating like a leaky balloon jabbed with a needle. "I haven't been avoiding you," he said, but there was no conviction in it. "A case came up. I'm doing my job. Isn't that what you pestered me about for nearly a week last time?"

Adele crossed her arms over her chest, causing her suit to wrinkle near the creases of her elbows. "John," she said, "how stupid do you think I am?"

John leaned back, setting one elbow on the guardrail of the staircase. "Stupid? I'd never," he said. He met her gaze without yielding.

She clenched her teeth. "You know what," she said, "fine, if you don't want to talk, be that way. I know what happened last time we spoke. Don't pretend like it didn't."

At this, John's cheeks flushed. "I don't know what you're talking about. We had some fun. Swam around that pool of Robert's. So what?"

Adele raised an eyebrow at him, "Oh? You didn't try to kiss me?"

It was like she'd shot him. John threw his hands to the sky. "*I* tried to kiss you? Right, *you* tried to kiss me."

Adult shook her head. "That's not how I remember it."

John glared now. "American Princess comes into France, steals a kiss, steals some of my booze, and then makes stories up. You live in fantasy land, little girl."

"You're insufferable. I can't even believe that I—"

"You what?" John's lips curled into a smile again, and he studied her with a sharklike expression.

Adele stared back, refusing to give in to his predatory gaze. She hesitated, then said, in a gentler tone, "I didn't avoid it because I don't like you; I mean I don't, not that way—I was just taken off guard is all. You didn't have to leave."

John snorted. "I don't know what you're talking about. If I did try to kiss you, I guarantee you it was the alcohol. I'm a man, you're a woman. You're okay looking, I suppose," he said, giving her a long, lecherous look.

Adele knew he was trying to make her uncomfortable, and she refused to give in. She kept her eyes fixed on his and glimpsed a flash of shame. But just as quickly, he set his jaw, his cheeks compressing a bit. "I'm not the sort to ask twice, American Princess."

Adele shook her head. "So you admit you did try to kiss me?"

He guffawed, and this time he leaned back, crossing his arms. "You missed me. No, don't deny it. I can tell. You missed me. Do you dream about me?" He wiggled his dark eyebrows again.

Adele snorted. "Look, let's forget that for a moment. Maybe I shouldn't have invited you over to Robert's. I don't know. I didn't mean to wound your fragile honor or anything."

Adele knew it would injure his pride when she said it, which was exactly why she did. Two could play this game. It was probably best they kept things professional anyway. He was a reliable partner. Nauseatingly unprofessional, but reliable. He'd saved her life after all.

"Look, I don't know what you're working on," she said, "but I could use your help."

John cleared his throat. "Look, Adele, I wish I could, but I really am working another case. I'm quite busy. I'm not lucky enough to have multiple agencies supplying me with intel."

"Fine," Adele, raising her hands. "No, really, I get it. Whatever you're working on is probably more interesting. I'm sure it's something really fascinating. Not financial crime or accounting or a bunch of numbers on a screen or anything—I'm *sure.*"

John's eyes narrowed. "I'll have you know, I'm investigating a very serious, important case of embezzling." He tugged at his black shirt, realizing the top button was undone. Before he finally had done it though, he seemed disgusted by his urge for modesty and left it unbuttoned, putting his hands on his hips in a defiant posture. "It's an important case," he insisted.

Adele hid a smirk. "Never said it wasn't. I'm sure it's very important. Very interesting. You can go over the numbers again, and again, and again. You get to talk to all sorts of interesting bankers and accountants." She nodded. "Fascinating."

He glared. "I like it better when you speak in English," he said. "At least that way I don't understand your drivel half the time. Actually, no, I like it better when you don't speak at all."

Adele smirked now, returning the same grin John had flashed earlier. "Oh?" she said. "Pity that. Because if I could speak, I would tell you we have a case with three dead girls." She fixed her eyes on John, some of the humor fading from her tone. "He's killing them at a three-day pace. We're on track for a lot of bodies if we don't do something quick. There's no physical evidence, no DNA, no fingerprints. He steals their kidneys. Last crime scene had a video, but we couldn't see his face. He wore gloves. Found a pool of water suggesting perhaps he had ice in the toolbox. The working theory right now is that he's been harvesting their kidneys to sell on the black market. It's an organ harvesting case. Which, of course, compared to embezzlement is boring. It's nothing."

John's lips tightened the more she spoke. He was now frowning. As she trailed off, he grunted, "Interpol have any files?"

Adele nodded. "Robert is combing through them right now. Due to the nature of this new task force, they're only giving one of us access at a time. But by the end of it, I think we'll find a connection. There has to be."

When she looked back, John was watching her with a slight smile on his lips. When he noticed her looking, though, he quickly coughed and turned away, glancing up the stairs. "Look," he said, hesitantly, "have you thought to look in organized crime?"

Adele shook her head. "We discussed it, but thought to start with Interpol's cold ones."

John nodded. "Makes sense, but I've actually worked a couple of cases. Three years ago . . ." He hesitated, trailing off.

"Three years ago what?"

He looked her straight in the eyes. "I didn't try to kiss you. I just got a little too close. It was the alcohol."

"Fine," Adele waved her hand, "you didn't try to kiss me. Totally professional. What were you saying?"

John seemed to settle. "Three years ago I worked a case with organ harvesting. A group of Serbians operating in France. They offered twenty-five thousand euros for a good set of lungs, kidneys, liver, anything."

Adele stared. "A group? How proliferate?"

John shook his head. "Not entirely sure. We didn't get all the books. We did, however, shut down the ring. We caught the Serbians. A lot of desperate and poor in France were coming here, some of them offering their own kidneys, or whatever organs they could spare without dying. Twenty-five thousand euros is a lot of money."

Adele felt her stomach churn. "Right," she said, "and so you shut them down?"

John nodded. "It was messed up, Adele. I saw some things . . . and I've seen a lot."

"What do you think this has to do with my case?"

"The Serbians often didn't pay. People would come, go under, have their organs removed, or bring some poor hapless victim who didn't know any better, and prey on them. They would take the organs, sometimes killing the person, and then leave. They wouldn't pay. They left these people poor, broken, no money, with injuries and poorly done stitches. Sometimes they wouldn't even stitch them back up, and would just leave them on their operating tables in a back warehouse, bleeding out; when they would wake from the anesthesia, they would be in pain, minus an organ, and no money to show for it. There were more than a few of those cases where I had to visit someone in the hospital and watch while surgeons repaired the messy job of the organ harvesters."

Adele shivered in horror.

He sighed. "You know what . . . fuck those guys. Fine, I'm in. I'll help. But I can't tell you anything it sounds like you don't know. There is one angle, though."

Adele watched, waiting for him to continue.

"I did have a contact. A French criminal. Not Serbian, but he worked with them, adjacent. He turned informant to get off without penalty."

"So he gave up a crime ring in order to avoid a prison sentence?" Adele asked. "Bold move."

"Anyway," said John, "I think I know where to start."

"If you want, we can meet up tomorrow morning and—"

John snorted. "Who said anything about morning? Come with me, American Princess." He turned and began hurrying up the stairs; Adele fell into step. She felt like he was moving faster than necessary, just to force her to jog to keep up with his lanky strides. As they moved, John fished his phone from his pocket, and pressed it to his ear.

"Who are you calling?" she asked, following him onto the first-floor landing and moving toward the sliding doors that entered the parking lot.

"My contact," said John. "He still works in France."

Adele frowned. "We're going to go meet with a criminal?"

"Hush," said John. He held out a finger and actually pushed it against her lips. Adele slapped his hand away, glaring, and John smirked again as he moved through the doors into the parking lot, gesturing she should follow.

CHAPTER NINETEEN

By the time John pulled his sports car to a grumbling halt along the ridged curb outside the café, night had fallen.

Adele was still staring at the luxurious interior of the vehicle, shaking her head. "This can't possibly be government issue," she said, glaring at John.

He smirked back at her, tapping the steering wheel. "No?" he said. "I thought Yankee Doodle Dandies liked cars like this."

She rolled her eyes. "Some of us think cars likes these are compensating for something small." This time it was her turn to give John a significant glance and flip her eyes down.

His expression became rather fixed. "I can assure you, American Princess, there's nothing small about—"

"Right, fine," Adele said, hurriedly. "Who are we here to see then?"

Still glaring at her through narrowed eyes, John said, "My contact. Name of Francis. No given second name—learned that when we arrested him. He just goes by Francis—I don't think his parents could bother giving him another."

Adele nodded. "You guys friendly?"

John winked. "Come now, of course. Everyone likes me."

"That does nothing to put me at ease," Adele muttered. Stomach twisting, she followed John out of the sports car. She shut the door behind her, glancing back at the tinted windows and the glossy black paint. Vaguely, she wondered how on earth John had gotten permission to use this as his official government vehicle. DGSI allowed operatives to bend rules for the sake of collaring criminals, but she would've loved to be at the pitch meeting for this gas-guzzling excuse for a mode of transportation.

Then again, this was the same man who had a speakeasy in a government building's basement. John's lengthy gait picked up as he moved toward the seedy café's door. Adele could practically see smoke coming from within, twisting up past the low roof. Four panes of glass occupied the wooden green door, but the paint was chipped, and one of the sections of glass was missing.

Adele stared at the café. She only knew what it was due to John. Otherwise, she couldn't see any sign or name suggesting this was a place of business. A series of red umbrellas hemmed in the front porch, wrapped in straps like leather above a few round tables.

Beer cans littered the ground around the sidewalk, and the windows of the café itself were painted black. They weren't tinted; it was as if someone had actually spray-painted them from the outside. The adjacent red brick building displayed all sorts of obscene drawings and graffiti. But the café itself hadn't been vandalized. Adele frowned. She'd once been on a case with Robert, years ago, where he'd told her that any place in a seedy part of a neighborhood which wasn't tagged meant the owner had a reputation.

"What is this place?" she said.

John, though, stepped through the small, rusted gate circling the makeshift porch and headed for the door with the missing glass section. "Try to look less like a cop," he called. "And if anyone tries to make a move on you in there, shoot them."

Adele stared after him, but then fell into step, the unease in her gut only rising. The tall agent pushed open the door. No bell announced his presence. As Adele followed after him, she was assailed by the smell of smoke. She forced herself to breathe through her mouth in slow, puffing breaths.

On their left, a low bar was occupied by a few patrons nursing drinks. They drank straight out of their respective bottles. John nodded toward a large, rotund woman behind the counter. She wore a white apron streaked with yellow and red. The woman glanced back at John and didn't return his greeting. Her eyes flitted to Adele, and her impassive expression remained as emphatic as a slab of granite. Her eyes tracked them across the room as John and Adele moved through the café.

On the other side of the room, small, circular tables occupied a space in front of neon vending machines and fridges lined with soda bottles. The bottles themselves were half empty, as if people had drunk them before putting them back in the fridges.

"Can I help you?" the large woman behind the counter called out. She had addressed the question to Adele. Adele shrugged and gave a small nod toward John.

John looked over. "Where's Francis?"

The woman's expression softened a bit. Instead of distrustful, now she looked curious. She waved a hand toward the stairs in the back of the café and then returned her attention to a customer who was banging his glass against the marble counter. Besides the smoke, the cafe smelled like a locker room and talcum powder. A few of the men sitting around tables made eyes at her. Most had strange tattoos up and down their arms; some had even tattooed their knuckles, their fingers, and their faces. One man had tattoos like tears down the sides of his eyes.

"Like I said," John said, "if any of them try anything, shoot them." He spoke loud enough so the patrons heard, and most turned back to their drinks.

"What is this place?" Adele repeated, keeping her voice low.

John said, "A hangout. For the sorts of people we put behind bars." He added this last part in a quiet voice. "They've seen me here before, but they don't know where I work. Probably best they don't find out either," he added, still quiet.

He winked, as if to offset the words themselves, but Adele only felt more at unease. She kept her jacket buttoned in the front, the length covering her weapon and her badge. Her Interpol temporary credentials were still in her suit pocket.

"Should've told me before we got here," Adele growled, eyes still fixed on the staircase.

John reached the top of the stairs and looked at her. "Just don't let them see the cuffs, right?" Then, he turned and took the steps. She noted he didn't reach out to touch the railing. The metal bar looked greasy. She kept her own hands at her sides as she too descended. The smell from downstairs, if at all possible, was less offensive than upstairs.

A pool table occupied a back wall with no windows. A couple of arcade slot machines and a poker table were populated by a group of men and a couple women. No one paid attention as they entered the basement save two men in black suits.

The men both stepped forward from where they'd been stationed against a square pillar, frowning at the newcomers. Their suits bulged near their waistbands, suggesting they carried weapons which Adele guessed were probably illegal. Both men held out halting hands. "Names?" they asked.

John eyed them both. "I'm here to see Francis."

The larger of the two suits grunted, adjusting his jacket. He turned his head and shouted, "Francis! Visitors."

There was a pause, then a groaning sound from behind a black curtain in the back of the room. The curtain cordoned off part of the basement behind both the billiards and the poker table. The groaning sound became a resigned sigh, and a frail hand poked through the curtains, brushing aside the fabric.

A man emerged, wearing a hoodie and sweatpants. He had sallow cheeks and a skeletal face. He looked like he might have had Korean and French heritage, but when he approached, he spoke seamless French. "What is it?" he asked, looking around. Then his eyes flicked from the guards to John. His expression became rather fixed.

"How's it going, Francis?" said John with a wink. "Tried calling." The sallow-faced man named Francis stared. A pink tongue darted out to wet his lips.

He sniffed a couple of times and wiped his hand across the back of his nose. "What are you doing here?" he said, quickly.

Adele glanced between the man and John, trying to get a read on the situation. The guards were also doing a quick survey, and they didn't look particularly pleased. "Do you know this twerp?" asked the muscular guard, jabbing a thumb at John.

"That's right, do you know me?" John said, putting a weight of significance behind the words. "Because, if you don't, I can introduce myself. I can tell everyone where I'm from, what I need, how we know each other..." He trailed off, allowing the words to linger.

With each subsequent phrase, the man named Francis seemed to pale even more. He adjusted his hood, tugging at the drawstrings and twisting them. At last, he let them go, allowing them to unwind with a twirl. "I know him," Francis said jerkily. "He's a guest."

Francis beckoned at John with a jerking motion and the guards stepped aside. Adele watched as Francis slipped a finger into his hoodie pocket and pulled out a crisp role of hundred-euro bills. He peeled off a few of the bills and tucked them into the jacket pockets of both the guards. "No need to tell upstairs, hey?" Francis murmured beneath his breath.

The guards looked away now, their eyes fixed on the staircase as if John and Adele weren't even there.

John strolled past, giving each man a wink, and he allowed Francis to guide the two of them to the back of the room, past the poker table and the billiards room. They reached the black curtain on a shower rail. Adele glanced up and down the room and spotted more tattoos she recognized as gang affiliated.

"Never a dull moment," she muttered.

John chuckled and brushed the curtain aside, gesturing gallantly for her to enter. Francis, though, moved forward first, glaring at John and muttering beneath his breath in a language Adele didn't understand.

He led the two of them into a small booth, sheltered by the curtain, hidden from the rest of the room. Immediately, Adele spotted rolls of euros and other money scattered across the table. Just as quickly, the money seemed to vanish, as with three quick, practiced sweeping motions, Francis shoved the bank notes into drawers, a leather bag, and a backpack behind the table. He then moved over and sat in a large, comfortable reclining chair. It wasn't a desk chair, so much as a lazy-boy. Still, he leaned back and placed his hands behind his head, glaring out at them.

A white shelf next to them displayed jackets dangling from hangers.

"We're in the coat closet?" Adele asked.

"Don't worry about it," Francis grunted. His nervous, twitching eyes set in his sallow face darted from John to Adele. "Who are you?"

"My name is Agent Sharp," Adele began, "and I'm—"

"Shush!" Francis interrupted fiercely, a finger pressed painfully to his own lips, and his eyes darted toward the gap in the curtains. John was in the middle of pulling the drapes closed with a rattling sound as the rollers moved in the tracks above.

"Stow it with the agent talk, hey?" Francis muttered, his voice barely a whisper. "What do you want?"

"Answers," John said, turning to face the small man behind the desk.

Francis crossed his legs and glared sullenly up at John from his cushioned chair. "I don't know if I have any answers," he snapped. He began twisting his hoodie's drawstrings once more.

"John," said Adele, "this is your contact? The one involved with the organ traders?"

John nodded once, and Francis quickly protested, shaking his head. His sallow cheeks seemed even less healthy in the darkness of the closet, shaded by the dangling jackets. "Hang on," he said quickly. "I'm not *involved* with organ traders. I had some dealings with their accountants—when I figured out what they were up to, I got out. Right quick," he said. He adjusted his hoodie as if it were a jacket. "I have a reputation to maintain," he muttered.

John grunted. "You owe me, Francis. I got you out of prison."

Francis stuck out his chin and clenched his fists around the ends of his hoodie drawstrings. "I told you everything I knew last time. Organ traffickers are the *worst*. I'm not involved with those folks or anyone they work with anymore."

John leaned put one foot on Francis's desk, supporting his chin with an arm lodged against his upraised knee. "You know things, Francis. It's why I got you out of prison, and it's why they pay you."

The informant didn't blink.

"I'm not asking you to sell out anyone you're in bed with—see? You dislike the traffickers as much as me. A little bit of information—that's all I'm asking."

Francis tried to speak, and for a moment it looked like he would refuse, but then his eyes flicked to Adele and he sighed.

"The Serbians?" he asked.

John nodded. "Are they back?"

Francis frowned. "Most of them are still in prison after last time." This time he spoke so quietly Adele had to lean forward to hear. "And, I might add, if they ever find out I was the one who—"

"They won't find out," John said, shaking his head. "I'm not going to let that happen, okay. I just need to know if any of them are setting up shop again."

Once more, Francis glanced between Adele and John. "Do I get a bonus for this?"

Before John could reply, Adele interjected, "We'll see what we can do. Look, if there's anything you can tell us, I'll owe you one."

Francis studied her a moment longer. "All right, Interpol," he said, steepling his fingers beneath his chin. "But don't think I won't collect."

John frowned at Adele, but she kept her gaze fixed on the informant.

"Look," Francis said with an audible swallow, "like I said, most of those psychos are still in prison. Thank God…as you well know," he added, with a look at John. "And, like I said, I'm not involved at all with any illicit business like that."

John waved his hand in a quick circle, as if to say, *Get on with it.*

"But," Francis said, dangling the word like a baited worm in front of a famished trout, "I have heard there are a couple of the old Serbs getting things back up and running. They don't have the same connections as before, mind you," he added, "but I hear they're working with someone else now."

John raised an eyebrow. "Who?" he demanded.

"Look, I told you. I don't know much. You bastards keep a close enough eye on me as it is." Francis trailed off, glaring at John, but then his shoulders sagged. "Most of them are still in prison. But a couple of the nephews of the lead guy are running their own chop shop out in a warehouse district. There's another shop, a motor place, but it's a front. The real business is in the back."

"What's the place called?" John growled.

"Debosselage et Automobiles," he replied quickly. He kept his voice low, whispering now. Adele glanced from the curtain back to Francis.

"They're paired up now," he said, quickly. "A German doctor. I don't know who."

John snorted.

"I'm not lying," Francis protested. "Seriously, I don't know who. I wish I did."

John hesitated, then raised an eyebrow toward Adele.

"I..." she began, still watching Francis, then trailing off. She frowned at the informant. "A German doctor? Why German?"

Francis shook his head. "Damn if I know. I didn't pry much. Trust me, there are people asking questions that I don't want to have answers to. It's not like it's safe for me out here anyway. People already suspect me."

"They should," said John, cheerfully. Then he turned to go, but before he left, John reached over and began rummaging through Francis's pockets.

The informant protested, shouting, but John held up a quieting finger, and Francis fell silent. Then John fished out a roll of bills they'd spotted earlier. He took the money, bounced it a couple times in his hand, examining the rubber bands wrapped around the money, and whistled softly. "That's a lot of dough," he said.

Francis cursed beneath his breath, shaking his head.

"John," Adele said, frowning at the money, but John ignored her and pocketed it.

"Look," Francis protested, "I need that. If my boss doesn't—"

"I'm sure you'll come up with something," John interrupted. "Debosselage et Automobiles, hmm? And you say they work out of there?"

Francis glared at the table. "That's the last I heard. Look, I promise—"

"Thanks, Francis," John said with a wink. He turned away, the money still rolled up in his pocket. He glanced at Adele and then pushed through the curtains, moving back out into the basement.

Adele inhaled deeply and shrugged at Francis, resisting the urge to apologize. Then, with a weight in her chest, she moved after John, pushing through the curtains as well, and following him to the bottom of the stairs.

John was a loose cannon, but either way, they had their next lead; Adele only hoped it would pan out.

CHAPTER TWENTY

Four blocks from Debosselage et Automobiles, under the cover of darkness, with midnight cresting the horizon, Adele and John sat in his vehicle, staring out the angled window.

"They coming?" John asked.

Adele checked her watch for the second time. She looked down at her phone, adjusted the dashboard radio, and shook her head. "Should be." She click the radio comm and said: "What's the ETA for Hazel Street?"

A pause, a crackle, then a voice, *"I'm sending the backup I have. They should be there within a few minutes. Hang tight."*

Adele clicked the speaker again and shrugged.

John growled, shaking his head. "It's been a few minutes for the last half hour. What are they doing? Eating donuts?"

Adele shook her head. "I don't know. Could be bureaucrat stuff. Maybe there's more red tape when working with an FBI agent."

John sighed and leaned back in the chair, stretching his legs beneath the steering wheel and heaving a breath toward the convertible ceiling.

"John," Adele began, glancing toward his pocket where he had stored the role of stolen money. John raised an eyebrow at her.

She paused, considering her words, but then shook her head. Perhaps John wasn't what she thought he was. Sometimes distance brought clarity. When she was in France last time, she'd been annoyed by John for the most part. He was unprofessional. Adele knew people like John weren't the type to change. The way he'd acted back there with Francis, taking that money . . . she wasn't sure what she thought. She'd gone along with it, but was starting to regret that decision.

"John, I just want to say," she began, "if I did anything to offend you, I hope you know that I didn't mean to."

John interrupted. "We don't need to. All right? Maybe we both made mistakes."

Adele shook her head, turning to glance out the window again.

"I'm not sure what you expected," he said, quietly.

Adele looked back at him. "Do you mean about this case, or—"

Instead of answering, he frowned, then said, "Sharp, I think I need to be clear. I'm not a good man."

Adele's eyes traced the scar on his chin. She thought of the pictures back in his secret bachelor pad, showing the image of his military buddies. She also thought of the serial killer last month standing over her. The gun shot from outside. The killer dropping dead. With that one bullet, John had saved both her and her father. She remembered asking for help on the radio, giving cryptic clues. She remembered John's voice at that time, when he'd heard she was in trouble. The sound of racing footsteps, gasping breath as he rushed to her aid. He was a confusing person.

"You shouldn't have taken it," she began, still staring at his pocket now, but then trailed off, shaking her head.

"Taken what?" John asked.

She raised an eyebrow, then her shoulders sagged. "Never mind, it's not important."

John seemed unsatisfied with this answer. He also turned to stare out the window. They waited for the next few minutes, but still, no backup came. Every couple of moments, Adele listened to dispatch's voice over the radio, mentioning backup was on its way.

"This is taking forever," John grunted.

The silence between them extended into awkwardness, then discomfort. Adele wanted to say more, to put her friend at ease. They were friends, weren't they? But she didn't really know John. Not well. She didn't even know how he'd gotten that scar.

"Damn this," John said with a growl. Agent Renee flung upon the door, swinging out of the car and pushing to his feet. He slapped his large hands on top of the sport car's roof. "You coming?"

Adele stared, her eyes darting to the radio.

"Bah," John said, "they'll never get here. Who knows what they're doing in that shop though. Might be cutting up some poor bastard while we sit out here twiddling our—"

Adele pushed open her own door and exited the vehicle. Backup would just have to hurry.

Satisfied at Adele's reaction, John turned, sauntering up the street, his weapon in his hand, the piece of metal seeming an extension of his body. As Adele watched him move, she felt a familiar sense of ease. It wasn't like back in the states, hunting the motel suspect with her new partner Masse. John knew how to use his weapon. Perhaps better than anyone Adele had worked with. She watched as he rounded the end of the street, heading down the block in the direction of Debosselage et Automobiles.

They had parked far enough away not to alert attention. But now, John made a beeline toward it.

Adele picked up the pace, her own weapon gripped in her hand as she followed John past fire hydrants and a bus stop. They reached the auto shop together, weapons raised.

"Gate," John said quietly.

Adele's eyes flicked from the front of Debosselage et Automobiles to the side alley.

The lights were dim from within the auto shop. The dull glow in the back of the store illuminated a few rows of old auto parts, and a space with a carjack where vehicles were likely worked on. Thin glass tubes displayed inside the dark windows of the shop, which Adele guessed could light up into neon letters. According to Francis, the real chop shop, as he'd called it, was in a warehouse behind the auto store.

No sounds arose from the establishment.

Adele watched as John tried the handle to the alley gate. It didn't budge.

Adele waited as John stowed his weapon. He then took two running steps, his hands grabbing the top of the fence, and he pulled himself bodily over the top. For a moment, his lengthy frame straddled the gate, and he winked roguishly at Adele. Then he dropped over the other side.

He smirked at her through the bars and waited, crossing his arms expectantly.

Adele glared at him, but then, without making a sound, she stowed her own weapon. She refused to be outdone by John. She took a few extra running steps, picking up pace, and then flung herself, leaping at the last moment. Her fingertips grazed the top of the fence. But she missed.

Her arm jolted as she fell, and her knees knocked painfully against the metal bars. Adele cursed wildly beneath her breath, slamming her forearm against her mouth to stop the flow of sound.

Adele glared through the gate at John, who was chuckling now. He kept his arms crossed as he leaned against the alley wall, waiting. Adele's eyes narrowed even further. Propelled by nothing more than a desire to wipe the smirk off John's face, she took another running start, breathing out at the last moment and then jumping.

This time, her fingers scrambled on the metal lip of the fence again, but instead of being discouraged by the sudden strain in her arms, she locked her elbows.

With an exerted grunt, far louder than she would've wanted, she pulled herself up, struggling and kicking her legs for momentum. The whole process was less smooth and much louder than John's had been.

He watched, amused, as she kicked, the metal gate creaking and shuddering beneath her. At last, she managed to pull herself on top. Gasping, her hair disheveled and in her eyes, she stared down at John in triumph.

"The look suits you," he said with a smirk.

Vaguely, Adele wished she'd worn sweatpants, or something a bit easier to move in. With a sigh, she threw a leg over the gate, sat for a moment, then dropped into the alley.

John caught her arm as she fell, giving her something to grab to soften the fall. Her hand caught his shoulder, and he hunched just as she hit the ground, absorbing some of the impact.

Adele stood, dusting herself off. Old dumpsters rested against cracked stone walls. Piles of trash, which someone couldn't be bothered to place *in* the adjacent dumpsters, lay scattered on the ground. Adele stepped over broken bottles and a low wall that smelled distinctly like human feces. The odor of garbage and old rot met her nose, curdling the air around her. The sounds had been louder than she'd wanted. Hopefully, it hadn't alerted anyone to their presence.

In near perfect synchronicity, both agents' weapons appeared back in their hands, and they began to move down the alley in the direction of the warehouse. John took the lead in a hunter's crouch, his gun raised, his eyes unblinking, fixed ahead. He moved in such a way that turned his body to present as small a target as possible.

Adele adjusted her own posture. Together, they crept around the edge of the alley and emerged near a white drainpipe with two busted fixtures of silver wire circling plastic.

Ahead, an old, worn warehouse sat on the lot behind the auto shop. Dark, brooding windows peered out into the gravel courtyard. Adele felt a chill creep up her spine, but then she set her grip on her weapon and moved toward the warehouse with John.

CHAPTER TWENTY ONE

John kept his eyes forward, his mind fixed on the task at hand. A sudden *crack!* He glanced sharply over, noticing a glass bottle and an alley cat looking up at him, the creature's eyes glowing in the dark. John flicked his attention to the windows of the warehouse once more. He rounded the edge of the alley, bracing his shoulder against the drainpipe in case he needed a stabilizing lever. His eyes switched from the windows up top down to the ones below. Up to down, tracking them as he'd been trained. *Clear*, he thought to himself.

He held his fist, gesturing for Adele to stop. He paused, shooting a look toward the American agent.

She really was quite beautiful. Perhaps not in a traditional sense, but there was an exotic allure to her. She came from France, Germany, and the US. A strange combination. She had long blonde hair, and skin weathered by sunlight. She also kept in good shape—a fact not lost on him.

Her eyes zeroed in on him, following his every motion.

John felt a sudden burgeoning anxiety in his chest. Quickly, he shrugged it off. He preferred doing missions like these on his own. Having someone like Adele along only compromised things. He would have to look out for her, to keep her safe. And as far as John was concerned, that was a nearly impossible task with this many variables. He gave another quick scan of the windows, never letting five seconds pass between attending zones of control. Outlooks from an enemy position could shift every few moments. Attentiveness was key. Eyes forward.

Ripping his gaze away from Adele, he looked back at the building, gesturing for her to take the left approach. No sense splitting up now. A pincer movement wouldn't work here. It would only isolate and allow the enemy to contain faster.

Surprise then. The only advantage they had. He hesitated, wondering if they should wait for backup.

But he gave the faintest shake of his head. Backup would only result in more people he had to look out for. The kind of backup that arrived this late wouldn't be useful in a firefight anyway.

John felt the steady weight of his weapon in his hand, and he inhaled through his nose, calming himself. He quickly moved across the courtyard, into the shadow of the warehouse behind the autobody shop. The shade from the building obscured them as they moved around the edge of the red brick.

His skin tingled as he maneuvered. He felt alive. If Adele hadn't been there, this would have been as easy to him as a dance, as beautiful as making love. He'd been in this position before; he adored it. Others complicated such matters, like voyeurs in a bedroom.

He could feel the bulge in his shirt from the rolled up bills he'd taken from Francis. He hadn't done it out of greed so much as a desire to punish Francis. John hated that man. He hated how he'd gamed the system. He'd been allowed to escape with his crimes. John had seen firsthand what Francis and his crew had done to their victims. They had preyed on the homeless, and those with little more than the shirts on their backs. They had taken the bloody organs, and then refused to pay the money they'd promised. Half the people they'd operated on had died. Not that they had cared. They'd made their profit regardless, selling the organs on the black market to whoever would buy them at an exorbitant fee.

John aligned his body so it presented as small a target as possible as he moved with his left shoulder ahead of his chin. He kept his gun raised, moving towards the side metal door pressed into the red brick of the warehouse. Above them, steel plates had been welded into place over a gap in the wall as a temporary fixture against weather damage.

He could smell the odor of water and damp. He could also smell something else. He frowned, taking another long whiff. Chemicals.

A slow trickle of excitement crept up his spine. The burn mark along his throat and down his chest began to itch. It often did when he found himself on the verge of conflict. Some people said their hair would curl when rainstorms came. In John's case, his burn would itch when heralding imminent violence.

He couldn't resist the small smile tugging up his cheeks as he moved toward the metal door, and with his elbow, he lowered the handle, pushing the door with his shoulder. It didn't move at first. Stuck.

He exerted an extra push—a quiet *creak*, and the door dislodged. It swung open, ushered forward by his body. He followed it in, using his shoulder while keeping a grip on his weapon, swinging his line of fire which revealed the area before him.

He could hear Adele moving behind him.

For a moment, caught there in the doorway, halfway in and half out, he considered the American agent. He wasn't sure what to think of her. The last time they'd met, things had been strange. Perhaps he had been avoiding her. He had jumped at the first case that arrived when he heard she was coming back.

John frowned, pushing the door open even more. The first room was clear. No sign of adversaries. Small stone steps led up to an office building with glass windows.

He pointed with his head toward the stairs, hoping Adele would understand the quiet message. And then he continued forward, keeping his gun braced, and moving toward the rectangular stone pillars jutting up and holding the warehouse aloft.

Four doors occupied the back wall, two of them large, like barnyard doors. Footprints scattered the dust everywhere. The smell of chemicals was even stronger now.

"They're in here," he said quietly, his voice a ghost of a whisper.

Adele's eyes flashed in the dark, and she nodded once. She moved along with him, also trying to follow his posture, trying to remember her training. John knew amateurs when he saw them. And while the Adele was no amateur, she wasn't comfortable with her weapon. This concerned him even more. She knew how to use her firearm, though, and there were few investigators as sharp as she was. He admired her for it. She would follow the lead wherever it took them. Whatever the cost.

His brow furrowed. No, perhaps not whatever the cost. She had boundaries. Another thing he admired about her. She was a woman of conviction. There weren't many of those left.

For a brief horrible, tantalizing moment, he thought of their swim back in the private pool on Robert's estate. He thought of coming near her, breathing the smell of chlorine on the air, but a faint, vague residue of her perfume still lingering on the breeze. He remembered leaning in, trying to kiss her. He thought of the way she had recoiled, surprised. He wasn't sure if she'd been horrified, or simply stunned.

Did it really matter? Either way, she'd drawn back. Clearly she hadn't wanted the attention. He'd misread the cues. She thought of him as a buffoon, a jester. Someone she didn't take seriously.

That was fine. What did John care anyway. Colleagues were just that, colleagues. Women were just that, women. A source of companionship, perhaps. In the same way a sip from his distillery was a source of companionship. Forgettable, replaceable.

He nodded, trying to convince himself of thoughts he didn't fully believe. The last time he had a team, the last time he had any real friends, anyone he was close to...

John shook his head, forcing his mind away from the desert, the chopper blades in the air, the shouting, the gunfire.

No, this wouldn't be like that time. He would make sure Adele lived. If he had to die for her to survive, that would be a fair trade. He'd experienced the alternative before, and it was no way to live.

John continued to move forward, pressing toward the double doors that served to occupy the center of the warehouse wall.

He didn't look back at Adele this time. Distractions now would prove fatal. Distractions would cost them. He would have to trust her to pull her weight.

John moved foot over foot, stepping with movements more rehearsed than those of any ballerina. He noticed a glimmer of light, a blue sliver through the crack in the door. He nodding his head, to see if Adele had also noticed.

She returned the nod. Together, they eased against the door, pressing their shoulders and putting their eyes against the slit.

John peered into the room and gritted his teeth.

A familiar scene of horror.

He could feel Adele next to him, tensing. She held her breath and took a couple of steps back, weapon raised, body tensed as if preparing to surge forward and kick the door in.

John held out a hand, halting her, then returned his guiding hand back to his weapon. He shook his head. And held up a finger against his gun. *Wait.*

❖   ❖   ❖

Adele breathed, but it was a difficult chore. She could feel her heart pounding in her chest, and she continued to stare at the crack in the door, witnessing the horrible scene within.

A single, bright blue light from an umbrella fixture stared down at an operating table in the dank, dusty warehouse. There were two IV bags, one filled with clear liquid, bubbling, the other with a strange brownish-red substance. There was a heart rate machine, with blue and green lights zipping across the digital face. Four men stood around the operating table. Two of them had guns, which they held against their hips, waiting impatiently. The other two men wore white masks and the blue-green outfits of operating surgeons.

Adele heard quiet murmuring from within. She wanted to burst in, but John was still holding up his hand, the finger resting against his gun, telling her to wait.

Adele watched as one of the men leaned over the body on the table. The doctor had a scalpel in his hand. He was murmuring quietly, and Adele realized he spoke German.

The doctor began to press the scalpel against the victim's flesh. The patient, though, was moving slightly.

Adele heard more muttering. The second man, also with a face mask, muttered in German as well. Adele leaned in, listening, translating in her mind.

"…anesthesia hasn't fully taken effect," the man said, quietly. "He's still conscious."

Adele shivered, and the sensation had nothing to do with the cool air of the room. The first man, with the scalpel, hesitated, glancing back. His voice came faded, distant from the room, but Adele could still make out the words. "How much longer until he's out?"

"No telling; I've never operated in this setting before." The second man was fidgeting with frantic movements, glancing up and down, his eyes especially settling on the guns in the hands of the two men behind him. He looked uncomfortable; clearly, he was younger than everyone else in the room, perhaps only in his mid-twenties.

Despite his face mask, Adele could tell he was panicking. "Calm yourself," the first doctor said in German, his voice calm, soothing. A voice practiced in eliciting whatever emotion he needed in volatile situations. "It's fine, it's going to be fine."

The younger doctor was shaking his head, but seemed to settle at the pacifying tones from the first.

Adele brushed against John, glaring. But John held up a finger, still waiting, still shaking his head.

"We need to go in now, before they start cutting," she whispered in a hiss.

John turned on her, his eyes wide, scary. Adele had seen this before. John was usually carefree, irreverent. But sometimes, in moments of action, he would zero in, focus. It would be like adrenaline possessed his body, and he wouldn't fully register what she was saying. He shook his head again. He held up two fingers, then gave his gun a shake. Then he held up four fingers on his guiding hand.

She frowned. Of course there were four of them. She could see that. Five if they counted the one on the bed.

She began to protest again, but just then, she heard more voices. The sound of boots against dusty floors heralded two more men with guns emerging from behind the separating wall where they had been standing out of sight.

John nodded now, his eyes narrowed, his gun still raised.

Adele felt her heart skip. She hadn't even noticed them. That's what John had meant. Four attackers. Four. If it had been up to her she would've gone right away. It would have cost them both.

She felt a tingle along her fingers and noticed her hands trembling. Adele squeezed her fingers around her weapon, trying to settle the sudden surge of horror.

John pressed his hand against the door, easing it open even further.

One of the new arrivals shouted in French, "What are you waiting for?"

The older doctor replied, his French accent broken from German syllables as he tried to speak. "The patient isn't under yet. Anesthesia is still taking effect. He's not numb."

There was a pause and a muttered exchange in a language between the gunmen which Adele couldn't understand. One of them, a bearded fellow with dark, dangerous eyes, shook his head with a quick jolt. "Start now. We don't have time."

The doctor, in a wheedling tone which threatened condescension, said, "You don't understand. The man will feel it. It will compromise the kidney. His body could go into shock."

The bearded Serbian paused a moment, trying to understand the words, despite the broken accents. Then he snarled, stepped forward, and raised his gun, pointing it at the doctor's forehead.

The doctor squeaked, quickly raising his hands, the scalpel glinting in the floodlight from the umbrella fixture. "Okay," he said quickly, "just give us a few minutes. A few minutes and the anesthesia will take effect."

"No," said the man with the gun and the beard. "No minutes. Now."

The older doctor shook his head, muttering to himself. The younger man in scrubs was trembling, shaking his head from side to side.

The older doctor tried to speak again in a reasoning tone, saying, "You don't understand, if I start cutting now, he will feel it. Anesthesia hasn't taken effect." He spoke slowly this time, with deferential tones, as if hoping a sudden courtesy in his posture would elicit the response he wanted.

But men with guns, in Adele's experience, weren't particularly fond of manipulation. The bearded man glared at the doctor, paused, glanced at his Serbian friends, and muttered something. One of the others replied. And then the bearded man turned his gun on the second doctor and fired. A loud blast boomed in the warehouse.

John didn't even flinch, his hands still steady. Adele, for her part, jolted, her own weapon tapping against the metal door. Thankfully, the sound was drowned out by the response from the room. The three other Serbians seemed to have known what was coming. The doctor, though, yelled in horror as his assistant fell over, a bullet hole in his left eye, blood spreading out on the dusty floor.

"What did you do?" the doctor shouted. But the older German surgeon quickly fell silent and backed up again as the gun leveled on him once more.

"Now," said the Serbian in broken French.

Muttering to himself, the doctor turned toward the trolley, trying to soothe himself with quiet, muttered comments. He raised his knife and pressed it to the chest of the man on the table.

The man fidgeted uncomfortably and emitted a quiet croaking sound. Not quite words, but they had the cadence of speech, as if he were trying to talk but couldn't.

"I'm sorry," Adele heard the German doctor mutter. He pressed his scalpel against the victim's chest.

"John," Adele said in a deadly serious voice, "*now.*"

John was already on the move. He shoved the door open with his shoulder, pushing it into the well-lit section of warehouse.

John fired once, twice. Two bodies hit the ground in quick succession. The two men whom Adele had spotted last, including the bearded man, collapsed onto the doctor he'd shot, their blood mingling with that of their victim's.

For Adele's part, she shouted at the top of her lungs, "DGSI! Hands in the air—we have you surrounded!"

A brief moment of consideration passed where everything seemed to freeze for that fraction of a second where vital decisions were made.

The two remaining gunmen had half-turned, facing John and Adele. But at Adele's shouts, they both seemed to reach the same decision, and their hands jolted to the sky, stiffened.

"Weapons down!" Adele shouted, voice swelling the room. She spoke with far more confidence and authority than she felt.

The men with the guns slowly began to lower the weapons. They bent at the waist, and at last put their weapons on the ground and straightened up again, their hands skyward.

Adele and John moved further into the room. The two Serbians turned, scowling when they realized it was only two agents approaching. One of them began to move toward his gun again, but John barked, "Don't." The gunman's eyes met John's and he went stiff, as if staring into the reaper's own gaze.

Pale-faced, he retracted his hand from the weapon and put it back in the air.

"Interlock your fingers behind your head!" Adele continued to shout. Again, the men seemed reluctant to comply, especially now they realized they weren't outnumbered, but again, John's weapon and Adele's presence forced compliance. They interlocked their fingers, and after another series of instructions dropped to their knees, still glaring daggers.

Once they were both on the ground, John moved with three rapid strides, far faster than Adele thought anyone his size should be able to move, and he reached the men. He kicked out twice, sending both of them sprawling onto their bellies, their hands still behind their heads. The tall agent dropped on the first man, shoving a knee deep into his spine and then pulling out his cuffs.

"Keep them there," John said, looking up at Adele. His eyes were still vacant, swimming with adrenaline and rage.

Adele steadied her weapon on the second man. Her gaze flicked over to the heart-rate monitor. The doctor still stood by the operating table, his scalpel having been discarded moments ago. Two shallow cuts slashed the bare-chested man on the table, but beyond that, he seemed unharmed. Adele pointed to the victim. "Is he hurt?" she demanded.

She spoke in German, and the doctor's eyebrows rose. He replied in German, shaking his head. "This is all a big mistake; no, he's fine. This is voluntary. He volunteered," the doctor kept repeating, pointed to the man on the table.

"Shut up," Adele snapped.

The German doctor began to protest even more, but then her gun swiveled from the second man on the ground toward him, and he fell silent. Adele reached back and unhitched her own cuffs from her belt, lifting them from behind her jacket and tossing them to John.

The tall agent had already moved over and was jamming his knee into the back of the second Serbian. The men in cuffs were looking at their fallen comrades, muttering beneath their breaths in a foreign language.

John's aim had been true; he'd caught two corpses with bullets straight to their heads.

Adele shifted, turning away from her partner and glancing to the table with the victim. He had dirt beneath his fingernails, and his hair was matted. His clothing looked old, where it lay discarded beneath the table, next to an open cooler.

Adele stared at the clothes and her eyes darted back to the man. "I think he's homeless," she said to John.

But at just that moment, John let out a shout. Adele whirled around to face him, but realized he was lunging toward her. She took a startled step back, then felt a sudden flash of pain across her cheek, and rounded again to find the German doctor breathing heavily, scalpel in hand.

He was cursing at her in German, shaking his head wildly, declaring, "A mistake! Just a mistake."

John was cursing and clutched at his hand. Adele glanced down and noticed he had caught the brunt of the scalpel against his palm. Blood seeped through his fingers from where he had inserted himself between the blade and Adele. She leveled her weapon on the doctor and began to shout, but at the same time, the gunman who John had been trying to secure only had one wrist cuffed.

Seizing this opportunity, the gunman lurched for his weapon. Adele spotted this the same time as John, and both their eyes widened. The Serbian, screaming at the top of his lungs, raised his weapon, aiming at John, and he fired.

Adele didn't have time to think. She didn't have time to plan. Like a coin flip, at the same time as the Serbian's weapon rose, Adele's own hand brought hers up. There were simultaneous blasts of gunfire.

A bullet found its mark.

The Serbian dropped dead to the ground.

John stood, frozen, staring at the heartbeat monitor directly to his left—a bullet hole buried into the vibrant screen. Unlike the movies, there were no sparks or smoke. It had simply died.

Like the three Serbians on the ground.

The final mobster was trembling now, cursing and shaking his head. He was staring at the third man who had fallen, a look of pain in his eyes.

A brother? A cousin? A friend? Adele wasn't sure. A part of her cared, but another, angrier part of her wished she could've put him down as well.

Adele scowled, keeping her gun trained on the man on the ground as John secured the doctor. He used a discarded IV bag to tie the German doctor's hands behind his back, securing the bonds tightly until the doctor grunted in pain.

"Don't try that again," John snarled beneath his breath.

The doctor replied in French, but John ignored him, shoving him to the ground and sending the man stumbling next to the corpse of his fallen friend. Four bodies. Three of them their doing. Adele felt sick. She resisted the urge to turn and stare at the corpses. She wasn't sure she could keep her lunch if she did.

In the distance now, she heard sirens approaching.

"Does that make us even?" she said, in a trembling voice. John looked over from where he stood by the operating table and murmured quietly to the man strapped to the cold metal. The homeless man looked out of it.

"What was that?" John asked, glancing up at her.

Adele shook her head. "Never mind."

John regarded the Serbian who had fired at him, then back at Adele. He seemed stuck for a moment, but then his head bobbed. "Yes, I guess it does. I appreciate it."

Adele wanted to say something clever. But all she managed was a shuddering sigh, her own emotions rising like a wave in her chest.

Three dead. Two suspects. Hopefully they would be enough to find the killer.

Still, something about the scene just felt too real. Adele was used to investigating people *after* they had died. But this time, she had arrived to save someone's life. That was rare. Somehow, it left her with an uneasy feeling in her gut.

She tried not to think of the scalpel or how close it had been to the homeless man's chest. She tried not to think of the Serbians. What if they had acted sooner?

The young doctor was dead.

He'd been part of it, but still, there were bodies on the ground, and Adele hadn't been able to prevent it. She wasn't looking forward to explaining this to Ms. Jayne or Executive Foucault. She could only imagine what Agent Paige would say.

She looked at the empty cooler next to a pile of dirty clothes. She shivered again and looked away, in the direction of the open doors from which the sound of sirens grew louder and louder. Adele swallowed, suppressing the rising bile in the back of her throat. John held the hand of the homeless man on the table, murmuring quietly to him. She watched as John turned and crouched next to the man's clothing. For a moment, she thought perhaps he was checking the cooler.

But then, when he regained his feet, Adele noticed the bulge of money he'd stolen from Francis was no longer in his pocket. She frowned, and glanced toward the victim's clothes.

Adele sighed and turned away, her thoughts spinning as the sirens approached, stopped, and the scatter of rapid footfalls came near to the warehouse. Backup had finally arrived.

CHAPTER TWENTY TWO

The small red jalopy trundled down the street, observing every speed limit, using the turn signal when necessary and coming to a full stop at every sign. The driver of the red jalopy whistled quietly as he drove, his eyes fixed ahead, his hands ten and two.

"We'll be there soon enough, Daddy, just hang on," he said quietly over his shoulder.

He glanced up into the mirror, smiling at his father in the back seat. The old man hadn't aged in a year. He still had the same dusting of gray hair around a balding head. Wise eyes peered out from a face creased with smile lines. The driver noticed similar crow's feet forming around his own eyes in the mirror.

Wrinkles are a small price to pay for smiling. That's what his father often said.

"Are you feeling okay?" the driver asked, still glancing in the mirror. After a moment, he turned his attention back to the road, putting on his blinkers as he merged into the left lane and continued up the street. He kept his eyes fixed on the street signs, trying to keep track.

His father often teased the younger generation glued to their phones and GPS. The driver of the red jalopy didn't want to be like everyone else. He spent a lot of time reading maps, studying streets. He knew six of the seven streets down this stretch of road alone by name.

He hoped to memorize all the streets in Paris in time for his father's seventieth birthday as a bit of a surprise.

"It's been a nice day," the driver said with a nod. "If you'd like, we can stop by that bakery you enjoy."

His father just turned, glancing out the window. His father didn't speak much anymore. Not after his health had begun to decline the previous year. The young man frowned, then just as quickly tried to smile.

"If you'd like, I could sing that song you enjoy," he said. "The one we used to sing before bedtime." He again looked in the mirror toward his dad.

His father still didn't speak, but instead inclined his head and gave the faintest of nods.

The young man began to hum beneath his breath, picking up volume as he did. He'd always been able to carry a tune. A skill he had learned from his mother, before she had left them. A delighted expression curled his father's lips as the driver hummed.

The young man began to hum louder, whistling in between, the red jalopy filling with the swell of music. A modicum of peace settled in the young man's chest. These were trying times for their family. His father could be saved, of course. The driver knew enough about physiology to know what was wrong. They'd confirmed it with doctors. But the medical professionals hadn't seemed to think surgery would be successful.

The son's smile began to fade, turning into a scowl, but just as quickly, he corrected his expression. There was no point in alarming his father. He continued to whistle, considering the words of the doctor from the previous year.

"I'm afraid he won't make it. No, not even with a kidney transplant."

"Dialysis worked," the son had replied, desperate. "If you look at his levels—fluid retention is down. The swelling around his ankles diminished. That has to be a good sign. CKD is moderate—shows signs of dropping. I'm sure it will work!"

The doctor had looked surprised at this. "Did you read that somewhere?"

The young man remembered the doctor's office, the way the walls had seemed to close in, constricting his breath. He had wanted to hum then too, but hadn't found the nerve.

"No," he had told the doctor. "I'm a medical student. Or, at least, I was. I dropped out last month to take care of my father. You have to understand, this is important. The surgeries can work."

But the doctor had just shaken his head and repeated the same word, "No."

The young man gripped the steering wheel, staring through the window. He set his teeth, wanting to shout.

"It's fine," he said, preempting his father. The old man began to open his mouth, noticing the frown on his son's face. "It's fine," he said, a bit more calmly now. "We're going to figure this out. Trust me."

Three more doctors. Three more refusing the transplant. They hadn't even considered putting him on the list. They said it would be a failure of a surgery. But what did they know? The young man had been top of his class at medical school. He, of course, planned to go back and finish, once all of this was put behind them. Once his father was okay.

"Look," he said, pleasantly, "we're here. This is where the nice girl lives."

The old man in the backseat raised his eyebrows.

"I know, I know," the driver said, shaking his head at his father. "It's uncomfortable. But there are genuinely good people in this world." He turned around, reaching out, holding his father's hand. It was tender to touch. He thought back to when he'd been growing up an only child. His mother had left when he was only eight. His father would sing him to bed, every night. He thought of the way his father would hold his hand, or rub the back of his shoulders when he was sick.

"There are kind people," he repeated. "She's kind. I promise you. She's going to be happy to help."

His father nodded and settled back, reclining his head against the seat back. The young man pulled the red jalopy over to the side of the road, parking beneath the shade of a tree.

He peered at the townhouse, then glanced back at his phone, which he had placed on the passenger seat while driving. He reached over, sliding it from where it had lodged beneath the toolbox, then held the phone up, scanning the contents and moving over to the message he'd received from the man he had hired.

"32. Recently arrived. Blood type unknown. Michelle Lee."

The young man read the message again. He frowned for moment. "Which unit?" he muttered beneath his breath. He glanced up again, peering toward the old white and blue siding of the two-story structure. There were three garages he could see curling around the side of the townhouse. A private driveway with an electric gate blocked any passage. This would be trickier than the others. But no less doable. There truly were kind people in this world. The driver's faith in humanity had been restored.

He paused for a moment and frowned. He reached down, rubbing at his side, wincing. He felt a flash of a chill across his spine, and he shifted uncomfortably. He glanced in the back seat and stared. His father's eyes stared back at him. For the faintest moment, memories surged in his mind.

Memories of his father in the bathtub. Memories of his own surgical scalpel in his hand. Memories of excruciating pain. He'd been certain he could do it. Certain he could. They had to have been a match. Father and son.

Memories of approaching his friends, asking for help. Memories of their refusal. Memories of rejection after rejection. Memories of despair, then desperation. Then came the memories of cutting his own abdomen. Memories of anesthesia applied locally. Memories of the pain. Just so much pain.

The young man's whistling faltered for moment, his humming ceased, replaced by the urge to scream. Why—why scream? They were here to meet a nice lady. A volunteer. Someone who wanted to help his dad.

He could feel sweat beading on his upper lip as the memories continued to flood in.

Memories of the cold tile of the bathroom floor. He had managed to extract it for the most part. But the pain had been too much. He'd fallen—he'd hit his head, slipped on his own blood.

He woke. Found his father in the bathtub. Palliative care be damned—he could cure this! His father trusted him!

The young man shook his head. Trying to focus, trying to calm himself. He smiled; what a strange memory. Just make-believe.

He looked back at his father. For the vaguest, faintest moment, he saw faded eyes, milky; he smelled the scent of decay; beneath his hand, which was still gripping his father's soft fingers, he felt something clammy, cold, like a dead fish. Something hideous was sitting in his back seat. But just as quickly, the young man began to whistle again. Humming softly to himself.

The fear faded. The memories—because they couldn't have been memories, they weren't memories at all—also disappeared.

The young man's smile returned, and he reached out, patting his father once more on the hand.

"I'll be right back," he said, softly. The kind-eyed old man stared back and nodded once.

The driver exited the red jalopy. The windows were tinted. His father had been bothered by the sunlight as the worst of the disease had come on. He'd had the windows tinted. It had cost €300. Most of what he had saved up for rent that month. Money was the main reason he'd been forced to quit medical school and come back to live with his father.

But the young man didn't care. It wasn't a sacrifice. His father had sacrificed far more.

He took his toolbox as he exited the car and adjusted the hat he grabbed from beneath the front seat. Still whistling, he moved up the street, toward the townhouse.

He wouldn't enter today. Today was time to get to know the place. Like a surgeon familiarizing himself with a patient's body, going over the operation in their mind, rehearsing.

The young man nodded, his eyes crinkling in the corners. It was a good thing to rehearse. Soon, though, soon he would meet the volunteer in person. Very soon. And then everything would turn out just fine.

Chapter Twenty Three

Adele watched as John reached up, growling, as he wiped spit from his cheek. He glared down at the Serbian, his fist clenching at his side.

Adele's own hand shot out, snaking forward and grabbing John by the wrist. "Don't," she said quickly. "It's not worth it."

She glanced uncomfortably at Foucault. The executive stood in the interrogation room with them. After the shootings in the warehouse, Foucault had wanted to keep a closer eye on the interrogation. They'd already spent nearly three hours briefing what seemed like everyone in a suit in the office.

Adele swallowed and looked away from the French executive.

They still needed information, but the Serbian had yet to provide any. This was the second time he'd spat on John.

"I don't think this is working," she said, quietly, moving John away from the suspect toward the corner of the room. Foucault stood against the mirror, glaring between the two of them. The Serbian smirked in Adele's direction, and John growled, making toward him, but Adele caught his arm again.

"Hang on," she said, quietly. "Don't. Just hang on."

John cursed the Serbian with a series of obscene remarks. The man replied in kind, and added a few words in his own language. "*Kucka?*" John parroted. "What did you call me?" he shouted, spittle flying. He jabbed a finger over Adele's shoulder, beneath the glare of Foucault. "You're *kucka*," he shouted! Hear me?"

At last he settled, and seemed to hear Adele. "What?" he demanded, rounding on her.

She kept her voice low, trying not to make eyes to where Foucault still leaned against the mirror, watching everything.

"What does *kucka* mean?" John demanded.

"I don't speak Serbian," she said tight-lipped with as much patience as she could muster.

"You don't?" John snorted. "You speak everything."

"No, I don't. Look," Adele said, turning her shoulder to shield her mouth and dropping her voice to a bare murmur. The Serbian continued to watch them with a contemptuous glower from where he was handcuffed to the interrogation table. "It's not working," Adele whispered. "He's clearly organized crime. He's not going to tell us anything."

John made no effort to whisper. He stared over Adele's head, returning the Serbian's glower. "Just give me a few minutes alone with him. I'll get him talking."

Adele shot a look at Foucault. The executive's frown had only deepened as he watched the two of them. He said nothing, but Adele felt like she could read the disapproval in his hawk-like eyes. Comments like these from John did little to mend fences.

John grunted, glancing between Foucault and the Serbian like a hound sizing up the greater threat. "What about the German?" he said.

Adele regarded the naked bulb above the suspect illuminating the metal table. "Fine," she said, quietly. "But let me do it alone." She spoke so quietly John had to lean in to hear her over the churn of air through the vents above.

Foucault's frown deepened, and he crossed his arms, still staring. "This is the sum of it then?" he asked, across the room.

Adele turned from John, dropping her shoulder and raising her voice. "Sir, if you just give us a moment."

Inwardly, she felt a flash of frustration. Foucault's presence wasn't helping anything. If anything, it was giving the Serbian further motive to stay quiet, if only to see the executive's temper rise. At this thought, the mobster began rattling off in his language and making rude gestures in Foucault's direction. For the briefest moment, the executive's ire rounded on the suspect.

Adele took this interlude to glance sharply at John, reaching out for his forearm and whispering, "I'll talk with the doctor. Just stay here. And . . . please, don't do anything dumb."

John shrugged her hand off and approached the Serbian once more as Adele moved toward the door. "Who do you send the organs to?" John demanded in French.

The Serbian grinned, flashing a row of yellowing teeth.

Adele sighed and spoke to Foucault. "I'll be right back. I just need to get a drink."

The executive's dark gaze glanced between Adele and John, as if he wasn't sure who he should keep an eye on. But then the Serbian made another remark and John lurched forward, slamming his open palm into the back of the man's head and sending him tumbling over in his chair, clattering against the ground with a shout.

Foucault whirled around, yelling, and John held up his hands, muttering something about having slipped. Adele winced, wondering how many weeks of unpaid leave John had just earned himself, before slipping through the door and shutting it behind her, cutting off the continued yelling from all three men.

Two agents were standing outside the door in the hall—they'd come with the executive. One of them, a woman with short hair, raised her eyebrows at Adele.

"Productive?" she asked, nodding at the interrogation door.

Adele flashed a clenched smile. "Very." Then she turned and hurried up the hall. Adele made her way down to the first floor and past the front desk, nodding at the clerk. The agent behind the desk returned the nod. She moved toward the hall where they kept the holding cells.

In the holding cells, unlike the interrogation rooms, there was no audio, but there would still be cameras. She approached a row of bars set in the wall and flashed her credentials to the man behind the desk. The desk sat in a bulletproof, sealed glass room, and the man reclined in a small chair, reading a comic. He glanced up, then lowered his head, peering through the thin slit in the bulletproof glass. "Yes?" he asked.

She pointed toward the metal door. "Have to talk with the doctor."

The attendant nodded once, glanced at her Interpol credentials—paused for a moment, frowning.

"Foucault's in an interrogation," Adele said. "He's fine with it."

The attendant considered this for a moment and then pushed the button. There was a buzzing sound, and the attendant held up a hand. "No firearm," he said.

Adele unclipped her holster and slid it in the slot beneath the bulletproof glass. The attendant took the weapon and placed it on the counter, jostling it up against a wooden box filled with folders. He nodded toward the door, then returned his attention to his comic.

Adele entered through the metal door and continued down a hall framed by rows of barred cells. The DGSI didn't keep many people in custody for long. All the cells were empty except for the one at the far end of the hall on the left.

She heard a buzz and a click, and turned back to see a green light had turned red above the door she'd entered; she watched as it slammed shut. For a moment, she stood at the end of the hall and glanced toward the glinting lenses of the cameras above.

She heard a voice murmuring ahead of her from the cell at the far end. Foucault had instructed them that he wanted to be present for all interrogations, but this, she determined, would only hold them back. Especially with the German doctor.

"Hello," said a voice in heavily accented French, "please, this is all a misunderstanding. I was just a volunteer. Please."

Adele move forward and then came to a stop directly in front of the cell.

Whoever had placed the German had been kind enough to give him the only cell with a window. The window was high in the ceiling and sealed with bulletproof glass, but it still allowed a beam of sunlight into the dark hallway, illuminating the cell and mingling with the fluorescent light.

"You," the man said suddenly, switching to German. "Please," he said, "it was all a misunderstanding. Just one big—"

Adele held up a hand, rubbing at her palm. She thought of John's injury— the scalpel he'd caught protecting her.

"Look," she said, softly, "I'm not going to lie to you. It's not good." She watched the German. Now, without his scrubs or operating mask, he just looked like a man. He had gray hair and wrinkled cheeks, but was in impressively good shape for his age. Perhaps he was a runner. Adele shook her head. "You're in France now. Germany can't help you. You broke the law—you were about to murder a man."

The German doctor began wagging his head wildly. He had a thin, trembling jawline—his chin like that of a woman. A large, pronounced nose protruded above pressed lips. Stubble had sprouted along his lip, but Adele judged, by the look of it, that he preferred to keep it shaved.

"Please" the German said, "there has to be something you can do. You're German? BKA?"

Adele shook her head. "I work with Interpol. And others." She leaned back, pressing her shoulder blades against the metal bars of the empty cell behind her. "I want to help you. Don't believe me? What if I told you that if you admit to anything, somewhere *else*, it can be used against you. In here, there's no audio. There is a camera over there," she said, pointing, "but whatever you say isn't being recorded."

The German doctor snorted, but tried to cover it in a cough.

She frowned. "Let me give it to you straight. Your only shot of getting out of this without a life sentence is me. I don't like you. I think you're a vile human being. But I also know a greedy man when I see one. You did this for money, yes?"

The German doctor studied her. Adele had to remind herself this wasn't a stupid man. He was greedy, evil, perhaps. But not stupid. He stared at her, still frowning.

She shifted. "I told you, you're not being recorded. Look, let's do this; I'm going to ask you a question. Say the French word for apple for yes and the French word for tomato if your answer is no. There's no way even if you're being recorded that a court would accept the words for produce in a foreign language as an admission of guilt."

The man looked bemused now, watching Adele as if he weren't sure if she were joking.

She tried to remain patient. "I need you to talk. I'm looking for information, not a confession, understand? If you answer my questions and put me on the track to find the person I'm looking for, then I'll make sure you get a deal."

It twisted her insides to say it, but Adele meant it. If someone like Francis could get a deal, she had little doubt the French authorities would put up much of a fuss in providing a similar one for a German. There was no need for an international incident here. Sometimes the job had unsavory components to it, but as far as Adele could tell, the only way they could make sure they got the information they needed was to give the man something in return.

He had been in that warehouse for the money, the same as the Serbians, but he didn't have the spine the gangster did.

"I'll make a deal," Adele pressed, "and I'll speak to the executive. I'm with Interpol," she said, flashing her credentials through the bars. "I have connections with the BKA too. If you'd like, I'll talk with them. None of this is a confession. You just need to tell me yes or no. Apple or tomato. Understand?"

Silence fell. The German doctor gnawed on the corner of his lip, and then glanced up the hall towards the cameras. He held a hand up to his mouth, and in as quiet a voice as he could muster, he said, *"Pomme."*

Adele tried to hide her relief. She stared unblinking through the bars. "Look, I'm tracking a killer. Someone who deals in harvesting kidneys. I need to know what you were going to do with that man's organs."

The German doctor frowned at her and didn't say anything.

Adele closed her eyes, focusing, then said, "Did you have someplace you were going to take the organs?"

"Pomme," he said, holding a hand over his mouth to shield it from view.

This time it was Adele's turn to glance toward the cameras; she turned her back fully to them now, her neck prickling as if from a sudden chill.

"Do you know anything about the murders of three girls from America?"

The doctor scowled and shook his head rapidly from side to side. *"Tomate."*

Adele stared at him, considering his response. He had seemed intent on keeping the homeless victim alive back at the warehouse. The doctor, as far as she could tell, was a coward. He didn't seem the sort to break into someone's apartment, kill them, and steal a kidney all on his own. At the warehouse, he'd had privacy, protection, and assistance. No, she decided, the killer she was looking for was too brash. It was one thing to prey on the homeless, where no one would see them missing. But quite another thing to hunt Americans in their apartments, attracting all sorts of media attention. She asked, "Where were you last week?"

The doctor's eyes widened, but then he quickly said, "Home. Germany. Check my travels. I don't know anything about killings!"

"Have you killed anyone else?" Adele said, slowly.

The doctor immediately shook his head again. *"Tomate,"* he insisted, a desperate look in his eyes. He stared at her through the bars. "Please, please, I've never. I've never. I was a volunteer. A volunteer," he whispered.

Adele studied him. The man was greedy, not stupid. Then again, how smart could someone be who got tangled up with Serbian mob? "All right, tell me everything."

The doctor frowned. "*Tomate*," he said.

Adele leaned in, pressing her face against the bars and glaring at the man. "I told you, nothing is recording."

The man just shrugged, his eyes wide like an animal in headlights. Panic emanated from every gesture.

Adele tried to steady her temper. "Fine," she said through clenched teeth. "Were you going to take the organs to a hospital in France?"

The man shook his head and then quickly stopped the motion, holding a hand to his mouth before whispering, "*Tomate*."

Adele's eyes narrowed. "Not Paris?"

The man kept his head very still this time. "*Tomate*."

She tried not to think how ridiculous this might look to anyone on the outside looking in. Instead, she pressed further. "Fine, if not here, then where?"

The man frowned again and said nothing. Adele breathed heavily, half wishing she had John here to beat the truth out of him. "Germany?"

The doctor fidgeted uncomfortably. "*Pomme*."

Adele felt a flash of excitement. "You are working with the Serbians, for money. The organs would be harvested here, then taken to Germany? Where? A lab, a hospital?"

"*Tomate*."

Adele set her teeth. "How many people are in on this?"

The doctor stared at her.

"A hundred?"

The doctor continued to stare.

"More than a hundred?" she said.

"*Pomme*," the doctor said, and then gave a slight shrug. "Even medical students need money," he said, quietly. He glanced toward the cameras again and shifted.

Clearly he didn't trust her. Adele leaned in. "What do you mean? There are other doctors in France doing this?"

"I didn't say that," the doctor said, loudly now, glancing toward the cameras. He lowered his voice again. "What sort of deal are we talking about? I don't want jail time. Promise me that. I want it in writing. I'm not saying another word."

Adele glared back. "Answer me this then. You said medical students. Why are they doing this? The money can't be that good, is it?"

The German doctor said nothing.

"Fine!" she said, frustrated. "So who was that young man back there? A med student? Someone you knew?"

Still no reply.

"Are there others?"

The doctor scowled. "I don't know what you're talking about. But if I did, I'd say that medical students often have large loans. Not all of them can afford those loans."

Adele stared, sick to her stomach. "Students are doing this with you? Why?"

The doctor just shook his head. "I don't know what you're talking about. I need something in writing."

Adele set her teeth. "I'll get you your deal." She hesitated, then looked up, her eyes narrowed. "You and your accomplices have to know what you're doing is wrong though, don't you? They pay off loans with the organs of homeless people? Don't you get how sick that is?"

The German doctor returned her glare. "*Tomate,*" he said, without flinching. "They volunteered."

"Fine," said Adele, attempting to hide her disgust. "Tell me, what hospital in Germany? Tell me that, and I'll go get you a signature right now. I'll talk to my executive; he's in the interrogation room next door."

"Look," said the German. "Here." Instead of answering, he reached into his pocket and pulled out a thin piece of paper. Adele frowned; normally possessions weren't allowed in the cells. She supposed whoever had frisked him had missed it. He was still in his own clothes, minus the scrubs.

She glanced at the paper and realized it was a business card. She accepted the paper and turned it over. "Berlin Medical Depot?" she said, reading the generic name. "Never heard of it. This is where you work?"

The doctor just stared at her. "Where's my deal?"

Adele waved the business card. "Clarify this. What is it?"

The doctor hesitated, then said, "A facility in Germany. Near a hospital. Obviously . . . the main hub of the," he cleared his throat and glanced away for a moment, unable to meet her gaze, "business," he continued, "can't take place in the hospitals. Too much oversight."

Adele examined the business card again, then tucked it into her pocket. She turned and began to march away.

"What about my deal?" he called after her.

Adele gritted her teeth. Everything in her wanted to deny the man his deal. To leave him hopeless, like he left his victims bleeding, terrified, on the verge of death. She'd seen firsthand that he'd been about to operate on a man without anesthesia. He had hesitated, though. He had tried to reason with the Serbians. There'd been a glimmer of humanity, though not much.

"I'll talk to the executive," she said. "But look at me," she said, from across the hall. He did, staring through the bars. "You're going to tell them everything. What medical students are involved, where the Serbians work out of, every facility, every hospital. Everything you know. Understand?"

The man winced and said, "No prison time, and I'll give you everything."

Adele felt a surge of disgust, but said nothing further as she turned and left the holding cells, waiting for the metal door at the end of the hall to buzz and the green light to flash over the frame.

She pressed her hand against the pocket with the business card. They were headed back to Germany.

"Funny that," said the voice echoing in her mind. *"Especially given where you worked."*

She stared into the eyes of the man with a knife to her father's throat. She heard the laughter, the jeering tone. They'd locked gazes for a moment, then a gunshot.

Given where you worked.

Funny that.

A new scene confronted her, playing across her mind's eye.

Three women, lifeless, their eyes vacant, their necks slit, all of them missing a kidney, standing naked before her in the black, staring out like ghouls in a graveyard.

"Funny," the corpses kept repeating, *"Funny that. Funny. Funny."*

Adele turned away, trying to hide her eyes from the gruesome sight, but her gaze only leveled on a fourth person. Another woman. Also young, also dead.

Her mother. Elise.

"Given where you worked," her mother said, her voice crystal clear, exactly how Adele remembered it. A soothing, gentle voice. Coming from dead lips above a

tapestry of cuts and slits and scars and swirling patterns gouged in her mother's flesh. A corpse whittled from tortured remains.

Adele tried to close her eyes, and it took her moment to realize she was sleeping. A nightmare. But still she couldn't wake.

"Funny," the voice kept echoing behind her.

Her mother had been brutalized. A sadist had set to with a knife, a psychopath creating some form of hideous art on her mother's flesh. She'd been left to die, bleeding out in the park.

But those three other women, their throats had been slit clean. They had died quickly. There'd been no joy in it, no pleasure.

Adele gritted her teeth, and she heard the voices now, louder, coursing in her skull; at last, she jerked away, trying to sprint free.

She heard someone in the darkness, drawing nearer. She couldn't tell how she knew, but she could hear ragged gasps. She glimpsed a flash of silver, of metal in the night.

"Who is it?" she shouted.

"Funny," a voice whispered out at her, like tendrils of mist in a graveyard, creeping through her ears and sending chills across the back of her neck.

She jerked upright, gasping.

The airplane. She was on the plane.

She continued breathing heavily, her head pressed against the slight incline of her headrest, her eyes fixed on the seat in front of her. She could feel a cool jet of air gusting down from the small nozzle vent above, and a glimmer of sunlight ushered through the open shutter of the small, oval window to her left.

She struggled to compose herself, inhaling the odor of peanuts and pretzels from the seat ahead of her, listening to the overly loud sound from the headphones of a passenger in the seat across the aisle. Ahead, near first class, she heard a stewardess offering drinks, followed by the quiet clink of glass.

Adele kept her head stiff, her eyes fixed ahead, her hand sliding into her suit pocket.

She pulled out the thin piece of paper, struggling to push the nightmare fully from her mind.

The Berlin Medical Depot. She examined the business card again, listening to the sound of the engine. The plane inclined a bit, suggesting they were preparing to land. Some folk disliked landing, but to Adele, the noise of the engines was a welcome familiarity—an appeasing hum heralding their descent from the clouds. She peered out the window, across John's chest, watching the great span of blue, then, eventually the patches of cottony white flit by.

Her weapon was back on her hip. A comforting weight. At her side, John provided a similar comfort, though a bit less predictably. She studied him. He had an almost peaceful air about him as he slept; his eyelashes were quite long for a man.

Her gaze traced his cheeks, down his bold nose, along his chin, and toward the edge of the scar beneath the hem of his shirt curving the underside of his neck.

Executive Foucault had every intention of punishing John for slapping their suspect. He'd approached the table, according to John, all brooding and bluster... And then the Serb had bitten the executive's hand.

Adele tried not to smirk at the memory of John's recounting. The nightmare had nearly faded completely from memory now.

Executive Foucault had forgotten all about John's indiscretion in the face of his own pain. The executive had kicked the Serbian's chair over, screaming for antiseptic and demanding they rush him to the hospital. Adele had only arrived as he'd rushed out of the room, his two lackeys flanking him as he muttered continually about germs and infections. The sound of the Serbian's laughter had spilled out from the interrogation room behind them.

Adele leaned back in her seat, still staring out the window. At least this way John hadn't been punished.

Adele had been forced to communicate with Ms. Jayne. After talking with Robert, they had booked their tickets, and Ms. Jayne had informed them the BKA would be waiting for them in Germany. Adele turned the business card in her hand once more and set it on the tray table lowered before her.

They were headed to meet one of John's old military buddies. A German Special Operations officer who'd worked joint missions with the Commandos Marine when John had served. If this officer was anything like John... Adele shook her head.

She glanced at the medical card, eyes narrowing. If the German doctor was to be believed, the Berlin Medical Depot served as a launching pad for the organ traffickers. BKA was already running their own intelligence gathering to confirm the intel. Adele looked out the window once more as the plan tilted, circling for descent.

Below, she spotted the familiar, hunched glass and gray of the Berlin-Tegel Airport. The plane continued to circle, giving her a long look of Lake Tegel, the circling wood and concrete piers framed by the forest on the opposite shore. The plane continued to circle, and in the distance, Adele spotted the cream-tan structure of Charlottenburg Palace adjacent the Spree River.

Adele found her hands gripping the armrests, and she turned away from the window, staring sightless at the back of the headrest in front of her. The bastards were unaware and unprepared—if she had it her way, they wouldn't know what hit them until it was too late.

CHAPTER TWENTY FOUR

Major Hewer barked orders in German to the assembled officers. They all wore tactical gear—black—and carried heavy military-style weapons—also black, though one officer had spray-painted his camo. Adele tried not to yawn, as weariness descended; she forced herself to listen as the special operations leader continued to rehearse the plan with his men.

He glanced toward Adele, past the two rows of nearly fourteen fully armed and armored men. His lips tightened a bit and his eyes narrowed.

Adele didn't look away.

Twice, already, he'd approached her about staying back during the operation.

Adele looked up at the water tower above them; in peeling blue letters, it read *Kienwerder.* Nearly a mile from the facility with the organ harvesting ring. The residue of dust wafted on the air, churning past the two Humvees, also military—set in the cover and shade of the colossal gray structure.

John stood at Adele's side, listening intently to Major Hewer.

The two of them had greeted each other with grim countenance, but otherwise hadn't exchanged words. With men like this, old friendships and reunions took a backseat to imminent violence, it would seem.

"...alive, preferably," Major Hewer was saying in German, brushing a hand through his impressive, orange-brown beard. His eyes fixed on the men, peering out from beneath his helmet.

One of the officers at the front of the huddled group raised a hand and called out, "Are all occupants of the compound considered hostile?"

Major Hewer glanced over at John and Adele once more before answering. "The compound is owned by Bermer Solutions—a dummy corporation supposedly owned by an international conglomerate. Except, Bermer Solutions isn't a real corporation. Their employees, as they are—are heavily armed. Drone surveillance has spotted nearly twenty assailants with weapons."

"Armed how?" asked the same officer as before; he was taller than most of the others, though not as tall as John.

Major Hewer frowned. "Automatics—from what we could tell. Obviously, illegal in Germany. No weapon's licenses, nor reports to the labor department for security registrations. Whoever is at the compound—they know what they're doing is illegal." Major Hewer turned from the operative who'd asked the question and regarded the rest. "Two lines. Stick to the plan. Jones and Aufa, you are with Agent Sharp, yes?"

Two men glanced over to where John and Adele stood, but both nodded without complaint.

John nudged Adele and, in barely a whisper, said, "Maybe you should stay back," he murmured. "We're trained for this sort of operation. It's not like—"

"My case, my collar," Adele grunted, without whispering in return.

A couple more of the gathered team looked toward Adele, but then Major Hewer regained their attention by shouting, "All right! This is it. We've had final confirmation; it's green!"

He waved with his hand and the men split, hurrying to the two Humvees. Adele was swept up in the tide and the men named Jones and Aufa came over and ushered her toward the nearest mottled brown vehicle with a turret on top. Adele pushed into the back seat, watching through a gap between large men and an even larger metal machine, as John moved to the second vehicle, gripped Major Hewer's offered hand in a sort of macho embrace, and then took the front passenger seat next to the driver.

Then, with a low growl of engines and the whine of wheels on dirt, the vehicles jolted forward.

Adele sat, jammed between two enormous men, with six others also filling the vehicle, trying to stare out what little she could see of the glass ahead of them. All around, dust billowed up from the roads, making it difficult to see much.

Adele focused on her breathing, calming herself, adjusting the bulletproof vest and the chin strap to the helmet she'd been forced to wear.

This was bigger than a single killer now. Whatever happened next would put an end to all of this.

❧   ❧   ❧

Adele clenched her teeth, her eyes straight ahead as the military vehicle rushed toward the gates. Vaguely, she wondered why the driver was going so fast. They wouldn't be able to slow down before—

Crash! They slammed through the gates, and immediately, Adele heard shouting. She sat stiffly, her heart pounding, motionless between the two large men seated at her flanks.

"Two assailants!" shouted someone sitting next to the driver, his hand pressed to a radio receiver on his ear. "Weapons raised!" In response, she heard the *chug-chug-chug* of the large machine gun on the roof, as the gunner opened up on the gatehouse.

More shouts. Drone surveillance had confirmed the nature of the compound. The more Adele had heard, the more it had sounded like a military outpost rather than a supply depot. At least twenty armed men, from what she'd been told.

Still, though she'd been briefed, it still shocked her system as she watched bullets spray the windows, slamming into the glass and spider-webbing in crystalline cracks. Adele heard more shouting voices from outside the vehicle—Serbian by the sound. Another salvo of bullets. More *chug-chugging* from the turret.

Then a screech of tires, a cloud of dirt churning around the windows, and the vehicle doors flung open. Large men with large guns exited the military-style vehicle, following the shouted commands of the man in front with the radio receiver. The second vehicle pulled up in front of her, and, in the midst of the chaos, she watched as John emerged. He'd been supplied with an automatic weapon to replace his sidearm. She stared, half stunned, as John took aim, fired once. A pulse of bullets ripped from his weapon and tore through a window two floors up. A shout cut short—then no further sound came from beyond the shattered glass.

John moved like a tank, quick, efficient, deadly. The tall agent was a big target, but an even bigger obstacle. The men around him seemed to rally to his movements. None of them stepped in front of him, but seemed, almost like a swan's V, to set up on his flanks and move forward.

They hurried toward cover; a low brick wall, facing the main structures in the facility. There were three primary buildings in Berlin Medical Depot.

Two of them resembled charcoal-gray warehouses; the third almost resembled a hangar, or, at the very least, a loading dock for large trucks.

Adele spotted two men emerge from within one of the facilities. Both of them had white outfits and masks over their faces. The men were unarmed and screamed, hands flying into the air. Two of the German officers from Adele's vehicle surged forward, their weapons raised, their voices shouting at the white-clad figures to drop to the ground and show their hands.

They didn't take long to comply. Adele heard more gunfire from within the compound. She watched as Major Hewer hurried forward, his hand signals directing the men behind him; they complied in rapid, practiced synchronization. The Germans moved with precision and poise. They took the first building, stepping through the warehouse-style structure as Adele followed close behind. The two men in front of her created a shield from metal and body armor, their own weapons raised.

They emerged in this first building; most of the people in here had white masks and thick, anti-contamination suits.

More shouting. This time in German. Hands flung into the air, small test tubes, vials, or beakers full of sloshing blue liquid clattering to the ground. Adele stared, stunned, at the multiple rows of coolers centering the room. One of the coolers was open, and within, Adele glimpsed what looked like a human heart and a set of lungs packaged in ice and cellophane like an order from the fishmonger's.

Just as quickly, one of the men in white uniforms slammed the cooler shut. But at this motion, he was tackled by one of the special operatives and sent clattering to the ground with a painful *thump*. In the distance, from the other buildings, Adele heard more rapid gunfire, more shouts, more cries of pain, then silence. The German operatives were like antibodies, making short work of a bacterial infection.

For her part, Adele only had eyes for the thirty or so containers set up in the room like a row of pods or bassinets. Each of the containers had an aluminum lid with green rolling locks on the side.

She heard more gunfire from further down in the second building of the facility. Adele followed two of the men, moving with rapid pace. She spotted Major Hewer on one side of an open doorway, and John on the other. This second building looked like a hangar filled with large trucks. Some of the vehicles resembled, of all things, ice cream trucks.

Men had set up behind the trucks; bullets riddled the front of their vehicles, but they sheltered behind the engines, returning fire. There were loud shouts and the chatter of automatic weapons.

Adele felt herself shoved out of the way as she was pushed roughly behind an outcropping metal container. More yelling. The time for negotiation was over. Adele's own weapon was trained toward the door, but she couldn't get off much of a shot in the face of the automatic fire.

She wished she'd asked for a better weapon. Still, she watched as John and Major Hewer emerged from behind a low concrete wall they were using as a barrier and aimed—two bursts of fire.

No answer. Everything quieted all of a sudden.

The silence was shattered by more shouts in German as Hewer commanded the men forward. They circled the trucks, attentive, not lowering their guard for a second. They moved now from this second building and headed for the third and final one.

More men in white uniforms and chemical outfits were spotted trying to flee—they were quickly shouted down and apprehended. The trucks they passed all had open backs—most of them empty. But the one furthest from Adele was filled with the aluminum coolers with green locking mechanisms. She shivered again, staring at the items, but allowed herself to be led further into the facility. She followed after Hewer and John in a flanking motion.

One of the men had a riot shield in front of him, holding it braced against his shoulder as they headed toward the last building.

This one was the smallest. But it was two stories, with glass windows that had been boarded up. It looked like it might have served as an office once upon a time. But now, there were fewer entry points. Only one door Adele could see set into the unpainted concrete structure.

More yelling came muffled from within this building. Major Hewer hurried forward, a grenade in his hand. No, a flashbang, Adele realized.

He lobbed it at the same time as John shot a hole in the nearest window. The flashbang flew through; there were sounds of shouting from within, and then a blast of brilliant white that Adele just barely glimpsed through a crack in the boarded up window.

A few seconds later, men with hands in the air emerged from behind the wall, stumbling and rubbing at their eyes. A couple of them had blood trickling from their ears.

Adele slowly lowered her weapon, feeling a surge of relief. Just then, there was the chatter of more gunfire. One of the men next to her loosed a startled cry and slipped. He hit the ground with a thump, gasping. Adele turned sharply, gun raised.

She got off two shots of her own in the direction of a man who'd been hiding on the roof of the second facility. The man looked like he'd been hit in the hand, and he clutched his injured arm, trying to raise his gun again at the same time.

At least six men with machine guns rounded, aimed, and fired in a matter of a split second, dousing the roof with bullets in a downpour of lead.

The mangled corpse of the Serbian fell, collapsing to the ground in front of the warehouse.

Finally, Adele breathed.

The man at her feet was rising slowly with the help of two of his compatriots. The bullets looked like they'd hit his vest. Ashen-faced and shaking as he was, this didn't deter the other men—once they'd determined he would survive—from teasing him and making fun of his expression.

For her part, Adele felt sick.

She stood in the middle of the compound, between the three buildings, inhaling and enjoying the sudden quiet. No more gunfire, no more shouts. Major Hewer was rapidly issuing orders still, but in a controlled way now, sending men to sweep through the buildings once more in teams and guarantee they were clear.

Adele glanced at the second building, finding her fingers trembling where they gripped her weapon.

That had been a lot of organs in those containers. She could only imagine how many shipments had come through this place. How many times they had packaged the organs and shipped them off around the world. She shivered, staring ahead, stunned. Adele felt a hand on her arm and glanced up at John. He gestured to the roof and said, "Good shot." She nodded, numbly.

Adele swallowed. She was determined to be professional. This felt more like a military invasion than anything, but it didn't matter; she was still on the job. She steadied her breathing and then followed after John toward the second building, her weapon raised once more, her expression determined.

Over the next couple of hours, she watched and helped as more arrests were made. She listened to the chatter of Major Hewer as he relayed information back to base. Not long after, there was the sound of sirens, and regular police showed up, preparing to take the traffickers into custody. It wouldn't be long before the news would start arriving as well, Adele surmised. From what she was hearing, though, from the mutterings between Hewer, John, and a man in a pressed suit who'd arrived with the police, this was *big*. The police were finding more and more evidence suggesting this thing had been international.

Adele glanced around, staring at nearly twenty men now on their knees, handcuffed, waiting to be escorted to prison wagons.

"Dear God," Adele said, watching as more and more suspects were escorted off by police officers. The sound of sirens had nearly drowned the sky at this point.

Eventually, Adele found herself in the back of the military vehicle she'd arrived in, alone, trembling. She clutched her hands in front of her, staring at the facility through the bullet-cracked glass.

She shook her head, exhausted.

A quiet tap on the glass dragged her attention to the side. At first she was startled, but then she relaxed a bit as she recognized Major Hewer. His large, bushy beard jutted out past the chinstrap of his helmet.

He unbuckled the helmet, pulled it off, and opened the door, glancing at her. "Boss wants to speak with you," he said. He gestured with his helmet to the man in the suit. The sky was darkening now and it was difficult to make him out against the backdrop of the gray warehouse buildings. Adele glanced past Hewer. "This seems like a big deal," she said, quietly, trying to hide her nerves.

Hewer examined her from beneath his dark brows. He nodded once. "You're a friend of John's?"

Adele thought about it for a moment, then nodded. "Yeah. I am."

Major Hewer cleared his throat. "Friend of John is a friend of mine. You did good work. Thing is starting to look international. Boys found discrepancies on the truck's license plates." He passed a hand over his face, streaking his forehead with dirt. "Looks like this might span several countries." He shook his head, rubbing his chin. "Spain, Hungary, France," he nodded toward her, "Germany..." He rubbed his chin. "That's only what we've found in a couple hours. There will probably be more."

Adele stared incredulously.

"You did good work," he said with a very John-like wink.

Adele tried to return his smile as the large, muscular man turned and began stalking back toward the suited fellow.

She would have to talk to him, but for the moment, she just tried to gather herself, to breathe. She could smell the gun smoke in the air.

It took her a moment, in the back seat of the Humvee, to realize she felt glad; glad they had put a stop to this. She tried not to think of all those organs in the coolers. What would be done with them? Would they be put to waste? What a terrible thought. Could they possibly be returned to their owners? She doubted it. She wondered how many people had died to amass that collection. Could the German government use them? They could save lives still...

These were questions far above her pay grade, and Adele felt a flash of relief she wasn't required to answer them.

She watched the traffickers taken off one at a time into the back of police wagons. And while this was a victory, she couldn't shake the notion that there was just one problem.

They still hadn't actually found the murderer in Paris.

Scowling at the thought, she emerged from the back of the vehicle and headed toward the suited man with the mustache.

CHAPTER TWENTY FIVE

"You made the news," her father said, looking up at her.

Adele smiled, studying the Sergeant. "Thanks for making the drive."

Her dad nodded once, scratching his chin. He looked as he always did—straight-backed, straight-nosed. A bit of a belly. If anyone could claim the title Sergeant, it was a man who looked like this. He was even wearing his uniform, pressed, clean. He smelled of soap, not unlike Sophie Paige.

The thought alarmed Adele. She sat in the corner booth of the café, a mile from the airport, watching her father. The smell of cheap coffee and even cheaper food floated on the air.

"They send you on your own?" her father asked, adjusting some of the silverware beneath a napkin.

Adele shook her head. "No, my partner is out in the car waiting. Plane doesn't leave for a bit though; we're fine."

Her father raised an eyebrow. "Tell your partner to come in. I'm sure she doesn't want to sit out in the cold."

Adele shifted uncomfortably. "I'm sure he's fine. How are you?"

Her dad sighed and then waved over the waitress. A woman in a pink apron with red polka-dots approached, smiling. "Can I help you, sir?" she asked. Adele's father pointed without speaking toward the coffee on the menu.

The woman nodded once. "Cream?"

"Course not," her dad snapped.

The woman shifted a little bit, her smiled turning down a few watts. She looked at Adele, her friendly expression seeming rather fixed all of a sudden. "And you?" she asked.

Adele shook her head. "I'm fine, sorry."

The smiled completely faded now as the waitress turned away, grumbling to herself about tourists as she headed to get the Sergeant's coffee.

"Doing good work," her dad said with a nod. "I don't know the extent of it, but from what's coming across my desk, you had your hand in a nice series of arrests."

Adele shrugged. She and John had spent the night in a hotel following the bust—separate rooms. They had waited on instructions from the DGSI and sat through interviews with the BKA. By all accounts except for Adele's, it had all been a huge success. The trafficking ring had been shut down. Evidence suggested that Interpol would have many more busts to make in other countries. John was confident the Paris murderer would be among them.

But Adele shifted uncomfortably, twisting a napkin beneath her fingers and tearing it off a piece at a time and watching the fragments fall to the table. She didn't think it would be so easy.

"What is it?" her father asked, studying her.

She looked up. "Nothing. Just something about the case. It's not a big deal."

Her father shifted. "Right. Okay then. Well, it's good seeing you."

Adele smiled. "Good to see you too. You're looking healthy."

Her father brushed the front of his uniform and nodded. "Thanks. You too."

"How are—"

Before she could finish, her father blurted out, "You're not dating your partner, are you? Is that why you don't want him to see me?"

Adele slumped, trying not to rub her eyes in frustration. "Dad, I'm not dating my partner. I don't want him to see you because he's an ass."

Her father scowled.

"Sorry for swearing. Look, let's talk about something else."

They drifted into silence again, and the woman in the pink apron came over, depositing the coffee, black, in front of Adele's father. Adele tried to smile sweetly after the woman, but the waitress stormed away, still muttering about tourists.

The sound of airplanes taking off and landing could be heard in the distance.

"Well," her father said, "you've been talking a lot about your mother's murder. You said you had a lead."

Adele tried not to let her exhaustion show as she shook her head. "Look, we don't have to talk about work. How's life? Are you seeing anyone? Have you made any good soup recently?"

"Soup is fine." Another pause. "You shouldn't go after him," her dad said.

"Dad," Adele said, "just let it go."

The Sergeant nodded as if he saw the sense in this. Another pause. "It's not safe, Sharp. You shouldn't."

Adele frowned. She wanted to look away out the window toward the parking lot where John waited in their loaner, preparing to take them to the airport before their flight.

But her father had a look in his eyes that gave pause. A haunted, heavy look.

He was staring at his hands, his eyes vacant as he shook his head, murmuring, "Not safe. It's not safe."

Adele watched the Sergeant for a moment, realizing it was almost as if he wasn't even speaking to her. For the briefest moment, it seemed as if he didn't realize she was there. He kept repeating, "Not safe, it's just not safe."

Adele felt a prickle across her skin as she watched her father. She had often thought her mother's death didn't bother him. But now, as she watched him, she felt the unease spreading, now prickling up her spine and down to the tips of her fingers.

"Dad, are you okay?"

Her voice seemed to jolt the Sergeant from whatever had come over him. For a moment, his expression softened, and she thought she saw tears forming in his eyes as he looked at her. But then his face turned stony, and he said, "You can't solve your mother's murder. Don't go after him. There's no point. I forbid you!"

Adele glared at her dad. "You forbid me? What do you think I am, six?"

Her dad shook his finger at her and began to raise his voice, but Adele pushed away from the table, shaking her head. "I can't believe you," she snapped. "Could we have a nice visit, just once?"

She tossed a ten-euro note on the table and said, "Goodbye, Dad; I have to catch my plane. Thanks for coming."

The Sergeant was still scowling after her as she pushed out the café door and stomped over to their waiting vehicle. She didn't return his look as John glanced over at her, opened his mouth to likely make some sort of snarky comment, but then seemed to think better of it, and gunned the engine.

"You okay?" John said, quietly.

Adele scowled at the dashboard. "Just drive," she snapped.

John held up one hand over the steering wheel. He turned out of the parking lot and onto the street. For a brief moment, Adele felt a sudden flash of guilt.

"Wait, hang on," she said. "Turn back . . ."

John raised an eyebrow at her. He put on his blinker and began to turn, but just as quickly Adele changed her mind. "Wait, no, never mind. Keep going. It's fine."

John muttered beneath his breath but turned off the blinker and directed the vehicle toward the airport.

Adele wasn't paying attention to her partner. She had wanted to go back . . . to what? To apologize to her father? But apologize for what? Her father was still treating her like she was a child. Granted, storming off didn't exactly speak of some huge maturity. Still, what was the point of sticking around to be yelled at? To be commanded like she was somehow employed by him?

That man was insufferable. She shook her head, still glaring at her fingers.

"Everything okay?" John said hesitantly, his eyes fixed on the road ahead.

"It's fine," she said, sullenly. "Just used to the men in my life causing trouble, I guess."

John hesitated, seemingly stuck between two options. At last, he said, "Well, I mean, I haven't known you nearly as long as your father, but I'm not trying to cause trouble for you if that's what you're implying."

Adele looked over and did a double take. "You, no, I wasn't talking about you. I'm sorry."

She shook her head. She had been thinking of Angus. Of her father. Perhaps John. Was John worth the thought? It wasn't like she knew him that well. He was unpredictable. Dangerous. He had struck a witness in front of the executive for the DGSI for crying out loud. He'd shaken down an informant for money. He'd given the money to a surviving victim, but did that make it any better?

"Look," John said, softly, "I'm not trying to cause pain. If . . . if this is about . . ." He waved his hand in the air between them and winced. As he spoke, it sounded like he was choking on the words. He paused for a moment, his cheeks tinged red, and stared through the windshield resolutely as if determined not to look at her.

"John it's not about *that*," Adele said, the exhaustion from a lack of sleep weighing heavily on her. "We'll just keep it professional and friendly then, fine?"

John frowned. He didn't answer one way or another, still staring out the windshield. For her own part, Adele wondered at the words. Was that what she really wanted? Professional? Did it matter? She allowed the silence to swell in the cabin as they moved closer to the airport.

"I—" He continued to struggle to speak as if the words were lodged in his throat. "I'm just not the best at getting close to people, all right?"

Adele hesitated. She didn't look at him, knowing that this would only agitate his discomfort. But as she considered his words, this brief flash of vulnerability from her otherwise stoic partner, her frown deepened into something akin to thought.

"What?" John asked abruptly.

She glanced at him.

"What are you thinking?" he said. "I know that look. You're on to something? What?"

She shifted uncomfortably, adjusting the seat belt across her chest into a more comfortable position. "It's nothing," she said, softly. "Nothing, not really. Except, well..." She paused. "Just what you said..."

"I am very wise," he said, nodding.

"Funny. No, about getting close."

John's jaw clenched and his look of discomfort returned.

But Adele began speaking quickly now, her eyes narrowed, fixed on the road speeding by. "It is hard to get close sometimes. Hard for a lot of people. Especially if you're moving to a new country, yes?" she asked, tilting her head.

John shrugged, seemingly still disgruntled by the vulnerability of the moment.

"It's lonely moving to a new country. I know it myself. It's hard to get close. But you can make it easier. Especially in the day of the Internet," she said, picking up pace as she spoke, nodding to punctuate each word.

"I don't get it," John grunted.

She turned to him now, staring at the side of his face. "It was obvious. All this talk about online forums, about groups. We didn't chase that trail enough. We should have focused on it more. Expats are victims. Especially from America. Why America? I've been so caught up in this trafficking angle that I lost sight of a valuable clue—both those women were members of that forum, Yankees in Paris. But what about the third one? Was she just another expat—a coincidence?"

Now John glanced at her, taking his eyes off the road for the briefest moment. "What are you getting at?"

"What if this isn't just about them being from America? Or them needing online groups for company and all that. What if it's that *specific* forum? Yankees in Paris. A stupid name, sure. But what if it's that group where the killer is finding his victims? With Waters, or whatever his real name is, we thought he'd been contacting the woman to lure them. We thought he was just targeting expats. But what if it is that specific group?"

"You think the third victim was a member of Yankees in Paris also?"

Adele shrugged. "It's worth looking into."

"It's a shot in the dark is what it is."

"Well, if you ask me, we're on a lucky streak."

Adele fished her phone from her pocket, no longer looking at John, her heart beating. It was an obvious clue. Just sitting in front of her. The sort of clue Robert would've seen immediately. Except Robert hated computers. He hated technology. So she should've seen it. Maybe Foucault was right. Maybe she wasn't cut out for this.

She staved off the storm of self-doubt, though, and quickly dialed Robert's number, preparing to give instructions to her old mentor.

CHAPTER TWENTY SIX

Back in France, they clustered in Robert's office. Adele sat behind her own desk, and Robert behind his. When John had followed Adele into the room, Robert's eyebrows had risen slightly, but he'd made no comment besides, "Hello, Agent Renee."

John had grunted in return.

Now, as they discussed the case, John's expression only seemed to darken. Robert shook his head once more and said, "Look, Adele, there's no connection. We've been over that list five times. I even had Ozil from upstairs double check me. There's no way anyone on the online form is a killer. No past convictions, nothing suspicious. No connections with the victims outside the internet. But," he held up a single finger, like a judge's gavel, preparing for a pronouncement. "You were right. That woman, the third victim, she wasn't in the group, but she'd been sent an invite. There is a connection there at least."

Adele straightened her posture and tried to wipe the sleep from her eyes with the back of her hand. She stared at Robert. "Yankees in Paris sent an invite to Shiloah Watkins?"

"The one and the same," Robert said with a quick nod.

John crossed his arms from where he stood by the window between the two desks. "This is over," he said. "Your killer, whoever he is, was either shot back at that facility, or will be arrested in the coming weeks. We have list after list of names. Almost a hundred arrests will be made."

He extended his hands like he was weighing a scale and shrugged at the end of it. "The chances of him getting away are slim. We may not be able to find exactly who he is," he said, "but I'll bet my bottom dollar that he's either dead or in custody."

Adele studied the tall man, her mind flashing back to images of him moving into the facility in tandem with the special operations unit. He'd moved so seamlessly. He was a man built for violence. She wasn't sure why this bothered her, and at the same time, it gave her a level of comfort.

She sighed and shook her head. "You could be right. There's no doubt in my mind that you could be one hundred percent correct. *Could.* But what if you're not? What if he got away?" She interlocked her fingers, cracking her knuckles absentmindedly. "Did you see how big that place was? The number of people working at that facility? The hundreds of containers?"

John glared. "So what?"

Adele shrugged. "Seems like they had no shortage of supply of victims. Homeless, the destitute—why start going after higher profile targets? The expats are vulnerable, but conspicuous. Why jeopardize their operation by committing such public murders? Not only that—they *only* took the kidneys. I'm not sure how their grotesque business model works, but . . ." She cleared her throat, considered the thought, but then didn't finish the sentence, allowing the men to fill in the blanks themselves.

John tapped his forehead against the glass a couple of times, bending over slightly to do so, keeping his hands at his hips in a posture of frustration. "You're not listening," he said. "Whoever this killer is, he's done. Done. Understand? Besides, listen to what Robert said, there's no one they suspect. No one with priors. No one who had connections to the three women. Yes, a couple of the administrators on the online board would've known their names, but we've vetted them."

John looked at Robert and raised an eyebrow as if seeking confirmation.

The older mentor nodded once. "You're not wrong, we have. The moderators who contacted the murdered women, other than Melissa Robinson, are both women in their sixties. They also have no past convictions and airtight alibis on the days the victims were murdered. One of them was even in London."

Adele shrugged. "Maybe it's not someone in the group. But someone getting their information *from* the group. I don't know. But I have to be sure."

"And how exactly do you plan on doing that?" John demanded.

Adele shifted, then clasped her hands in front of her. Her eyes were heavy, and her eyelids felt like sandpaper. She wanted nothing more than to go to sleep, to get over with it. But, at the same time, she wouldn't let this killer get away.

He didn't deserve her complacency. John might think the operation in Germany would catch him up, like a fish in a net. But she felt otherwise. This killer was no minnow. She was starting to suspect he might not even have been involved with the organ traffickers at all. But if not, what was he doing with the kidneys?

In a ghost of a voice, Adele said, "We're on a clock here, gentlemen. The killer strikes every few days. He's due for another kill—*soon.* I can only think of one way to lure him out for sure. It's risky," she said, shrugging, "But like I said, we're out of time. And if, like John thinks, he's already caught, or is going to be, then we shouldn't have to worry about anything. But if he's still out there..." She trailed off.

Now it wasn't just John frowning at her, but Robert too. His trimmed eyebrows rose over the top of his computer and he leaned over, staring at her across the room.

"I'm going to pose as an expat," Adele said. She nodded with finality. "It's the only way. I'm going to pretend to be new to Paris. I'll make a cover story, something he can't resist. Hell, I'll even post my address."

"Your address?" said Robert through thin lips.

She looked at him and shook her head quickly. "Not your place. I've already talked with Foucault. He's willing to give me a safe house for a couple of days, just to see if it works. He didn't like the idea at first either. But he knew I was right. We're against the clock. We can't have another body drop." John and Robert were now frowning so hard Adele could barely make out their eyes from beneath their eyebrows. Both of them began shaking their heads at nearly the same moment.

"No," John said, "that's stupid. You're just putting yourself in danger."

Robert didn't say anything, but he echoed John's sentiments with his scowl.

Adele shrugged. "What is it? Either he's captured or dead, or he's still out there. Why would I be in danger if he's captured?"

John huffed, his hands jammed in his pockets. "You're playing with fire, Sharp. This is stupid."

Adele shrugged. "I mean, I wasn't planning on going there alone. That's just what he's going to think. That is, if you're willing to spare another day from your super important embezzlement case."

John, with fire in his eyes, glared at Adele. "You're damn right I'm gonna be there." He turned away, muttering beneath his breath about stupid Americans and their stupid plans.

CHAPTER TWENTY SEVEN

He whistled softly, allowing the notes to calm his mood. It wasn't going to work. The last volunteer who'd been interested in donating to save his father couldn't be met with. Her routine was too erratic. Her housemates were always home. No, it was a bust.

The young man glared at his computer. He stood, rather than sat. He knew well enough the problems with circulation if someone sat too long. He was nothing if not health-conscious, especially given what had happened to his father.

What had happened?

He glanced over his shoulder toward the couch where his father sat watching TV. He smiled in the old man's direction, still whistling, still humming, and giving a little wave.

His father waved back.

"Soon," the young man said, loud enough for both of them to hear. He saw his father nod, a sleepy expression on his face.

The young man winced and reached down, pressing his fingers against the tender portion of his abdomen. It would be fine. He would be fine. His father would be fine. He clicked through the computer, scanning the information the man he'd hired had sent him.

It would have been too risky to join the group himself. But thankfully, his time at university had connected him with all sorts. One particularly smart fellow, who wasn't as interested in following the law as most, was willing to hack into any site for a certain fee.

That had been the rest of the man's savings for medical school. But it was worth it. It was how he had found the last three volunteers. This fourth one wasn't going to work out, though. There had to be someone else. Someone else, who . . .

The man paused, reading the messages through the wall of black and green text which his hacker friend had supplied. He leaned in. Just this morning, someone had posted something about a party at their house. They were only newly arrived in France. They would be having the party tomorrow.

"Hello there," he murmured quietly. The man began to hum, murmuring to himself like a mother swaddling a child and putting it to sleep.

"Oh dear, would you like to help my father?" he asked beneath his breath.

He clicked on the woman's information and went to her profile. Thirty-three, golden hair. She gave her name as Adele Vermeal.

She had a pleasant face. Younger women had smaller bodies. This meant less strain on their organs. They would save his father.

"Thank you," he whispered at the computer screen. He reached out a trembling finger and touched the face of Adele Vermeal. His finger trailed along her chin, and he found that he was starting to cry. "Thank you," he said with a sob.

He looked back to his father.

A flash of pain shot through the son's abdomen. He blinked, and, for the barest of moments, instead of his father, a ghoulish, skeletal face stared out from the couch. He blinked again. And the horrible visage was gone just as quickly as it had come. The faded, wrinkled, shriveled flesh was replaced by healthy, smooth skin. The sunken, empty, milky eyes reformed again, replaced by his father's tender gaze. The crushed, broken fingers returned to their soft, trembling fleshy form, gripping the remote to the TV.

The young man shook his head. He winced as another flash of pain jolted through his right side, and he reached down, clasping it with his hand.

"This will all be over soon," he murmured. He started humming again, whistling. She said the party would be tomorrow. But she had posted her address already.

Perfect. The man would just have to prepare his tools.

He loved volunteers.

Chapter Twenty Eight

Adele sat in the dark upstairs room of the safe house. Her eyes glazed over as she reclined by the window, staring out into the street. No traffic. Earlier, she'd seen a red jalopy with strangely tinted windows trundle by. But it hadn't parked, and instead had continued around the block.

She'd been avoiding sleep for days, but now it seemed intent on collecting its due. She could barely keep her eyes open.

John was in the other room, hidden, waiting. He still thought this venture foolish. She was starting to think maybe he was right. She had posted on the message board hours ago. But nothing since—no surprise visits, no messages in return, no one seemed to care save a few likes on her post.

"Just a few more hours," she said, trying to talk herself awake.

And yet, still, sleep drifted on her shoulders, weighing her down where she sat by the silent window. Her head lolled ...

... her eyes closed ...

... A sound jolted her awake.

Adele's eyes snapped open. From the direction of the side room where John was hiding, she could hear snoring. So much for attentiveness. They'd both fallen asleep.

She immediately pushed out of the chair by the window and stood in the small, cloistered bedroom, glancing around. Vaguely, she wondered who had lived here before. There were small drawings on the wall, against the paint itself. The DGSI hadn't taken the time to cover the sketches. They looked like the drawings of a child. A lot of blue, and monsters with fangs.

Adele smiled at the etchings. She glanced around the darkened room, then paused. She thought she heard a quiet engine, a rattling sound and a red streak moved up the street, visible through the window. She peered out at the car, but it disappeared around the block.

She stood still for a passing moment, but then shook her head, reaching up to wipe sleep from her eyes. She turned toward the window again, looking out into the streets once more.

No one. Not a soul moving along the smooth asphalt or segmented sidewalk divided by benches, bus stops, and natural ornamentation. She glanced at her smart watch: 3 AM. The dead of night.

She could still hear John snoring and made a mental note to tease him about it later.

She inhaled the still room's air, her nose twitching. Whoever had used the safe house before had worn a powerful cologne. The lingering odor of a far too sweet citrusy smell clung to the walls and circulated the vents. Adele thought she detected mothballs as well.

She winced, scratched at her nose, moving away from the chair toward the door. She needed a breath of fresh air. Night was safe. The killer only struck during the day, posing as a maintenance man. His victims had died in the afternoon.

Convincing herself, Adele moved out of the room, and with quiet steps took the stairs, then turned down the short hall to the front door.

She checked the locks and the security camera array set up by the door. Four screens watched all four directions. No movement. On the camera facing the backyard, she thought she glimpsed the edge of a bumper behind the garage. A red bumper? Adele leaned in, peering closer, but shook her head. The car wasn't moving. It was hard to tell anything. Probably just one of the neighbors. The killer struck in the afternoon. He wouldn't change his MO.

He was harvesting organs. People in the business of greed and murder for profit were often reliable. They were scared of being caught. And they would remain predictable, because they thought their routine made them invincible.

She pushed out the front door and found her first step onto the patio sent a jolt of trembling up her spine.

Adele reached up, placing a hand against her cheek, half preparing to slap herself out of it. She was not a fearful woman. So why was she acting so scared all of a sudden?

Adele lowered her hand and rubbed her arms in quick, jerking motions to get the blood flowing once more. She needed to stay alert. She couldn't believe she'd fallen asleep on the job. She thought of John's snoring and smirked to herself. So much for the killing machine she'd partnered with. Her expression softened as she took the two steps onto the sidewalk and began moving up the empty street.

France at night was beautiful, but eerie. The large, looming structures in the distance cut jagged shapes of shadow against the skyline. The quiet of the sidewalks and streets, the empty businesses, and the silent houses stood sentry in the dark, witnessing her progress up the sidewalk. She traced the cracks, stepping over the gaps in the stones, circling the planted trees, her eyes fixed ahead.

She heard something.

Adele turned sharply, her hand darting to the weapon on her hip. Someone was coming toward her. Someone in a hood. She stared and began to raise a hand, calling out.

A flash of silver in the person's hand. Her weapon jerked from its holster, pointing toward the oncoming aggressor. "Don't," she began, but then she froze, and just as quickly stowed her gun before the person noticed.

A young woman was staring at the sidewalk, hood up, earbuds in, muttering to herself beneath her breath as she strode purposefully up the nighttime streets. Suddenly, as if catching a look of Adele out of the corner of her eye, she pulled up sharply and stared, wide-eyed from beneath her hood. It didn't seem like she'd noticed the gun.

The young woman stopped a few paces away, took one look at Adele, then cautiously moved across to the other side of the street, making a big deal as if she'd intended to cross all along.

Adele watched the young woman put earbuds deep in her ears again, adjust her hood, then set off at a jog. Adele wanted to call out, to tell her it wasn't safe wandering the streets at night. But another part of her knew most people didn't live in her world. Most weren't confronted with murder and death on the daily. The chances of something happening to that young woman in this part of the neighborhood was relatively low. Adele couldn't protect everyone. People had to make their own choices.

She turned back to the house, still inhaling deeply through her nose and wandering up the street.

It took her a few more minutes to gather her breath and completely rid herself of the scent of strong cologne and mothballs which lingered on her clothes. Finally, brushing her sleeves and turning back to the safe house, Adele moved once more.

A sudden scraping sound drifted down the street from behind her; again Adele whirled around, heart in her throat.

This time, though, it was just a metal sign across the way, advertising a shoe store on the other block. Buffeted by the pawing wind, the sign scratched against the sidewalk, one of its rope fastenings having loosened.

Adele stared at the metal sign and smiled grimly to herself. This time, she did reach up and slap gently against her face. *Focus,* she thought. She shook her head and then turned, moving back to the house and taking the patio steps.

Just seeing ghosts, she thought. Adele grabbed the door handle and turned it.

She stepped into the dark house, wishing she had left a light on. But she hadn't wanted to alert anyone. If the killer *did* decide to change his MO, she had wanted to catch him off guard.

Darkness was a close ally of ambush.

She stepped further into the hall, felt a sudden breezy chill, and quickly closed the door behind her. Perhaps it wouldn't be the worst idea to get at least a little light. It wasn't like she'd seen anyone on the streets anyway. Adele reached toward the light switch by the living room door frame.

Then, a sudden sound of shuffling movement.

Her heart invaded her throat.

A pale hand snaked around the doorway and snared her wrist. With a powerful yank, the hand dragged her forward.

Adele yelled in surprise and horror. She caught a glimpse of a young man, wearing a bright hat. But she couldn't see much else except for a flash of metal arcing toward her neck.

She yelled and jerked back.

Adele managed to dodge the swiping blade, but the man still gripped her by the wrist. For the briefest moment, they struggled, and Adele heard something . . . something strange.

The man was humming.

She winced, her blood pumping, terror fueling her.

"John!" she screamed. "John, downstairs!" Adele wanted to move, but she couldn't distance herself. The young man's grip was too strong.

The strange humming continued, interrupted only by grunts of exertion as he began tugging at her. His eyes were vacant as he stared at her and smiled like a jack-o'-lantern.

"Let go of me!" she screeched.

Her off-hand reached for her gun. Despite his grip, she still twisted, trying to reach across her waist to the holster on her opposite hip. She had to stop, though, as the blade sliced toward her neck a second time, but this time Adele kicked out, catching her assailant in the knee. He released his grip and stumbled back.

Adele rapidly pulled her firearm from her hip and took aim, but before she could squeeze off a shot, the man lunged toward her again with a snarl. He tackled her, sending her clattering to the ground with a painful grunt. Her head whipped back, slamming into the floorboards, and dark spots danced across her vision. She lay stunned for a moment, but found it difficult to breathe.

As the fog cleared, she realized his full weight was pressed on her, crushing her chest, impeding her lungs. "Get—get off!" she tried to shout, but the words came out jumbled, and she continued to gasp, unable to draw breath.

The man's hand fumbled against the floorboards, reaching past her, his body still thick against her, holding her down.

"Thank you," he said in a wheezing voice, "thank you so much for volunteering! Thank you!"

Then he began humming again. Adele felt shivers up the back of her spine, angling her head and extending her fingers toward her weapon which had landed in the threshold of the dining room against the floorboards. Her fingers scrabbled against the wood, and her eyes widened. Even with shallow breaths, she could feel the fear flooding her. Her fingers brushed the butt of the gun, just as the man lashed out with his knife again.

This time, though, he'd seen her groping hand and had aimed toward her fingers.

A flash of pain. She jerked her hand just in time to avoid losing a finger, but the knife had sliced her middle finger and forefinger. A deep, deep cut, she could already tell by the pain and the sudden warm wetness pulsing down her fingers and hand.

The pain was secondary, though, to her need to breathe.

She no longer cried out or protested; she needed what little air was left in her lungs to stay conscious. If she passed out now, it would all be over.

The man's knife moved again, this time angling toward her throat. He sat on her, straddling her chest, his legs on either side of her, pinning one of her arms and trapping her abdomen. Her bleeding hand jutted forward, catching the knife before it sliced her throat.

It cut her palm this time, sending another spasm of pain through her already mangled hand.

A squeak of pain escaped her lips, and the man stopped humming to snarl in frustration. He sliced down again, but this time, with her bloody hand, Adele managed to fling her palm out and catch his wrist.

He was strong, but not unusually so. She held his wrist tight, shoving his hand back.

The man whimpered like a scalded child. He tried to dislodge her grip, shifting a bit, pushing even more air from Adele's body.

Now, the black spots had returned. She was gasping, but no air managed to enter her crushed, compressed lungs. *Where is John?* she thought, vaguely.

The man kept yanking his arm, trying to dislodge it. And, in one last, desperate play, as darkness closed in and consciousness fled, Adele released her grip and flung her bleeding hand toward the man's face. Hot droplets of crimson speckled his nose and cheek. Her hand slapped against his eyes and the blood pouring from her fingers drenched his face, momentarily filling his eyes.

The man howled and reflexively, his hands darted to clear his gaze. A human could always be expected to maintain their vision—it was a primal instinct Adele had been counting on.

Now, with both his hands arching toward his eyes, she had a brief window where the knife wasn't a threat. She lunged again for her gun, no longer breathing. Her head pounded in pain from a lack of oxygen. Her motion was weak—in this fading state, she'd overestimated her ability to move quickly.

With sluggish motions, though, her fingers, still slick with blood, grappled the butt of her firearm. But the blood made the gun slick. Her fingers slipped off it.

The man had managed to wipe his eyes now. And he took only the faintest moment to steady himself and blink, before slashing at her again with the blade.

Nothing for it. She simply turned her head and jerked to the side. A necessary sacrifice.

She felt pain across her cheek and down her ear. The slice was deep—the knife sharp. Still, if she'd tried to catch it again, she would have died in moments. Only a few seconds of air left. Her fingers scraped the slippery gun again. The man began to cut again, this time leaning forward a bit to reach her neck.

At the same moment, she finally managed to snare her gun—he was single-mindedly focused now on her throat.

A costly mistake.

Another cut now across her neck, shallow at first, but she could feel the blade dragging almost in slow motion as she brought her weapon around at the same time.

She couldn't angle her arm, due to his extended hands, to get a clean shot. Now, the sound was all she needed. Distraction. Wake John. Desperation.

She fired twice.

The man and his knife jerked back as if he'd been torched. But he moved too quickly to have been hit. Far too quickly.

Adele, gasping now, desperately gulping in air, lay on the floor, her vision still clearing. It took her a moment to clear her vision; as she did, she glimpsed a shadow of motion hurtling toward the kitchen.

Gasping, chest heaving, she pushed herself up as quickly as possible, but the rapid motion caused her head to swim and she jerked back down, half sitting, half lying, still gathering her thoughts in a pool of blood widening down her cheek and beneath her hand.

Still, pain was secondary.

The bastard couldn't be allowed to escape.

He'd fled toward the kitchen: a mistake. The windows in the kitchen were barred, the door reinforced per agency standards. He didn't have the key; he was trapped. Or was she the one trapped?

"John!" she managed to shout up the stairs in a strangled, rasping voice.

She could hear rapid movements. The sound of footsteps from the kitchen. Then, nothing.

Adele bunched her hand in her shirt, wrapping the fabric around the wound, and switched her firearm to her weaker hand. She'd never practiced off-hand shooting much, but now it was all she had.

Then, desperately hoping John had woken, she moved toward the kitchen doorway, eyes forward.

"Give it up!" she called, still breathing heavily. "There's only two ways out of that room. A body bag or cuffs. Don't be stupid—this is over!"

No answer.

Adele scraped her shoulder blades against the wall, approaching the kitchen. They'd locked the door? Hadn't they? She was sure they'd locked it.

"Give it up!" she called again, raising her voice louder than necessary in a hope to wake John.

Again, no answer. A pause.

Then, the sound of humming.

The strange, melodic noise sent chills up Adele's spine and she swallowed back the fear in her gut. Something about bleeding, gasping, caught off guard in a locked house brought out a more instinctual part of her. But she needed to remember he training, to suppress her emotions. Fear was the enemy.

"Come out!" she called. Her shoulder pressed against the ridged wooden frame of the kitchen doorway.

She hesitated, feeling her cheek sticky against the wall. From within the kitchen, the humming persisted, low, eerie in the dark.

It was coming from behind the fridge.

Adele leaned in, keeping her eyes fixed on the fridge. She licked her lips and moved into the kitchen, stepping sidelong. She kept her weapon focused on her off hand, her injured palm still snared in the hem of her shirt.

"Get out from behind there!" she barked.

The large, metal fridge was like the belly of a broad man, blocking her vision of the alcove behind it.

She circled the room, keeping as much distance between herself and the fridge as she could as she tried to gain line-of-sight. She checked her weapon and felt her hand trembling—for a moment, she felt like Masse. With her weaker hand, she did her best to maintain a shooter's crouch, but the strange whistling, the blood loss, the fear of the moment were weighing on her.

Finally, she rounded the wall across from the fridge, facing the darkness on the side of the appliance.

No man.

Still, though, the sound of humming.

A flash of silver. She yelped, but realized, a second later, as she peered closer, that a small recording device lay on the floor by the fridge.

She frowned, leaning in, then prickles erupted across her spine as there came the sound of rushing footsteps from the complete *opposite* side of the kitchen. A distraction. He'd been hiding beneath the table. She spun, weapon raised, and managed to glimpse a shadow bolt through the doorway, back out into the hall.

Adele cursed and spun from the recorder, racing toward the doorway as well. The man jerked out of the hall into the dining room. Adele didn't move forward immediately, fearful of the man lurking just beyond the doorway again, waiting to ambush her.

She heard the sound of heavy footsteps above her now from upstairs.

"Adele?" John shouted.

"Downstairs!" she called back. "He's armed. Knife!"

She circled, one step at a time, trying to keep her weapon fixed on the dining room doorway. But the room was empty. Adele cursed, her weapon still raised—then her gaze settled on the window behind the table.

It was open, leading into the backyard.

She shouted, "Backyard!"

Adele hurried to the window, gun raised. As she reached the sill and aimed into an empty grass lawn, she heard the sound of an engine firing; the red vehicle she'd spotted earlier jerked away from the garage, the tires squealing as it took off up the street.

Adele aimed, eyes narrowed, then squeezed—once, twice.

Two loud retorts echoed in the dead of night. The first bullet didn't hit anything. But the second caught the front wheel.

A loud explosion—and the car suddenly veered sharply. The vehicle slammed into a fire hydrant, then rolled over it, sending a spray of water into the air.

Weapon in hand, Adele slithered through the window and sprinted across the backyard, racing toward the vehicle. She heard the back door to the house slam, and the sound of hurried feet as John made after her.

Adele reached the vehicle first.

A young man sat in the front seat, wearing a yellow hat. He was shaking his head dazedly, a thin trickle of blood creeping down the side of his cheek, but he was looking over his shoulder and talking to someone in the backseat.

"Get out of the vehicle!" Adele shouted. But the young man ignored her.

It was hard to make out much through the tinted windows. But the front window was rolled down halfway, and she could hear the words, "Hush now, Daddy . . . it's going to be okay. It's going to be fine. She's a nice volunteer. We just have to reach an agreement. A very nice lady."

Adele stared, stunned. "There's two of them!" she shouted to John.

His heavy footsteps reached her on the sidewalk. John circled the other side of the car, his gun raised toward the front seat, then swiveling to the back through the tinted glass.

"Hands up, or I'll spray your brains over the upholstery!" John shouted, his eyes wide as adrenaline coursed his body.

Adele kept her own eyes fixed on the young man behind the steering wheel, her gun leveled on his head. Her fingers trembled as she prepared to squeeze off a shot at a moment's notice.

The man glanced toward her, blinking as if noticing her for the first time. He frowned and shook his head. "Thank you," he said. He reached up, rubbing his eyes.

Adele grabbed the door handle, yanking the front side open. "Drop your knife!" she demanded, retreating a couple of steps now that the door hung ajar, providing a better view into the vehicle. The car was going nowhere from where it had stuck on the edge of a fire hydrant and jammed against a stone sidewalk barrier.

The young man glanced into the backseat once more. He began to whistle, soothingly, like a mother trying to placate a young child.

Adele felt a shiver up the back of her spine. She heard the back door open as John flung it wide.

Then there came a sharp hiss and a horrified gasp. "Adele, get him out of the car. Now!"

Adele felt chills, but reacted with the barest of hesitations, clearing her throat and shouting, "Get out, now!"

The young man was shaking his head, still looking confused. His eyes still had a vacant quality to them, but the more she shouted, the more alarmed he seemed to become.

"Get out of the car! I'm not kidding. I'll shoot!"

At last, the man, like he was moving in a dream, emerged from the vehicle, his hands raised, shifting uncomfortably, glancing between the two agents. "Don't hurt him," he said. "Please, don't hurt him. He's sick."

Adele shoved the man sharply to the ground; as he lay on the pavement, she kicked hard once, twice at his right hand, which still gripped the knife. The blade clattered free beneath the car. Adele twisted the man's arms behind his back, and in three swift motions cuffed him. Then, keeping her eye on him, she stepped back, leaving the suspect handcuffed on the ground.

She circled the car to where John stood, staring.

"Securing the second suspect?" she asked, breathing heavily.

But John was just peering grimly into the backseat, shaking his head from side to side, his teeth clenched.

At last, Adele circled completely and stared into the back of the old red jalopy. Her gun lowered, and she felt bile rising in her throat.

A corpse was in the backseat. It looked like the corpse of an old man, but it was hard to tell. The horrific stench assailed her the moment she circled the car and leaned into the back.

The corpse had shrunken eyes, the eyeballs milked over, the flesh putrid and decayed. The ghoulish, skeletal face leered out at her, and thin wisps of the final remnants of hair circled the old man's mottled scalp.

In the corpse's lap, there were three shriveled, decayed items.

Adele frowned, peering closer. "Oh, dear God," she said.

"Think we found the kidneys," John murmured.

The three kidneys, in different states of decay, were placed in the old man's lap, his skeletal fingers, still displaying some levels of flesh, arched over the kidneys like the talons of some bird of prey protecting its young.

"I'm going to be sick," Adele said, her voice strained.

"Don't hurt him," the young man kept repeating, pleading from where he lay on the ground. "Please, don't hurt him."

CHAPTER TWENTY NINE

A dele stared through the glass one-way mirror, watching the interrogation. John stood next to her in the viewing room. They hadn't been allowed in after the last time. Still, Adele studied the strange young man.

He was handsome, in a feminine sort of way. He kept tapping his fingers against the metal interrogation table as if he were listening to some unheard track in his mind. Adele fidgeted uncomfortably, examining the interrogating agent. If it had been up to her, she would've chosen someone else. Anyone else. But still, Agent Paige was good at her job, when she wasn't trying to get even.

Adele watched as Paige leaned in, and through the interrogation room speakers, she heard, "Why did you do it?"

No answer.

"What's your name?"

No answer.

John was bored, and had already maneuvered to the corner of the viewing room where he bounced an empty Coke bottle against the wall. For her part, Adele stood next to the third member of their viewing party.

This woman, standing next to Adele, had short, bristly hair and smooth, dark skin. Her expression was tender but intelligent as she peered through the viewing room glass, examining the suspect. Adele glanced over at the woman. "Well? Dr. Tyra? What do you think?"

The smaller woman regarded Adele, but then just as quickly returned her gaze to the spectacle from within interrogation.

"I don't believe the questions are registering," she said, softly.

Adele exhaled in frustration through her nose. "We found his dad's corpse in the back of his car along with three rotting kidneys. The fact that he's not riddled with disease already is a miracle. What makes someone do something like that?"

"Can I just say," John called from the corner, raising his hand, "there is a chance..." He trailed off for dramatic effect.

Adele glared.

"That perhaps..." he said, still dragging out his sentence.

"John!" Adele snapped.

"I maybe," he winced, "was wrong about the killer being arrested along with the organ harvesters."

Adele reached down to rub her hand. It was bandaged, with twice as much gauze and padding as John's had been. She also had stitches along her cheek and hand. Despite the pain and her frustration with Agent Renee, it would've been foolish to blame John for what had transpired that evening. She was the one who'd fallen asleep first. She had left the house, giving the killer opportunity for entry.

"Are his fingerprints in the system?" This question she directed at John.

The tall agent shook his head. He went back to bouncing his Coke bottle off the wall.

"It's hard to say," said Dr. Tyra, still peering through the glass. "He seems distracted, yes. Tired. But I need to be honest, I'm not sure how much I'm going to get just standing out here with you."

Adele scratched her chin and looked into the room, watching as Sophie Paige launched into another line of questioning.

"Go in," said John. He shooed his hands toward Adele. "I'm the one who slapped the Serb. You didn't hit anyone."

Dr. Tyra's eyebrows flicked up ever so slightly, but she kept her peace.

Adele considered this, still staring at the see-through mirror. They'd been instructed to keep John out of the interrogation room. When she'd seen Agent Paige, she'd decided to sit out as well.

Through the glass, Adele watched as Agent Paige growled and began to shake her head. "What happened to your kidney?" she demanded, glaring at the victim.

At this, though, the suspect started babbling, shaking his head side to side. "Couldn't help...Had to—he was going to die. I needed to, needed to save him. I was good enough!" He shouted this part. "I was good enough! Top of my class at Sorbonne! I was going to be a surgeon. I could do it. I know it. It-it was hard. But no one would help me. Please," he said, his voice cracking now, his lips trembling. The dazed look had returned to his eyes. "Please, I didn't know how painful it was going to be. I hadn't done the anesthesia right. I thought I did. But it was so . . . so painful. I tried. I really did." A sob creaked from his lips.

Adele stared at the suspect in alarm, trying to piece it all together. "Top of the class. He's a medical student. He removed his own kidney to try to put it in his father?" she asked, glancing at Dr. Tyra.

The psychiatrist didn't reply. She continued to watch through the glass as the man broke into tears which began slipping down his cheeks. "Of course," he shouted at Agent Paige, "of course. I would do anything for him. He's my best friend. Please, can I see him? I just need to speak with him."

Adele felt confusion fading to be replaced by a welling sadness and horror. She felt a heaviness weighing on her, and she shook her head, no longer looking at the suspect; she addressed John. "I'm sure you'll find his name if you talk to Sorbonne—ask for any dropouts from last year. I don't think he's lying."

She felt a hand on hers and glanced down. Dr. Tyra looked up, meeting her gaze. The young, kind-eyed doctor stared at Adele, her eyes unblinking, her lips pressed together. "A psychotic break, most likely. He thinks his father is still alive. He avoids the question, or discussing it when it comes up. He doesn't believe he's dead."

Adele ran a hand along the edge of her jaw, shaking her head in disbelief. "So he's been driving his dead father around for nearly a year? That's how long it appears he's been dead."

Dr. Tyra shrugged. "I don't know how long. But he thinks his father is alive. And it sounds like he tried to take his own kidney and put it in his father. I can't even imagine the psychological stress that would put on someone. Sounded like the operation didn't work. Maybe that's when his father died. Under his own son's knife."

Adele shivered, staring at the doctor.

The psychiatrist shrugged. "I can listen in for more—perhaps ask a few more questions. But I think you're right. I think he's telling the truth about medical school. About being a stand-out student. You'll likely find his name with registration."

Adele hesitated, then said, "Honestly, I might leave that up to Agent Paige."

Dr. Tyra studied Adele, then nodded. "It is sad."

They dwindled into silence once more, listening to the crying from the interrogation room. Adele felt her stomach twist, and she closed her eyes to stave off a dawning headache.

"Why?" she said, hesitantly. "Why was he calling me a volunteer? He said the same thing about his other victims—what was the point of the kidneys? Why did he kill them?"

Dr. Tyra hesitated. "Sometimes, with a psychotic break, you only see things you want to see, and you hear things you want to hear. For all I know, in his mind, he was in an operating room, with people willing to give their kidneys to save his father. I don't know for sure. But whatever he's been seeing this last year, isn't the same as everyone else."

"You're saying he's actually insane?"

Dr. Tyra paused. "I'm saying something broke. The weight of the world was put on his shoulders, and he couldn't carry it. And a lot of people got hurt because of it."

Adele swallowed, shaking her head. The whole business left a bad taste in her mouth. A few moments passed with her standing in the viewing room, staring into the bleak, gray interrogation room.

The young man hadn't seemed like a killer, and Adele had sat across from killers before. He had seemed like a worried boy, concerned for his father. Desperate. But he had also killed three people; he had almost killed Adele. It was like he didn't even remember. Like he didn't even think he had done anything wrong.

Adele muttered to herself, collapsing against the wall and passing a weary hand over her face. She had no doubt they would be able to find his name soon enough. But what was in a name? Did she even want to know it?

It would help them discover if there were more victims. There was some modicum of peace for the families to know their daughters' murderer had been brought to justice. But it wasn't much. The dead stayed dead, and grief only worsened.

"You okay?" a soft voice murmured from behind her.

Adele glanced back and saw John standing closer, leaning against the glass to the viewing room. As she regarded the tall, scar-faced agent, she felt her shoulders begin to tremble.

Strange, why was—

She realized she was crying. Dr. Tyra seemed mesmerized by the spectacle from within the room. But Adele still felt a flash of shame; John, though, didn't seem concerned by an audience.

"Oh, Adele, it's-it's fine," John began to speak, but then thought better of it, and instead gathered her in an embrace. Adele felt herself pressed against his warmth. She stood there, trembling, crying into his shoulder. Like a child.

She wasn't sure what brought it on.

She thought of the boy losing his father. She'd not been much older when she lost her mother.

There had been a lot of pressure then as well. She wondered what she would've done if she thought she could have saved her mother. If there had been a moment when she had warning of what was coming, and to what ends she might go to prevent the horrible inevitability. And if she tried and failed, would the guilt have been manageable, or would it have swallowed her whole?

Adele continued to cry, and John just held her, murmuring softly in her ear and pressing his hands around her shoulders. She felt small in his arms, and yet, somehow it still felt protective, and safe.

She stood like that in the corridor of the DGSI headquarters, listening to the quiet drone of muffled voices through the interrogation room.

Eventually, though, John began to guide her away, pressing his hand against her shoulders and leading her out of the room, down the hall, out the front of the office, into the parking structure. He didn't say anything, and neither did she. Her tears kept coming, hot, streaking down her cheeks.

They distanced themselves in body from the case, from the interrogation, from whatever was going to come next. Adele guessed Agent Paige would find the killer's name soon enough. Adele would have to sign some paperwork, would have to make a report to Ms. Jayne. But that could wait. They'd found the answers they'd been looking for. Bleak, dark answers.

And yet not everything about the world was so cold, or so dark.

She leaned even closer to John, feeling his warmth and allowing him to lead her in a circle around the small gray stone steps in the center of the parking structure, passing beneath the glint and glimmer of the windows from the bare-faced facade of the DGSI headquarters.

CHAPTER THIRTY

Adele sat in a red leather chair, facing the fire. She could hear Robert in the kitchen, whistling and preparing something. He'd promised he'd found the perfect tea, and while Adele wasn't the biggest fan of tea, she'd never been able to say no to one of Robert's adventuresome concoctions. She detected the faint fragrance of berries and some sort of spice wafting in from the kitchen.

As she sat in the leather chair, staring at the crackling fire, she heard a buzzing noise.

Adele jerked upright, startled. But then she relaxed, realizing it was just her phone. Was it John? They'd made plans to meet up in a couple of days, just to chat. Nothing weird. Purely professional. At least, that's what they were telling themselves. She reached down and pulled out her phone, peering at the screen.

No, not John. Her father.

The blue and green screen buzzed, displaying white letters spelling *Dad* across the front. Adele clicked the phone, holding it up. Her father's face displayed across the screen, his nose jutting forward.

Adele sighed. "Dad, you're too close. Hold it back a bit."

Her father moved the camera, and now she found she was staring at his hands in his lap.

"Dad, just a bit higher—can't see your face." It took a bit, but finally they were able to adjust, and Adele found herself looking into her father's gaze across digital space. "How are you doing?" she asked.

Her dad didn't respond at first. His face was red, his nose shining. He seemed to be breathing heavier than normal, and for a moment Adele felt a bolt of worry.

"Dad, is everything—"

But then, as the camera shifted again, she spotted the two empty shot glasses and the tall bottle sitting on the kitchen table.

She sighed. "Dad, maybe you should go to bed."

But her father was muttering to himself and shaking his head. His red nose glinted in the light of the camera from his phone. At last, he coughed slightly and said, "Dear, dear Becks." He slurred the words a bit, and stared lopsided through the phone.

Adele smiled slightly. "I think you need some rest."

Her father snorted and began to giggle, shaking his head. It was a rare thing to see her father amused. But this worried her more than anything.

"You're so much like her, you know," her dad said.

Adele's uncertain smile faded as quickly as it had come. She cleared her throat, shifting in her leather chair. "Look, I don't think we should talk when you're like this. How about—"

"You think I don't care," he said, tapping his finger against the screen with each word. He burped and shook his head. "But no—no, no, it devastated me," he said, releasing a breath. "You know, you know that," he said, with a hiccup. He wagged a finger to no one in particular and then pointed it, jabbing at the camera and blotting out screen for a second. Then his finger lowered, his reddish face revealed once more. "I-I'm not trying to force you—you to do—you anything," he said, still slurring his words.

Adele thought back to the last meeting at the café outside the airport in Germany. She sighed. "Dad, I shouldn't have rushed off. I'm sorry."

"I can't stop you," he said. "I can't. I want to. I do. I want to. But I can't." He giggled again and nodded rapidly, causing his head to bounce up and down.

Adele leaned even further back in the red leather chair. "You said it devastated you," she said, trying to settle her own emotions. "What did?" She spoke gently, trying to channel her inner Dr. Tyra.

Her father sighed. "When Elise died, I thought I lost everything. I know we were separated. I know. Still, it nearly ended me."

Adele stared at the screen. She felt a lump forming in her throat. She'd never heard her father talk like this before. She cleared her throat, trying to keep a grip on her emotions. "I'm sorry, but that's the same for me. It's why I want justice. I'm going to bring him in. For both of us."

But her dad shook his head. His eyes were rimmed red, and it looked as if he hadn't slept in a while either. "Sharp, I'm scared. I'm so scared. If I lose you too..."

The lump in Adele's throat had nearly blocked off her breathing for a moment. But she managed to swallow the blockage, and despite the wetness in her eyes, she said, "It's going to be fine. Look, I know it's scary. I know. But Mother deserves justice. You have to see that."

Her dad hiccupped again. "I didn't tell you everything," he said. He shook his head. "Honey, there's more about the case. Something, something I know I should've told you. I know. I just couldn't come—I couldn't bring myself..."

Adele stiffened, staring at the camera. The prickle across the backs of her arms and up the nape of her neck became more intense.

"Dad, what do you mean?"

Her father waved his hand, and the camera angled off again toward his lap.

"Dad, are you okay? What do you mean you didn't tell me everything?"

But her questions went unanswered. After a moment, Adele heard the quiet groaning sound of snoring. She sat like that in the red leather chair, facing the fire in Robert's mansion, listening to the sound of her father snoring, and also heeding the flow of the thoughts swishing through her mind, twisting one after the other.

She wasn't sure what her father meant by that last part. Had he withheld evidence? That didn't sound like him at all. Still, her father sounded scared. He didn't want to lose her. It had been a moment of vulnerability, and it touched her. But, though it mattered, though she cared for him, it didn't change anything.

Adele kept her grip tight on the phone, still angling it toward her face, still listening to the snoring, but as she stared into the fire crackling in the hearth and listened to Robert whistling in the kitchen, she knew without a doubt that she would hunt her mother's killer—and find him. Nothing was going to stop that.

But she wouldn't bring him in. No. Not this one. Her hand tightened around the phone. He had cut her mother to ribbons, enjoying her bleeding out at his feet. Whoever it was, wherever he was, when she found him, the DGSI, the FBI, Interpol—none of it would matter.

Adele's eyes narrowed, staring unblinking into the fire.

The killer wouldn't be brought to justice. Not if she was honest with herself. He would be brought to her. He would suffer. Of that, she was certain. And then—only then—would she end it.

Now Available for Pre-Order!

LEFT TO HIDE
(An Adele Sharp Mystery—Book 3)

"When you think that life cannot get better, Blake Pierce comes up with another masterpiece of thriller and mystery! This book is full of twists and the end brings a surprising revelation. I strongly recommend this book to the permanent library of any reader that enjoys a very well written thriller."

—Books and Movie Reviews, Roberto Mattos (re Almost Gone)

LEFT TO HIDE is book #3 in a new FBI thriller series by USA Today bestselling author Blake Pierce, whose #1 bestseller Once Gone (Book #1) (a free download) has received over 1,000 five star reviews.

An Italian couple vacationing in Germany are found brutally murdered, causing an international outcry. FBI special agent

Adele Sharp is the only one with the international expertise to cross borders and stop the killer—and she finds herself working alongside her estranged father, who knows far more about her mother's unsolved murder than he lets on.

Though still shaken from the recent events in Paris, Adele must embark on a wild chase across Germany, uncovering lies and deception at every turn.

Can Adele and her father heal the rift between them?

And can she track down the killer before tragedy strikes again?

An action-packed mystery series of international intrigue and riveting suspense, LEFT TO HIDE will have you turning pages late into the night.

Book #4 in the ADELE SHARP MYSTERY series will be available soon.

LEFT TO HIDE
(An Adele Sharp Mystery—Book 3)

Made in the USA
Middletown, DE
05 January 2021

30879567R00123